The Conscript

First published in Great Britain in 2021 by
The Book Guild Ltd
9 Priory Business Park
Wistow Road, Kibworth
Leicestershire, LE8 0RX
Freephone: 0800 999 2982
www.bookguild.co.uk
Email: info@bookguild.co.uk
Twitter: @bookguild

Typeset in 11pt Adobe Garamond Pro

Printed and bound by CPI Group (UK) Ltd, Croydon, CR0 4YY

ISBN 978 1913913 182

British Library Cataloguing in Publication Data.
A catalogue record for this book is available from the British Library.

The Conscript

A Story of Naiveté, Deceit and Betrayal

Alastair B. Davie

The Book Guild Ltd

Part One

In the beginning…

"One thing is constant through the whole story of Jarrow – through boom and slump, through so-called prosperity and consequent distress – and that is the poverty of the working-class people of Jarrow. They built vast fortunes for others. They remained at subsistence level and many are now below even that."

The Town That Was Murdered by Ellen Wilkinson, Member of Parliament for Jarrow from 1935 until 1947.

1

Tom Pearson's confession was dated June 13th, 1943 and was a long statement written in his careful hand in a 'safe' house in London. His inquisitor had finally left him alone to write it after his interrogation. He believed their aggressive questioning was unnecessary because he so desperately wanted to unload his unbearable burden.

His written confession began: "Call me naive if you like or call me a traitor, you'll have to decide, but first understand my whole story before you judge me, because you have to know the circumstances I found myself in in the 1920s and 1930s. I make no excuse for my beliefs because they were born of the pain I felt at that time and the need to right many wrongs as I saw them, even if this led me down a path of deceit and acrimony and to my eventual downfall.

"My life turned into a nightmare from which I couldn't wake. It was a relentless night of sorrow and regret as I was pursued by bogus friends and determined enemies.

"I'll always remember the first day of my metamorphosis from a happy-go-lucky child to an angry teenager and then a confused adult..."

* * *

Jarrow, north-east England, June 4th, 1926

In Jarrow, it was supposed to be summer, but that day it wasn't. North-east England was feeling nature's fury as a storm blew in unexpectedly from the unpredictable North Sea after several days of sunny weather. It had caught everyone by surprise, particularly a young boy as he ran from one sheltered place to another trying not to get too wet on his way home from school.

Jarrow is a town on the River Tyne in north-eastern England, close to the city of Newcastle, which is to its west on the north bank of the river. The town was known in the late nineteenth and early twentieth centuries primarily for its shipbuilding, although there was a working colliery in the nearby town of Hebburn. The town had suffered with a lack of work for most of the 1900s onwards. There was a renaissance of sorts during World War One when the British navy needed ships. But the ups and downs of work continued after this. Its population in the 1930s was about thirty-three thousand.

The ten-year-old boy was Tom Pearson and he was, what his teachers called, a prodigy. He was so advanced in his learning, particularly in mathematics, that he had skipped a year. This had caused problems with his classmates, who regarded him as an oddity. He was teased a lot by the other boys, although they weren't ashamed to ask his help with their homework. He took all their taunts in his stride and, kindly, helped them out. One thing they also respected him for was his physical skills on the soccer field. He wasn't a big boy but skilful in his ball handling. This, among all things, garnered respect from his peers.

One other thing they didn't know about him was his love of music. That fact wasn't known until his last term at school when he made his concert debut in front of the whole school. He played the piano every day after school on his father's old, rickety, out-of-tune upright piano, which his father wouldn't spend the money to have tuned.

When Tom reached home after dodging the rain, he had no idea of the shock that awaited him. This would be the second traumatic event in his young life and was to be one of many. Maybe the storm was precursor and symbolic of what was to come.

As he entered the house through the back door, he could hear weeping coming from the living room. He cautiously opened the door and saw his father, sitting in his chair, uncontrollably sobbing.

Tom had never seen his father cry before. He had always seemed emotionally strong and showed none of his inner feelings to his ten-year-old son. He had always been stand-offish and Tom never felt very close to him. But some would say that that was the schoolteacher in him. It was abnormal to see this big man sob like a child.

Tom didn't know what to do. Should he go up to him and put his arm around him? But his father wouldn't do that to him. He would only tell him roughly to suck it up and be a man. It was shocking to witness this austere and undemonstrative man crying, a man Tom respected more than loved. Should he sneak away and make a noise in another room to let him know he was in the house? In the end he did nothing and just stood by the door watching.

Tom's father was sitting in the living room with a glass of whisky in his hand and was staring at the fireplace as the memories flooded into his mind.

"Dad, are you alright? Why are you crying?" Tom finally asked.

"Hello, lad," he replied, as he tried to gather his emotions and thoughts. "Come and sit over here. I have some bad news and you'll have to be brave about what I'm going to tell you."

Tom didn't like the sound of that, but he sat down and faced his father, sensing something terrible was in the air.

"Where's Grandpa?" Tom asked, almost intuitively.

"Grandpa won't be coming home, I'm afraid. He is no longer with us, Tom. He died late this morning from what looks like a heart attack." He paused and took a deep breath and continued. "You remember he always went for a walk every morning come rain or shine past the Palmer Shipyards. He liked to stop at one of the work gates and talk to the men about what ships they were building or repairing. Well, this morning on his way back here he fell down. The hospital called me at school and I rushed to see him. When I got there he was already dead. I didn't get to say goodbye to him.

"I'm afraid there is just you and me now, Tom, and we'll have to make the best of it."

It took a few seconds for this news to register with the boy. He eventually burst into a flood of tears. His father didn't put an arm around him and hug him as most parents would have done. Instead he just looked sullen, swigged his whisky and stared at the boy.

There had been two people in Tom's life. There was his grandpa, who he adored and had a special relationship with. They would talk for hours and do things together like going fishing or watching soccer games in Jarrow and Newcastle. And there was his austere, stand-offish father, who he respected but did not feel any real warmth for. It did not dawn on him at this young age that there was any problem with their relationship.

Tom's grandpa was a life-long trade unionist, shop steward of the boilermakers' union and member of the Communist Party of Great Britain. He had been the bane of Palmer Shipyard's management for years, fighting for better conditions for his members. He retired in 1921, much to their relief. He firmly believed the worker-led Russian revolution of 1917 should be copied in Great Britain and, as a result of his contacts, speeches and magazine articles, the British MI5 security service followed his career very closely. He wanted to see the government and industry led by the workers and their unions so that the country would become egalitarian and a poor person's utopia.

Tom's father, forty-year-old Frank Pearson, was what you

would call a formal man, always polite, dependable and unruffled by most situations, but by no means warm or expressive. He was a tall man who stood at least six feet, but he was very lanky. His thinning hair was always combed back, hiding his balding head, and he had a well-groomed Charlie Chaplain-type moustache.

He always dressed immaculately in a three-piece suit, polished shoes and one of his tartan ties. Why a tartan tie no one knew because he wasn't Scottish or Irish, but he told anyone who asked that he just liked their designs. He was a science teacher at the Jarrow Grammar School and garnered a lot of respect from his pupils, because he was patient and good at explaining complicated scientific theories so they could understand. He was known not to have a sense of humour, although his pupils sometimes made him smile, but most of the time he was serious about making sure that they could be all that they could be in life. He saw this as his calling as a teacher.

Tom's father had fought his way up from his desperately poor background in Jarrow, gone to university on a scholarship and had become a teacher. He had been expected to join Tom's grandfather at the Palmer Shipyards and suffer the feast and famine of work that the ten thousand or so workers at the yards suffered over the years. And Grandpa Pearson was determined that Tom would follow in his son's footsteps and go to university.

Tom's father had met his future wife at the Victoria University of Manchester and they had married soon after they graduated. Jane Pearson had continued her studies there and gained a PhD in chemistry. At first, Frank taught in a school in Manchester, but he wanted to get back to Jarrow to teach because he saw a desperate need there. They moved back in 1913 and Jane took up a teaching post at the Royal Grammar School in Newcastle. Through an inheritance from Jane's parents they were able to buy the house in St. John's Terrace in Jarrow, which was a relatively more affluent part of the town.

Grandpa's sudden death wasn't the first time that tragedy of this kind had visited Tom's family, although he was too young at the time to really understand. His paternal grandmother and grandad lived in a dilapidated house on Clayton Street near to the shipyards. When grandma passed away in 1917 from pneumonia, Tom's parents had insisted that grandpa live with them in their house on St. John's Terrace. Now he was gone too.

His mother, Jane, had died from the influenza pandemic, also known as the Spanish flu, which hit Jarrow in 1918 when he was just three. She died in the Palmer Memorial Hospital and was one of 174 townspeople who died from the pandemic that year, and they joined the millions of people worldwide who had died from the disease.

When Tom's tears receded a bit, his father stood up and became his gruff self. "I've got to go to the undertakers now and arrange for a wake here and his burial at the Jarrow Cemetery. He wasn't religious so there'll be no church service. Do you want to come with me? The rain seems to have stopped."

"No thanks, Dad, I'll stay here."

"Fine. I'll see you in a couple of hours," he said and left.

Tom went out of the back door into the garden and sat on his swing. He always did this when he had things to think about. He was gently swinging when a voice called out, "A penny for your thoughts, young Tom."

He looked up and saw Mrs. Aldridge from next door, who was hanging some washing on her line.

"My grandpa is dead," he announced.

"I'm sorry to hear that," she said, but she couldn't resist smiling to herself. "I'm sure you'll miss him. When did he pass away?"

"This morning. My dad is at the undertakers right now. He's arranging for a wake here and his burial."

"You mean all his friends from the shipyards will be here on our street? Oh, this will be terrible. Why don't you have the wake at the union hall?"

Tom was not listening to her going on as she picked up her

clothes basket and disappeared into her house tut, tutting as she went.

Mrs. Martha Aldridge was a rotund woman in her late fifties. She had been a ward sister at St. Mary's Hospital in Manchester. She was self-righteous and very opinionated. She brooked no arguments from nurses, other sisters or even doctors. She bullied her husband Dr. Edgar Aldridge, who was a local GP and a good friend of Tom's grandpa. But the one person she couldn't verbally bully was Grandpa Pearson, who won many confrontations with her.

Mrs. Aldridge's views were extremely right-wing, supporting the Conservative Prime Minister Stanley Baldwin who had introduced martial law in Britain to combat the general strike that May. Britain's only ever general strike was called by the General Council of the Trades Union Congress to support the coal miners who had been locked out of mines and faced wage declines and job losses. The strike failed to reverse the mine owners' policies, but it effectively shut down such industries as transportation, some unionised manufacturing and the newspapers.

Tom's grandpa's extremely left-wing political views were anathema to Mrs. Aldridge and he spent some time enjoying winding her up whenever he saw her. She took the bait every time and it got so bad that Frank asked his father frequently to stop annoying their neighbour. Peace lasted for a few days before war broke out again.

As the French doors were open at the Aldridge house, Tom could hear an excited conversation going on. He crept to the side of their house and listened and watched from behind a bush. Mrs. Aldridge had bounced into her living room with an unmistakable 'joi de vivre', surprising Dr. Aldridge, who was sitting reading his newspaper.

"What's got you so excited, Martha?" he asked.

"The commie is dead. Isn't that wonderful?" she announced.

"Who is dead?"

"That old bugger next door, that's who."

"You mean Reg?"

"Sometimes I think you are so thick, Edgar! Of course. Who else?"

"Martha, I don't think you should be overjoyed by someone's death. Haven't you got any respect for this dead man? How do think Frank and Tom feel at this moment?" Dr. Aldridge reacted with unusual anger.

This took Martha aback for a moment, but then she carried on with her thoughts. "Now this street will be back to normal after the wake and it will be seen as a true middle-class one of professionals as it was before he came to stay. It's important that we maintain standards in this forlorn town with all these men hanging about whenever I go shopping on Ellison Street."

Angrier now, Edgar reacted: "You've no idea, woman, what the desperate families of these workers go through just to survive! I have seen kids in rags in my surgery, suffering from all kinds of problems from malnutrition, rickets to TB. They have no hope in life except to follow their fathers into the shipyards when there is work or down the coal mine in Hebburn. Reg and I often talked about this catastrophic situation when we used to go down to the Royal Oak pub."

"You did what!" she reacted, fuming. It was her turn to be angry: "You went down to the pub with him?"

"Yes. We went there maybe once or twice a week when I finished evening surgery. He was a very interesting man and well read."

"Why didn't I know about this?" she shouted.

"Because I didn't tell you, that's why. He always got the better of you in your arguments and, frankly, my dear, it was amusing to see you tangled in knots trying to win a debate with him."

"Well, I never thought you would ever deceive me like this!"

"You had it coming with your haughty-totty ways."

"Well, my sister was right, I should never have married you!

You're a monster!" She opened the living-room door, stormed out and slammed it shut behind her.

Dr. Aldridge just smiled and continued to read his paper. Tom retreated to his own back yard, delighted that his grandpa had had such a friend.

One day later a wake for grandpa was held at their home. It was the first time Tom had seen a dead body and what made it worse was that it was his grandpa whom he had loved with all his heart. He stared at the now-peaceful man, who was dressed in his Sunday best suit and tie. Here was a man who worked hard all his life, with his gnarled hands now across his chest. Here was the man who took Tom fishing and told him about the appalling conditions in the shipyards and coal mines. Here was the man who told him about the plight of the families of the working class in Britain. Here was the man who took him into the slum areas of Jarrow to show him how those people lived. Here was the man who had been a revolutionary in his thoughts about the unrestricted needs of working people so that Britain would become a classless society. Here was a man who was a dreamer about a better world for all.

Tom was just staring at his grandpa and was deep in thought when he felt an arm around his shoulders. When he looked up he saw Jake Ferguson, Grandpa's oldest friend. Jake was a wizened, toothless, little man who walked with aid of a cane, which he had used for forty or so years following an accident at the yards. Jake and Grandpa had grown up together, gone to school together and, at fifteen, started work at the yards together. They had been inseparable.

"He was a wonderful person, our Tom," he said in his thick Geordie accent and with tears in his eyes. "I will miss him terribly. Now, always remember him as he was, not like you see him now. That really isn't the man. He did so much good in this town and there are many families hereabouts who are thankful for what he did for them. Take a look out of the window and you'll see what I mean."

Tom walked over to front window and he saw lines of people snaking down the street as they shuffled along to pay their respects to Grandpa.

"I think your grandpa wouldn't have liked to see you work at the yards. We did so because we had to. There was no choice. Your da was able to avoid this and so should you. Your grandpa wanted you to get an education and become someone, but he wanted you to never, never forget the working man and where you come from. He wanted you to use your skills to better their lot in life. Now come and meet some of these people."

Grandpa's open coffin was on the dining-room table. The room had been cleared of most of its furniture so that mourners were able to file around the coffin and exit through a second door. Many people had brought small traditional offerings of cakes and bread, which they gave Tom's father as they walked in single file around the coffin. Frank shook the hands of each person and exchanged pleasantries with their condolences.

The wake started at five in the evening and didn't end until well past ten. When Tom eventually climbed into bed he was exhausted both mentally and physically. However tired he was he couldn't sleep because he was thinking about the man lying in their dining room. Lying there, he wished he had known more about his grandpa so he could have asked questions. For example, his ten-year-old mind could not grasp why people lived in such poverty and why the government didn't help them. He drifted off to sleep about midnight.

The next day at eleven in the morning, Tom, his father and Jake Ferguson followed the hearse in one of the undertaker's cars to the cemetery. As they turned the corner onto Monkton Road, there was small group of about twenty people gathered. They all began to clap as the hearse passed them. When they reached the Jarrow Cemetery, the three of them gathered around the freshly dug grave and they bowed their heads as the coffin was lowered into its final resting place.

The remembrance of Tom's grandfather and what he stood for was forever engraved on the boy's mind. It was something he would recall for the rest of his life.

2

Jarrow, August 10th, 1934

Eight years later, Tom Pearson was a strapping eighteen-year-old senior at Jarrow Grammar School and he was waiting to hear from the University of Leeds whether he had been accepted to study physics the next term. He really wanted to get into the field of wireless technology after university and he had read about the early development of radar, which had intrigued him.

Tom had grown to become thin like his father, but not as tall. Despite his lanky look, people said that he had an attractive face, blue eyes and a winning smile that beguiled those who were his friends. However, his clothes seemed to hang on him and many other pupils at school often teased him calling him a boffin and any other derogatory terms they could think of. He usually ignored them, but he had got into fights when he first went to the grammar school. Nowadays he was left alone. However, he got his own back as he often outshone his critics in the classroom as well as on the soccer field. His eyesight wasn't great as he was short-sighted so he had wear spectacles all the time, except when he played soccer, the game he loved.

Tom's music teacher, Miss Lomax, had cajoled his school's

headmaster to allow him to play the piano at one of the social evenings that was organised for parents. He played some Bach and Chopin to a rapturous audience who called for an encore. Instead of more classical music he played a medley of American jazz pianist Fats Waller's early jazz standards 'Squeeze Me', 'Ain't Misbehavin' and 'Honeysuckle Rose'. It was quite clear from their tepid applause that Miss Lomax and the audience were shocked. And he didn't care because he loved the music.

Since his grandpa's death, Tom began to worry about his father as he was acting out of character. For the past two years, his father had the habit of disappearing for occasional weekends or for long periods during the school's summer holidays. Whenever Tom asked him where he had been he was told gruffly to mind his own business and he did, but still he was intrigued because his dad was always in a good mood when he returned. His absences by this time had become routine and it didn't bother Tom, because he was so wrapped up in building a ham radio system, he didn't miss him when he was gone.

Little did he know that his father had a girlfriend near London and would spend time with her. He learned later that this father had met her at a teachers' conference in Harrogate and they enjoyed each other's company. Soon their friendship blossomed into romance. He would go to clubs and the theatre in London with her and they would spend the nights in each other's arms. Frank felt so exhilarated with their relationship and enjoyed the secrecy of it. He looked forward to their times together because it made him feel so young again. He never told anyone about this because he didn't want to be the subject of gossip in this small conservative community, where everyone knew each other's business, or thought they did. The other reason was that if the school found out about his illicit affair he would be sacked, such were conservative social standards of the times.

Tom had become an avid amateur electronics hobbyist and was now an ardent ham radio operator. He had already communicated with ham operators in Germany and France and was building an Eddystone short-wave radio that he hoped would reach the United States. His room was a veritable warren of radio equipment, valves, microphones, manuals and other parts that were lying on two work benches and on the floor.

He had started his electronics hobby when he was thirteen by constructing a simple crystal radio set and he had progressed from there to build more complicated and sophisticated systems. He eagerly read scientific magazines such as *The Wireless World* and *Practical Wireless* and absorbed the latest technical developments in the burgeoning field of modern electronics. His father, to his credit, recognised his enthusiasm and suggested that he should think of electronics as a career. That's why he chose to study physics at university and any day now he was going to hear from the University of Leeds whether he'd been accepted to study there.

One day when he was busy in his room, there was clatter of the letter box at the front door. He rushed downstairs and grabbed the envelope from the hall carpet where it had fallen. He opened it feverishly and, when he had read it three times, he let out a loud, "Yes!"

"Good news?" asked his father from the kitchen.

"Yes, Dad! I start at university in September," he said jubilantly.

"Congratulations, lad. Let's go out and celebrate."

"Sorry, Dad, I'm meeting Jason, but why not tomorrow?"

"Great. We'll make it then," his father said.

That evening Tom's father sat down in his living room with a scotch in his hand. He smiled and gave thanks that the boy was leaving. Now he would be free to make his own life, abandoning any responsibility now for his son.

Tom's best friend was Jason Cooper, who he had met at St. Bede's Junior School and they had both gone on to the senior school. His grandfather had insisted that Tom should go to a local school where 'he would get a real education into how the other half live and survive'. And he certainly did. The other pupils were often poorly dressed, dirty and hungry, and certainly not ready to learn.

The lessons were taught in an old schoolhouse that was made up of three large classrooms with two classes in the same room divided by a curtain. The condition in these rooms was unbearable with desks made up of long tables with just benches with no backs to sit on. In winter, the one fire in each room roasted those in front so they would fall asleep and those in the back were numb with cold. Things were better in the senior school as pupils were promoted there based on their abilities so there weren't as many schoolchildren to accommodate.

Tom helped Jason in class and with his homework and as a result they had become firm friends, despite being from very different backgrounds. They both loved soccer and played for the school. Jason lived on Clayton Street in a very poor slum and his father worked at the Palmer's Shipyard when he was not laid off, which happened a lot.

Jason was now a physically large, handsome young man and, over the years when the two boys grew up, he always watched over Tom to ensure he, a slight bespectacled boy, was never bullied by more physical peers. One day, for example, when they were twelve they were playing soccer on a street in Jason's neighbourhood when they were approached by girl of thirteen or fourteen in a ragged dress.

"Give me a penny and I'll show you my twat," she said to Tom as he picked up their ball and started to dribble it towards Jason, who was in goal between their two jackets.

"No, thank you, I'm not interested," Tom told her politely and carried on playing.

The girl stared hard at him, pursed her lips and ran off. A few minutes later she returned with her brother who was about fifteen.

He grabbed Tom by the throat: "I'm going to teach you a lesson you won't forget for asking my sister to pull down her knickers for a penny."

As he said this he suddenly collapsed on the floor as if he had been hit by a goods train. The train was Jason giving him a rugby-style tackle. The boy hit the road with a thud and Jason began to pummel him unmercifully. When he had finished the boy had a bloodied nose and was crying. His sister ran off shouting for help.

Jason turned to Tom and smiled: "I think we had better scarper." And they ran.

Jason and Tom left St. Bede's Senior School at fourteen. Tom went to the Jarrow Grammar School and Jason was apprenticed at the Mercantile Dry Dock & Engineering Company as a plumber/coppersmith. They still kept in touch going out regularly and playing soccer for Jarrow Football Club reserves.

That night they were to meet at the Golden Lion pub on Walters Street where they had become 'regulars'. Tom was excited to tell his friend about his good news, but when he entered the pub Jason was sitting there with a girl Tom knew called Edith Winslow.

"I've got some good news to tell you," Tom said as he sat down.

"I bet mine is better," said Jason with a Cheshire Cat grin.

"Alright, I'll buy it. What's your news?"

"Me and Edith is engaged and are getting married next month!"

"What!" Tom exclaimed, completely taken by surprise because he didn't know anything about their relationship. A few seconds later he recovered from the shock of this unexpected announcement.

"Congratulations! That is great news," he said, unsure whether that was the right sentiment.

Tom was completely taken aback by this news. Jason had never let on that he was seeing Edith seriously. He knew that they had been going out a few times, but Jason had many girlfriends and they tended to last a short while. Edith was from North Shields, about five miles away on the other side of River Tyne from Jarrow. She was a shop assistant there and lived with her parents. Tom couldn't think where Jason had picked her up from and then he remembered, it was at a dance at Jarrow Football Club they had been to some six months earlier.

"Would you be my best man, Tom?" Jason asked.

"Of course I would."

When Edith had gone to the ladies, he told Jason he was very surprised at the news.

"Are you sure you want to do this?" he asked. "I remember you always wanted to go out with as many girls as possible and never get hitched."

"Well, you see," he said shyly, "she is expecting my bairn."

This news completely floored Tom and it was some time before he could respond.

"How did this happen?"

"How do you think, man?"

"Didn't you take precautions?"

"It was kind of spontaneous, like. I didn't have anything on me. We were in my room and my parents were out at the pictures and it just happened."

"When is she expecting?"

"She's about four months along. We decided to get married after we had a talk with her parents, who insisted I do the 'right thing'. They were very upset with us but eventually they came around to the inevitable. The wedding will be at her church in North Shields."

"Do you love her?"

"What sort of question is that? I suppose so. I find her interesting," said Jason defensively.

When he got home, Tom was concerned about his friend Jason's news and he wasn't in a talkative mood. His father, sensing his mood when he walked in, asked: "What's troubling you, lad?"

"Jason's getting married and he is being forced into doing something he doesn't want to do because the girl is pregnant."

"In many ways he brought it on himself, but I see your

concern," said his father. "He couldn't leave her to bring up a child by herself so he has to do the right thing by her."

"I know, but it stinks."

"Unfortunately, sometimes life is unjust. We have to make our own future, just as you are doing," he answered knowingly.

Tom's father paused and then changed the subject: "Your grandfather gave me this envelope for you and asked me to give it to you when I thought you had grown into a man and you are ready to understand its content."

Tom took his evening cocoa to his room and opened the envelope. Inside was a letter from his grandad written in his careful hand and two books – *The Communist Manifesto* by Karl Marx and Charles Dickens's *Hard Times* – and various pamphlets written by Vladimir Lenin, the leader of Russia, and R. Palme Dutt, a leading theoretician in the Communist Party of Great Britain. He took out the letter and began to read it:

> Dear Tom,
>
> By the time you read this I will be six feet under and pushing up the daisies! I wanted to let you know my thoughts when you were old enough to understand them, so I asked your father to give you this when he judged you were old enough. I hope you will go to university like him and support your friends in Jarrow who only want to live their lives in reasonable comfort.
>
> I want you to carry on, if possible, my wish to see through a social revolution that will eventually come to this country where the ordinary person has a say in their work and life. These items I have left you in this envelope will help you understand my thinking and tell you about the plight of the working man in this country, and all over the world, for that matter.
>
> Now you know I have been a life-long communist and socialist. I have come to believe very strongly that

the wonderful revolution that happened in Russia in 1917, when the ordinary working people took over the country and are now successfully running it, will be repeated in Britain. Already in Germany there is strong, viable communist party which was born as result of the hardships of people after the Great War.

In my life, I have witnessed many tragedies here in Jarrow which have included steps by management to take shortcuts in work to make more of a profit for the bosses. These have often resulted in men's deaths with little or no compensation given to their widows. I've seen the hopelessness and despair in people's eyes when their breadwinner is laid off. I've seen children with barely any clothes on their back and with no shoes in the dead of winter because the bosses do not pay a living wage. Profit is the evil that ensures working people are downtrodden and slaves to their masters.

We read about the black slaves in American cotton plantations and their treatment or the serfs in the middle ages, but we face many of the same hardships that they did. We are 'owned' by the bosses, not in the property sense but by the fact we need the work to live and have to follow their demands. And it's not right!

So, Tom, always follow your conscience and help your friends in this town. Goodbye, my boy.

Your loving Grandpa
Reginald Pearson

Tom lay in bed that night and reread his grandpa's letter. Over the next few days he read and absorbed the pamphlets and the books Grandpa had left him. He was stunned by these books and recognised many of the problems these publications talked about in Jarrow. It was then he realised he had to fulfil his grandpa's wishes. But how?

Tom was mindful of his grandfather's life-long fight for the working men of Jarrow. Grandad was a communist through and though. He saw that communism would help alleviate the caustic environment in which so many lived. The Russian revolution in 1917 had given him some hope of changing the lot of workers. He saw it as a shining example of what could be achieved for the poor underclass in society. On the other hand, he had urged Tom's father to go to university to get away from his appalling existence. Tom knew that his grandad would have approved of his career choice, but he believed that one way or another he had to repay the old man's sacrifices and somehow help to realise his dreams and legacy.

The following month, Tom turned up at Christ Church in North Shields for Jason's wedding at eleven in the morning. He was feeling the worst for wear following a really boozy bachelor's party with Jason and two of his friends the night before. Edith's mother gave him a withering look as if he had been responsible for Edith's pregnancy. There were about thirty people at the service, mainly from Edith's side. Jason's parents and three or four people from his work filled the bridegroom's pews.

The wedding was a dreary affair. For a start the sky was dark and it was raining, not a hard rain, but a morbid drizzle. This made the town's buildings dark and ominous and added to their cheerless and dirty appearance. The ceremony was conducted by the church's curate and not by its vicar, who probably did not think the family was important enough for his presence. The curate ran through the ceremony as if he had a train to catch and his homily was short, talking about the sanctity of marriage as if he would know all about the subject, having just graduated from university. And that was that. Everyone trundled out of the church, putting up umbrellas as they went.

Edith's only bridesmaid, Angela, was very unattractive in a toothy sort of way and she was physically a large girl with acne covering her pot-marked face. She had made a beeline for

Tom at the reception at the Sir Colin Campbell Hotel. She was continuously going to the bar for more wine and in between she tried to make conversation with him, but it was an unintelligible slur. She stood as close as she could to him, breathing alcohol fumes at him when she talked, which was all the time.

After everyone finished eating at the buffet, Tom made his faltering speech listing the positive attributes of his friend and telling lame jokes about some of their antics. Nobody laughed except Jason and his other friends. Tom was very relieved that the ordeal was over when he raised his glass and toasted the bride and groom. Edith's father then made a very short speech and toasted the 'happy couple'.

The band then struck up. Well, it wasn't a band really since there were only two players, a drummer and, the star of the show, an ageing accordion player.

No sooner had they had started playing when a very drunk Angela whisked Tom onto the floor and started to dance closely with him. The only trouble was that he didn't know how to dance, but this didn't matter to Angela, who eagerly held him close and rubbed her rather fulsome body against him, much to the amusement of Jason and his friends.

When the music stopped, Tom told Angela he needed to visit the gentlemen's and he retreated as fast as he could to the one room he could claim as a sanctuary from her. By the time he cautiously returned to the reception, Angela was nowhere to be seen. With a sigh of relief, Tom walked to the bar and asked Jason where she was. Apparently she had been taken ill and her parents, who were also guests, had taken her home. He was relieved.

At five that evening, the bride and groom left for the station in a taxi. They were to go to the seaside resort of Redcar for their honeymoon. They planned to spend three days there and then move into their rented house on Walters Street in Jarrow.

As soon as they had gone, Tom quietly left the hotel unnoticed and walked to the station to catch his train home to Jarrow. Sitting in the waiting room at the station and then in his third-class seat he began to muse about the day and the life in which his friend had become trapped. Yes, he had made a mistake with Edith, but his work had also ensnared him in the malevolent roundabout of life in the impoverished world of northern England. How do you break out of this environment where you are expected to live in it until you die? Tom's father had broken out of this malicious cycle and he would. But, what about the people left behind? Would no one help them? He began to understand his grandfather's thoughts and theories.

Two weeks later, Tom left for the University of Leeds to begin his studies. He didn't know it then, but he would never see Jason again.

3

Leeds, October 3rd, 1934

Tom started to walk the short distance between the Leeds railway station to the university campus on a sunny but chilly day carrying two suitcases stuffed full of clothes and papers. As he got off the train he had seen about fifty or so young men such as himself and a small group of young women making their way along the street towards the university. A few of the men, who were obviously second- or third-year students because they looked older, were busy chatting and joshing as they walked along, whereas the first-year students, such as Tom, walked in silence in trepidation about what they faced.

Tom felt a combination of emotions. He was both elated and anxious about his future at the same time. He knew that his choice of a career in radio technology was the right course to take and that a degree in physics with electrical engineering would help him achieve his goal.

He had been determined to forge this career from the age of sixteen and he never wavered from this despite the conversations he had had with his remote father, who didn't seem to care and seemed happy that he was leaving for university. Tom had read many technical journals and had been captivated by the possibilities of the burgeoning field of radar.

Although he felt confident about his career choice, he was nervous as this was the first time he had lived away from home. His father had half-heartedly offered to drive him to the university in a borrowed car or accompany him on the train, but Tom had turned him down as he wanted a clean break from home and this decision was much to his father's relief. He knew that his father was relieved to see the back of him. They had become more estranged in the past few months.

The letter he had received from the university had told him to report to Devonshire Hall, which was an all-male residence hall on Cumberland Road. As he approached the university he asked other students where Devonshire Hall was and eventually found it. This building had been the Regent Court Hotel and was bought by the university in 1929 as part of its development programme as the number of students grew. Tom stood in the road looking at the Victorian building which would be his home for the next three years. It had three floors and in the centre was an elegant clock tower with two large bay windows on the second and third levels. The tower reached another twenty feet or so and dominated the design of the building.

Tom walked across the courtyard and through the front door. There was a hall porter at a desk who was checking off names from a list and handing out room keys.

"Ah, Mr. Pearson, you are in room thirty-two on the second floor," he said with military efficiency when Tom gave him his name. "Put your suitcases in your room and report to the Great Hall to register for your classes," he said as he handed Tom a key.

Tom climbed a rickety staircase to the second floor, found his room and was unlocking the door when a voice behind him gave him a surprise.

"Hello there! My name is Brian Onslow."

Tom turned around and shook Brian's extended hand.

"Tom Pearson."

"Well, let me show you around our digs when you've put you stuff in your room. This is my second year and I can show you some of the shortcuts to living here," said this friendly man who just happened to be passing.

Brian was an untidy man not only in his dress but in his thinking and work. He wore corduroy trousers which were too big for him, his jacket was too small and the sweater he wore showed old stains on it. When Tom got to know him better in the months ahead, he recognised that beneath his seeming nonchalance was a person of determination and steel. Once he'd made up his mind about something his willpower ensured he succeeded. He had a ready, warm smile and an ebullient nature, which was deceptive in that he was a street-smart man who could see through anyone's nonsensical arguments as baloney. He was physically unusually muscular in his squat frame and was the sort of person who was ardent about health and fitness despite his appearance. He was in his second year studying for a law degree and was from Bradford where his father was a well-known solicitor.

Brian showed Tom the bathroom on their floor which had a large Victorian bath with a water heater above it. Brian explained they were only allowed to take a bath once a week and pointed out the schedule for that pinned to the back of the door, and Tom saw his name down for Thursday evenings. There was a separate room with the toilets and four sinks that had large mirrors above them.

In the middle of each floor was a student common room with soft chairs around a fireplace and along the walls there were a number of desks. Brian explained that when it got really cold they were allowed to build and light a fire.

Brian and Tom walked over to the Great Hall to register for classes. He recognised the building as the place where he had sat his university entrance exams and where he had been interviewed by two crusty old physics professors. Today, replacing the silence and air of formality, there was chaos as hundreds of men and women, all talking at the same time, queued at the appropriate desks that had signs on them announcing the subject speciality.

Tom looked for the desk with a sign with physics on it and reported in to the staff member. He was again checked off a list and given details of his first year. Also, he was given a schedule of lectures, their times and location. When he got back to his room, he studied the papers he'd been given. The curriculum for this first year was an introduction to physics, mathematics and chemistry. All the classes were to be taken in the relatively new physics block which had been opened three years previously and had modern laboratory facilities.

Brian and Tom went to the refectory for dinner, which was the main meal of the day served between 12.30pm and 2.00pm. Again there was a cacophony of sound as hundreds of students helped themselves to food served buffet-style and then they sat down on long tables that accommodated twelve people. Tom chose a lamb stew, which, when he tasted it, seemed to have uncertain ingredients.

That evening Brian and Tom went to the Pack Horse pub which was nearby on Woodhouse Lane. This was a local hangout for most the students and that evening it was crowded, but Brian saw three students he knew sitting in a corner. When they had got their beers they joined them.

"Tom, I'd like to introduce you to Rodney Garfield, Roger Jackson and Simon Owen," said Brian, who knew them from their private school days in Bradford.

They shook hands.

"What degree are you taking, Tom?" Rodney Garfield asked.

"Physics with electronic engineering. And you?"

"Oh, I'm just one of those dunderheads taking commerce, not one of you bright individuals, I'm afraid. My old man wanted me to come here before I joined the family firm in Bradford," he replied, and his voice, Tom thought, was tinged with a lot of resentment. His first impression of Rodney was not good and something inside warned him to be careful.

"Where are you from, Tom?" asked Simon Owen.

"Jarrow."

"What's in that god-forsaken town?" asked Rodney.

"Not much these days. The main employer Palmer's Shipyard closed for good this summer," he replied sadly. He felt that he was being judged by the others and seen to be left wanting as someone you don't really want to know. He thought, maybe this was just him and his inferiority complex.

Despite the negative comments, he continued to explain Jarrow's predicament: "The unemployed workers in Jarrow are desperate for work, as some seventy-five per cent of working men in the town are unemployed. Their unemployment insurance money is dismal. Can you imagine trying to live on an unemployment benefit of fifteen shillings a week for a man and wife and about five shillings for each child? An American steel company is trying to get a plant opened there so we'll have to see."

"Remind me never to go there," Rodney Garfield commented in a sarcastic tone to his three friends and they all laughed except Tom's new friend Brian Onslow.

"I'm sorry to hear this, Tom. Is your family affected?" Brian asked.

"My dad's a grammar schoolteacher but my grandfather used to work in the yards and would have been shocked at their closing. Fortunately he's dead so he wouldn't see the distress it caused in the town."

"I think we all know all too well the tragedy that had befallen so many towns and cities here in the north of England. This was just another one. I hope the government can find a way to revive the town's fortunes," said Brian.

"Let's talk about something less depressing, shall we, chaps?" Rodney said after a moment's silence. Tom thought that Rodney was a selfish little rich boy who was only interested in himself. He knew that he shouldn't judge a person at the first meeting, but as the months went by he was only to be proved right.

Rodney then began to talk about the girls he had seen at the Oxley and College Halls and how he had already set up a date with one of them. They then began talking about soccer and all agreed they would turn up for the trials for the team the following week.

As the weeks passed, Tom began to enjoy his time at university and he was intellectually challenged by his professors. Apart from soccer practice and games on a Saturday, he was very absorbed in his studies and often didn't have time to interact socially with Rodney and his friends. When he did, they tended to tease him so he didn't join them on their pub crawls or go to dances at the student union. By this time, each of his so-called friends had girlfriends, whereas he was very shy and very awkward with the women the others tried to introduce him to. So he just gave up trying as he knew he had more important things to focus on.

Noticeably missing from the group, as time went by, was Brian Onslow. He wondered why and he was about to find out the hard way why he was boycotting the group.

One day after soccer practice Tom found himself alone in the changing rooms with Rodney Garfield, who looked very despondent and hadn't been his usual lively and obnoxious self.

"What's wrong, Rod? You don't seem happy."

"Oh, I'm alright. I just had some bad news, that's all."

"Anything I can help you with?"

"Truth is, I got a note from my maths lecturer today saying unless I buck up with my tests and work he is going to fail me. And that means they'll kick me out of university. My dad will be furious."

"What are you going to do about it?"

"There's much I can do. I'm not just good at maths and that's all there is to it."

"I'll tell you what, why don't I help you and tutor you?" Tom suggested. He didn't know why he ever volunteered to help him.

He didn't like him and only kept in the group because they were part of the soccer team.

"That would be great. But promise me one thing, you won't tell a soul about this."

"Of course I won't, I promise."

In the next few weeks Rodney and Tom spent time solving maths problems and he found out that he was quite bright but lazy. Tom supposed that this was because of his privileged upbringing and the fact that he hadn't been pushed to succeed. After a few weeks of working on his homework and tests Rodney achieved a slightly higher than passing grade in his exams.

Despite his tutoring and the help Tom had given Rodney, he felt that his so-called friends had grown to regard him as an oddity and that he was someone they tolerated. He was their working-class token who they put up with because they were 'open-minded' to people from all walks of life or so they thought in their arrogance. Tom never seemed to get close to any of them as he had done with his friend Jason Cooper in Jarrow. The girls in the group were particularly condescending towards him and would laugh at his views or social mistakes.

Rodney and the other members of the group of friends were gathered one night in the Pack Horse pub without Tom as he was busy working on a paper for his professor. It was a good thing he wasn't there because the group were talking about him and how he always, as one of them said, tried to get 'in' with them all the time. They laughed about his dress, large glasses and tousled hair.

"He's like a lap dog, always wanting to do something to please," said Rodney viciously. "Frankly, I'm tired of him."

"I bet he's still a virgin," said Roger Jackson, and they all laughed. "Maybe he's a pansy."

"He wouldn't know what to do if he a naked woman came on to him," said one of the girls in the group, giggling.

"That gives me an idea for a great joke, which we'll all remember for years to come," enthused Rodney. "Now listen to this."

As the weeks went by, Tom began to realise that whatever he did he wasn't really a member of their group. This had been quite clear when he wasn't invited away on weekends he knew they all went on. They all talked about what they had done that weekend in front of him as if he had been there. So he was surprised when in November he received an invitation to Simon Owen's twenty-first birthday party at the Wheatley Arms Hotel in the village of Ben Rhydding, just east of Ilkley in Yorkshire. He thought perhaps they'd changed their minds about including him and he was gullibly looking forward to the party.

The rest of the group had left the university in Rodney's car ahead of Tom on the Saturday morning of the party. He had to finish some laboratory work that morning and caught the train from Leeds to Ben Rhydding, arriving at about four o'clock in the afternoon. The small hotel was only a short walk from the station, which was good as it began to rain hard.

As Tom entered the reception, he heard the voices and guffaws of the others in the bar. He checked in with the receptionist and was given a key for his room on the second floor. He climbed the oak staircase and found his room at the end of the corridor. He unlocked the door and smelt a faint odour of perfume as he walked in. Standing there was a beautiful woman in her dressing gown smiling at him.

"You must be Tom. I'm Veronica and I guess we are roommates this weekend."

Tom just stood there in shock and all he could say was, "Are we?"

"Well, sweetie, I've just run a bath so I'm going to take it now. You're welcome to join me if you like," she purred. And with that she dropped her dressing gown and walked naked to the bathroom.

Tom had never seen a naked woman before and couldn't believe his eyes. She was beautiful and very curvaceous. He felt something inside of him he had never felt before and was very tempted to follow her into the bathroom. But why had she chosen him? He did not know her and then it occurred to him that he'd been set up by his so-called friends. It was then that he realised just how naive he had been about these people who lived in a different world from him. This class of people just take and take and never give, especially to the likes of him. They had shown him just how vicious they really were by playing this prank on him.

Tom left the room and went down to the receptionist to see whether there was another room he could use only to be told everything was booked. With a sigh he said to receptionist that it was just as well because he didn't really fit in with this group. She smiled at him knowingly.

He walked out into the rain again and started to trudge to the railway station. He had to wait for two hours in a cold waiting room for the next train back to Leeds and didn't arrive back at the university until ten.

When Tom reached his residence hall, he found Brian Onslow sitting by the fire in the common room smoking a pipe and reading a book.

"God, Tom, you look all in and thoroughly wet. Come and sit by the fire and warm up."

Brian left the room and came back with a bottle of Scotch whisky and two glasses.

"Now drink this and tell me how you got into this mess."

Tom then told him what had happened and that he was surprised to get an invitation to the party because he hadn't seen the group for some time.

"I expect you think I'm really naive."

"No, just inexperienced in the ways of this bloody world, especially with shits like them," Brian replied. "I'm not shocked by what you told me, though. I gave up seeing them weeks ago because I realised they were really shallow people who didn't give a fig about anyone else. I told them to their faces one night and they didn't like it. You'll find people like that here and in the wider world. My advice, don't let it worry you and just move on."

When Tom went to bed that night, he couldn't take Brian's advice to forget about what happened. As he thought about the trick they had played on him and the way they had treated him in the past few weeks, the more he burned with anger and was determined to exact revenge on these tormentors. Now gone was the easy-going boy he had been and what surfaced was an enraged and aggrieved human being. This vengeful side of him would plague him from time to time for the rest of his life.

4

One Friday night in a pub called the Crucible in Leeds, a group of friends gathered and Tom was with them. It wasn't Rodney Garfield's group, but friends of Brian Onslow. Tom had met them before and enjoyed their company. As Christmas was approaching, they were celebrating the end of exams.

"Let's have a singalong," Brian called out above the hubbub. "Anyone play the piano?"

"I do," said Tom as he sat down at the upright piano in the bar and lifted the lid that covered the keyboard. He sat down at the piano and they sang their favourite Christmas carols.

Late into the evening, Tom started to play his favourite jazz piano pieces. Everyone in the pub stopped talking and listened to his playing. People from the other bars came in to listen and soon he had a large audience. They applauded loudly when he finished and called for more. He obliged and it was closing time by the time he stopped.

As Tom was leaving, the pub's landlord asked him whether he'd be interested in playing on Saturday nights for his customers and he would pay him two pounds a night. Tom jumped at the chance of earning money doing something he enjoyed. And so started his Saturday gigs.

The university closed down for the Christmas holidays and Tom arrived home late on December 20th. He was looking forward to telling his father about his first term at the university, especially about the new physics experiments he was working on. Instead he was in for two surprises that would mar his news. Christmas had always been a dour celebration with just his grandfather, his father and himself. Now his grandfather was dead these gatherings had even been grimmer. He was not looking forward to it, although he was planning to look up Jason.

When he walked through the front door of his home all was dark and quiet. He heard voices coming from the living room so he opened the door and walked in. His father was sitting in his chair and, opposite him across on the other side of the fireplace with its crackling fire, was a woman whom Tom had never met. They were both deep in conversation with drinks in their hands and laughing. They were clearly enjoying each other's company, but when Tom entered the room they both fell silent.

"Hello, Tom, welcome home," said his blushing father, who obviously wasn't glad to see him. "For some reason I was expecting you home tomorrow. However, I'd like to introduce you to Patricia Hedges, who is a colleague of mine from school."

Tom shook hands with her, saying politely how nice it was to meet her. But he wondered what his father was doing with a woman in their house. His father was extremely uncomfortable because he clearly was not expecting his son to come home that night. The more Tom stared at him the redder in the face and angrier he had become.

It never occurred to Tom that maybe his forty-nine year-old father was in need of female company after the death of his wife some seventeen years previously and that she was his reason for disappearing so often not telling anyone where he was going. He never knew that his father and Patricia had been seeing each other for two years. Now their secret was out in the open.

Patricia Hedges was in her late thirties and curvaceous, but on the heavy side, as she tried to look younger than she was by wearing heavy makeup. She had a pretty face with sparkling blue eyes and she smiled warily at Tom as he approached her to shake hands. She was dressed in a beaded mesh evening dress that went mid-way down her calves. The dress had a revealing V-necked top that showed off the outline of her ample breasts. Her black hair was short, rather boyish, which had been fashionable in the 1920s but not now, and she had a curl of hair over each ear. Her long, elegant legs were fashionably crossed at the ankles as she sat in his grandpa's chair.

Patricia was originally from Ilkley in Yorkshire. She was a widow who had no children and she needed to support herself after her husband had eventually died. He had a lung disease caused by a mustard gas explosion in the trenches at Third Battle of Ypres during World War One. He had been a second lieutenant in the Second Middlesex Regiment and was gassed on his first day in the trenches in 1917. It had taken him ten years to slowly die in excruciating pain and all the time Patricia had nursed him constantly at a hospital for officers and then at home.

After he died, she showed no interest in men. She was exhausted and it took some time for her to determine her future. Their small savings had enabled her to go to university and get a degree in English literature. She was able then to pursue a teaching career first in London and she had returned home to Yorkshire to look for a position. Tom's father had found her one at the Jarrow Grammar School.

Tom didn't realise what Patricia's motivations were with his father. In her mind, it was called preservation. After her husband's death, she soon realised that in that day's society she needed to find a husband. Security was the key to survival and status in her middle-class world. The war had created too many single women and widows and she was determined not to be one of them. That sounded callous, but it was the reality of life in the economically depressed world she found herself in in 1934.

In her hunt for a husband, she had been out with several men and had actually been engaged twice, but none of them had met her exacting standards. Tom's father suited her fine. She wasn't really in love with him but respected him with his rather conservative ways and his sound professional reputation. She would soon mould him to her needs and the first step was moving from the depressed town of Jarrow. She knew Tom's father was besotted with her and she had made sure he had fallen in love with her as she made her plans.

"Why don't you take your things upstairs and come and join us?" said Tom's father. "You know where the beer is. We have something important to tell you."

Tom climbed the stairs to his room, puzzled about his homecoming surprise. He lay on his bed and started thinking about Patricia and trying to fathom out what he had just witnessed meant. She was not the image of a schoolteacher he had been used to. He certainly didn't warm to her at this first meeting because he sensed she was holding back something and she had not been amiable towards him. It was a very awkward first meeting. Irrationally, he resented her intrusion into his family, especially at this time of year. He was confused about what his father was doing bringing this woman into their house. In truth, he was jealous of her for usurping the relationship with his father, however distant it was. These thoughts tumbled through his confused mind.

"Tom, where are you, lad?" called his father. "We are waiting for you."

Tom reluctantly went downstairs, poured himself a beer in the kitchen and re-entered the living room.

"Ah, there you are, lad. Come and sit down because we have some important news for you," said his father, rather too enthusiastically. "The first is that Patricia and I are going to be married. We are planning a small wedding in April. What do you think of that, lad?"

To say that he was totally stunned at the news was putting it mildly. The shock must have showed on his face as he looked at them both smiling. Eventually, after what seemed like a long time, he blurted out, "I don't know what to say. It is all a big surprise."

"How about congratulations then, son?" said his somewhat irritated father.

"Of course. Congratulations. I never knew anything about this and it has come as a bit of a shock."

"You may kiss me, Tom," ordered Patricia. Tom got up from his chair reluctantly and obligingly pecked her on one of her cheeks.

"The other part of our news," continued his father, "is that we are moving to Durham. Patricia and I have been offered teaching posts there which we are taking up in September next year. We are busy trying to find a house near the school and we will also be selling this place as soon as possible."

"That's a lot of change, Dad. Your news has blown me away. I never dreamed that you would remarry after so many years alone."

"Nor did I, Tom, but Patricia swept me off my feet."

"Also, are you sure you want to leave your hometown?"

"I'm afraid Jarrow has become a ghost town. There is nothing here for us now. So it's time we moved on."

"What about me?" Tom asked. "How will this affect my university studies?"

"Not to worry. Your mother left money aside for this and your small allowance so that things won't change."

"What will happen to me during the holidays? Where will I stay?"

"You would be welcome to stay in our spare room," answered Patricia.

"I won't have my own room!" cried Tom.

"Listen. You will be finished at university in the next two years and starting a career of your own. And, as such, you will want to rent your own place," said his father soothingly.

"So I'm being kicked out! I'm to fend for myself because you're married again and don't want me anymore," Tom raged.

"It's not like that, son."

"Don't worry about me then. I'll just go and stay with Jason and remain in Jarrow."

"You ungrateful boy! After all your father has done for you, all you can think of is yourself!" Patricia responded angrily.

"Isn't that what you are doing?" Tom responded accusingly.

Tom didn't realise it, but that comment stung Patricia because it was so near the truth. She realised that maybe he had worked out her scheming towards his father. This was dangerous as his dad might get some inkling of what she was up to.

Tom felt quite sick and stormed out of the room. He went up to his bedroom and cried about the loss of his family as he knew it.

As he went upstairs, he heard his father angrily speaking to Patricia: "Don't say such things to my son again, do you hear me! I'll deal with him, not you!"

"I'm sorry, Frank, I just thought that it needed to be said as this situation affects us all."

"Look, please let me deal with my own son my own way. I know him better than anyone," he said calmly.

"Do you, Frank? It's funny how university changes people's outlook on life and their beliefs are sometimes re-formed. I wonder whether that has happened to Tom. Anyway, it's time I went home."

The next day, Tom left the house in the late afternoon as Jason wouldn't be home from work until about six. He had had the whole day to himself as his father was at the grammar school as its term time finished on December 23rd. As he walked along Monkton Road he was struck by the quietness of the town. There was a lack of Christmas cheer emanating from homes. They were not decorated for the season as they had been before, each home in the past trying to outdo the others on the street. What was strange was there weren't any children playing in the streets.

When he crossed Ormonde Street, which was one of the main

shopping streets of Jarrow, there were hardly any shoppers. At this time of year there was usually a sea of people doing their last-minute shopping. Outside of the new Woolworth's store there were six or seven members of a Salvation Army band playing mournful Christmas carols to nobody in particular and certainly nobody was there to appreciate them.

Tom found Jason's house in Walters Street and knocked on the door. After a while the door opened and Edith was standing there dressed in a black dress and looking very haggard with uncombed hair. Her face was puffy and her eyes were red with crying. She was heavily pregnant and had a look of desperation on her lined face.

"Edith, what's the matter?"

"You'd better come in, Tom."

He went into the kitchen and sat down at the table while Edith made tea without saying a word.

"Tell me what is going on. I got into town last night late so I haven't had a chance to talk to Jason."

Edith stopped what she was doing and looked at him and burst into tears. He went over to her to comfort her and he helped her to sit down.

When she gathered herself she blurted out: "Jason is dead, Tom. He was killed a week ago at work." And she burst into tears again and sobbed uncontrollably.

Tom was so shocked he didn't say a word. And then he gulped and, holding back tears that he knew would come, asked softly: "Why didn't you contact me? I would have been here for you, you know that."

"I didn't know how to contact you, but I did tell your father."

Tom grew angry at this, but he knew he had to calm down and help Edith the best way he could.

After a few seconds, he asked her what happened to Jason.

"I don't know exactly, but some of his mates told me a boiler was being winched across the workshop and the chains holding it just snapped. The whole thing came tumbling down on Jason and another man," she sobbed. "We buried him last week and I received this letter when I got back from the funeral."

She handed Tom a letter which informed her that she must vacate the rented home the following week.

"What are you going to do, Edith?"

"His company gave me fifty pounds' compensation so I will save it for the bairn. My parents have hired a moving firm to collect my things and I will go back and live with them. It's not the greatest of situations, but I have to do it for my bairn's sake."

"Only fifty pounds?" he asked, askance.

"Yes. I complained to the personnel people at his work and they told me I was lucky to get that because the accident, they claimed, was partly his fault. I know from his mates that this wasn't true. They probably blamed him because he wasn't there to defend himself."

And then she started to sob again and he put his arm around her.

Tom was livid at the treatment of Edith and the callous way Jason's death had been handled by the company. He knew something must be done to change the way employers treated their workers. He saw his grandpa's point of view about workers taking over the running of companies. He was determined to right the wrong he saw. His grandpa had mentioned the Russian Revolution as shining example of what could be done, so he planned to read what books or articles he could find at the university's library on communism. He owed Jason, Edith and their child that much to see if there was a better way for people like him to live.

Then there was a loud banging at the front door. When Edith opened it there were three rough men, who were the bailiffs, demanded she leave as they wanted to begin moving her furniture out into the street.

"Stop!" said Tom, standing in their way. "She has just lost her husband! Can't you show some compassion? It is Christmas, after all."

"Who are you then?" asked their foreman.

"I'm a family friend. Her father is coming to move things out after Christmas. Can't you leave it until then?"

"'Fraid not, lad. We don't get paid until we move her out and we have mouths to feed just like everyone else. Now get out of the way, four eyes, or you'll regret interfering."

Tom just stood there. The foreman grabbed by the labels and threw him out of the front door and the other two men punched and kicked him until he lost conscious. They then began to move Edith's belonging out of the house.

Then suddenly a loud voice screamed at them: "Oi! Stop where you are!" And about six of Jason's friends appeared armed with cudgels. They appeared seemingly out of the blue but in truth a neighbour had sent one of her children to warn the men about what was happening. They made short shift of the bailiffs who were beaten up and escaped.

Tom sat on the pavement feeling very groggy. He put his broken glasses back on and began to get up. Strong arms helped him to his feet and held him up as he wobbled from side to side. Finally, he was able to stand on his own.

"Thanks. It seems that we won the first round, but they'll be back," he said to the men. "Does anyone know anybody that has access to a lorry? We need to move Edith tonight."

After a lot of discussion among the men, the leader of the group called David Lambert said that he knew someone but it would cost money. Tom took out his wallet and handed David two pound notes. "Will this do?" he asked.

It took an hour before a lorry arrived. In the meantime most of the men remained and stood guard over the house. Once the lorry had been loaded with Edith's few possessions, they set out for her parents' home in North Shields. They had to cross the River Tyne on a ferry, which they just caught in time.

Their reception at her parents' house was frosty, to put it mildly, but after Tom explained the situation to her father they were more understanding. Edith went straight to her room to lie down because the strain of the day had exhausted her. Her mother fussed over Tom and cleaned up his cuts as the other men unloaded the lorry.

By the time they had unloaded Edith's belongings and driven back to Jarrow, it was just gone nine in the evening. Tom brought everyone a round of beer at a local pub and when he got home it was about ten thirty.

His father heard him come in and called out from the living room. When he entered the room his father was alone drinking whisky. This was unusual because he wasn't much of a drinker. He seemed to have had too much as his speech was slurred.

"What the hell happened to you, boy?" he demanded, seeing Tom's appearance.

"Jason's dead and you didn't tell me! Why not?!" This was all that he could say.

"You can stop yelling at me right now, do you hear?"

"Well, why?" Tom demanded.

"I did know, but I just forgot because when she told me I was leaving the house to go away to London for the weekend. It just skipped my mind and by the time I had got back I'd forgotten about it. I only remembered when you said you were going to see him so I thought I'd leave it for you to find out from Edith. I'm sorry, lad. You wouldn't have got back in time for his funeral even if I had told you because she didn't tell me in time. Anyway, why are you so bruised and dishevelled?"

Tom took a deep breath and calmed down. He then told his father what had happened and that he and a number of Jason's friends had moved Edith to her parents' home.

"This bloody town!" cried his father. "It'll be death of us all, you mark my words. It killed your grandpa as it has done with many good men over the years. Grandpa was obsessed with this town and wanted to do good to its people. Look what it did to him. He became more fixated with his politics and the more he tried the more he was stressed about life. It killed your grandma early too. Grandad was made of sterner stuff but it eventually got him.

"'Thank God I'm moving away. The only good news is that I've been able to sell this damned house today to a young solicitor who doesn't know any better. He has agreed that we can move out at the end of the summer term in July."

Tom didn't argue or respond to his father and he just let him ramble on. After a while his father fell asleep in his chair and Tom took his glass from his hand. He put a blanket over him, turned the light off and went to bed.

Tom lay in bed thinking about the grim sights he had seen that day. He had also seen the kindness shown by some men to someone who was in trouble and how they had gathered around to help. These were good people who would rally to help each other despite their own difficulties. They shouldn't be deserted.

Events in the last few months culminating in that day was the beginning of Tom's metamorphosis in his views of life and society. It made him more determined than ever to do something about changing the inequities in society as he saw them.

Christmas Day was a cheerless affair for Tom. There were just the three of them. He felt like an unwanted guest at a private party and was someone who everybody put up with because they had no option. Patricia and his father flirted with each other all the time and were heedless of his presence.

Tom was quietly angry at this as he scowled at them and wondered why his father ignored him. He felt they had lost the intimacy of father and son that they once enjoyed, or did they have it in the first place? He now realised that they had never been that close and he wondered why. His father's affection for him, if it was ever there, was now gone for ever. The more he thought about it, he realised that his father had gone through the motions of bringing him up and now he was at university his father had tasted freedom as he had never known before. But he still didn't know why.

As Tom pondered their relationship over the years, he realised that his father hadn't ever been warm and affectionate. In reality, the more he thought about it, his father had been quite distant at times with him. Truth was, it was Tom's grandpa who had taken care of him and had been his real father.

After church, they had a Christmas lunch of two small chickens with all the trimmings and celebrated with a bottle of wine. Tom had bought another tartan tie for his father, who seemed to be delighted with the present. However, when he was helping Patricia in the kitchen with the washing up and his father was upstairs having a nap, she told him that she was trying to wean him off wearing that type of boring tie and that she would appreciate it if he would not buy him any others.

"Tell me, Tom, what are your plans for the summer holiday?" Patricia asked, handing him a plate to dry.

"I hadn't thought about that. I'll probably be with you in Durham," he said, taking the plate, drying it and putting it away in a cupboard.

"That won't be possible, I'm afraid. My niece will be staying with us as she is a student at the University of Durham and we only have one spare room."

"Oh! So I'm being turned out without so much as any consideration from my father. I'll go and see him right now and sort this out!" He stormed out of the kitchen, slamming the door as he went.

His father was coming down the stairs, pulling his braces on as he went.

"What's all the noise about?" he asked.

"Is it true that I am no longer welcome in your house, Father?" Tom demanded vehemently with tears welling up in his eyes. "That woman in there said I can't stay with you in Durham in the summertime. Is that true?!"

"That woman is my fiancée and I will not have you speak about her like that," shot back a very angry Frank Pearson. "It's time you grew up, boy, and faced the world. You'll have to find your own place to live with the money your mother left you and make your own way in life, just as I've had to do. I have been trapped here like some celibate monk for years making sure you were properly brought up. I promised your mother that! Well, that's going to end right here and now! I've got my own life to lead and I'm not letting you get in the way of my future with Patricia. It's over between us!"

Tom had never seen his father so angry, but he persisted.

"So you plan to abandon your son because you've met this woman, is that it?! Where do I come into your plans, or do I?"

His father slapped him hard on his face and the force of the blow knocked him to the floor.

"I want you out of this house tomorrow and I don't want to see you ever again, boy! I've spent years rearing you as your mother wanted, but you aren't even my son, so now I wash my hands of you!"

"What do you mean I'm not your son?" Tom demanded from the floor, rubbing his swollen face.

"Your wretched mother left me soon after we were married and lived with someone at the university where she was doing her PhD. She got pregnant with you and her so-called lover kicked her out. I, like a fool, took her back and I've regretted it ever since. So pack your bags and go and let me enjoy what's left of my life!"

"Did Grandpa know the truth?"

"No. We were living in Manchester at the time and he wasn't aware of what went on. He was too busy with his politics anyway to understand!"

Frank Pearson stormed into the living room and slammed the door behind him.

Tom spent the night in a daze of disbelief as he packed his belongings into cardboard boxes. But many questions remained unanswered as he put his few possessions in boxes and sobbed. What had turned this usually calm man so viscerally against him?

Maybe Tom's reluctance to accept Patricia was the last straw that made him finally break.

As he thought about his upbringing, he realised that his so-called father had treated him like one of his pupils at school, distant but always helpful. He got used to this and didn't think it was abnormal, although his grandfather had sometimes admonished his father for not showing any affection towards him. Why had he been living this lie? Tom realised that he must have really loved his mother to have put up with this shame all these years. These thoughts whirled through Tom's mind.

Tom had never really had a comforting or fulfilling family life, particularly after his grandfather had died. He had spent most of his time in his room with his electronic equipment. His so-called father had made no effort over the years to understand and befriend him or to take him on trips to, for example, the seaside or to see London with its vast history and museums. On reflection, Tom felt that his now-stepfather had been cold and only did the minimum to bring him up. He supposed the man resented him and saw this other man's child as a burden he had to bear in order to keep the home he had inherited from his wife. He certainly could not afford to live there on his teacher's salary.

When he got up the next morning, the house was empty. On the kitchen table was an envelope addressed to him. Inside there was a cheque made out to him for fifteen thousand pounds, but there was nothing else like a note from the man that had been his father.

When Tom left the house later in the morning with his luggage, he turned and looked up at it for a long time. He knew he would never see it again but recognised he would retain fond memories of growing up there and of his beloved grandfather.

5

It was Boxing Day when Tom caught a train from Jarrow with connections to Leeds. As it was a public holiday, the train service was spotty so that he arrived very late in the evening at New Station in Leeds. He checked in at the Old Griffin Hotel on Boar Lane in the Leeds city centre for two nights because the university's residences were closed. He ate a solitary meal in the only pub he could find open.

That night was worse than the night before. He tossed and turned in bed trying to sleep, which did not come, and by the three in the morning he was still awake. He eventually got up and started to make a list of what he had to do the next day. The university term did not start until January 8th so he had some time to get his new life somewhat organised.

It was strange, but he felt a sense of relief that his life had changed so dramatically. The emotions he felt when he first learned of his predicament were put in the back of his mind and now he had become cool and calculating. He wondered who his biological father was, but he felt that he did not want to know, at least not at that moment, especially because of the way the man had treated his mother. He thought that his biological father certainly did not want to meet his son and had probably forgotten about his affair with his mother. Tom knew he was better on his own, but he felt a tinge of sadness for the man who was his stepfather. He believed that Frank's new-found love was calculating and had an agenda for him which he would eventually find out about too late.

The next morning, Tom walked into the nearby Midland Bank on Boar Lane and opened a current account with the cheque his stepfather had given him. Armed with a new cheque book, he walked to the university and received a list of their approved lodgings and started to look for somewhere to live. Most of the places had been taken because it was the middle of the university year except for an attic room in a house which was about a mile from the university. The room had just come on the rental market and was larger than most he had seen. He paid his new landlady a month's rent in advance and told her he would be moving in the next day and that he wanted the room on a year-round basis until he graduated. This suited Mrs. Price, who was recently widowed and needed the income. She was a very friendly, jolly woman of about fifty, and she and Tom hit it off almost a once.

Tom then looked for a bicycle shop. After asking passers-by and after a few wrong turns, he eventually found one. He bought a second-hand bike and a lock and chain. Now he was ready for his new life.

That night, Tom went to a local pub near his new home and was enjoying a beer when someone touched him on his shoulder. He turned around and there smiling at him was Dr. Gerald Young, one of his lecturers on his physics course.

"Hello, Tom. What are you doing back here so early?"

He explained that because his stepfather was moving to Durham he had decided to come back early and find a place to live. He told Dr. Young where he was now living and it turned out that his professor lived nearby in a Georgian terraced house.

"I'm glad I bumped into you," Dr. Young said. "I need some help with an experiment I'm doing about sound wave oscillation. You were top of the class last term and I was very impressed with your work. I was wondering whether you could help me. I'd like to pick your brains."

"I'd be delighted," Tom said. Inside he was excited and couldn't wait to start work.

"Good. Meet me at the physics and chemistry labs tomorrow morning at nine. I'll be in Room 231."

They talked further about Dr. Young's experiment.

"What do you plan to do after university?" Dr. Young asked.

"I'd probably try and get a master's degree in electrical engineering so I can work in that field," he replied.

In the next week and a half before the university term started Tom was busy with Dr. Young working hard on his various experiments. He had made a few suggestions which turned out to be successful and Dr. Young was very impressed with his work.

On January 8th, the new term started at the University of Leeds and Tom was busy with the round of lectures and homework. However, he spent some time in the laboratories working on his own and Dr. Young's projects. He occasionally saw Rodney Garfield and his friends in the refectory, but he avoided any contact with them and they him.

One evening Tom was invited to dinner with Dr. Young and his wife, who told him he needed feeding up because he was too skinny. He liked Susan Young and, as time went by, he had a number of dinner dates with their home, which sometimes included other university faculty members or PhD students.

Conversations at these dinners usually centred on left-wing politics and growing discontent with the government's handling of the chronic unemployment situation in the north of England. A major topic was concern with the rise of the far-right British Union of Fascists (BUF) led by Sir Oswald Mosley, particularly this movement's antisemitism. A BUF rally at London's Olympia in 1934 had led to serious and vicious attacks on anti-fascist demonstrators. Known as the Blackshirts because of the black uniforms they wore, the BUF at this time (1935/36) were expanding their recruiting efforts in the north of England.

Tom always enjoyed these dinners, especially when Dr. John Rivers, a history professor, was there to launch into erudite criticism of world affairs as he saw them. One particular evening he voiced his concern about people being drawn into what he called the poisoned web of fascism.

"These fascists appeal to some of the desperate, unemployed workers in that they give them the false hope of a better life," he said angrily. "They boast about their right-wing movement cousins in Italy and Germany as shining examples of what could be achieved. It is true that Mussolini is beginning to turn around Italy's dire economic fortunes, but his military aspirations are a real cause for concern. But at what cost to their people has this turnaround been? How has he done this? He has stifled and eliminated opposition to his plans. Hitler, with his Brownshirts in Germany, does the same. Alright, he is leading a resurgence of that county's economy despite the depression of the early 1930s and retribution for the Great War, which was placed on it by the victorious allies in 1919 at the Treaty of Versailles. But at what cost to people in the long run? Again they are telling people 'Do it my way or suffer the consequences' and so we have assassinations and imprisonment for those who oppose him.

"What do we have today? All pretence of democracy in Germany and Italy has vanished and they have become true dictatorships. And what we do about this as a country when Hitler tramples on the Versailles Treaty? Nothing! The French are useless as well! They are all frightened of upsetting the applecart and starting another war. Our newspapers are full of articles about the rise of fascism in these countries and still the government does nothing! I thought Stanley Baldwin, when he took over from Ramsey McDonald as Prime Minister, would take action, but no! So what are we going to do?

"The only challenge to this dire political situation is strong opposition from socialists and communists such as most people around this table. We need a government with backbone to put a stop to these fascists. What do you think, young Tom?"

There was a palpable silence around the table as all eyes turned to Tom, and he quickly gathered his thoughts.

"We have to show people there is another way instead of forcing them against their wishes and telling them what's good for them. The only way we can turn our country around is if workers take over the economy and succeed in providing for everyone, not just a few. In other words, we need to lead by example and show the rest of Europe what can be achieved. I'm not insightful enough, but my thought is that this fascism would eventually destroy itself."

"Well said, Tom. I hope you're right, but I think it is going to take some years of sacrifice to achieve this," said Dr. Young.

Tom's remarks were noted by a pretty young lecturer, Jane Harcourt, who was in her first year in the faculty of the arts. Little did he know at the time that Jane wanted to hear more from him about his political ideas as he might be a possible recruit to help in her cause.

Several days later, Tom was in the refractory for a hurried lunch and on his way out he looked at the university union noticeboard. There was a mess of papers pinned haphazardly on the board announcing such activities as sport clubs, the debating society dates, bazaars and dances, some of which were past due as no one bothered to take them down. In a lower corner there was a notice about the Leeds University Socialist Society which met monthly on the first Wednesday of each month.

When the next month came around, Tom set off to the meeting not knowing what to expect. He was the first to arrive in a meeting room in the Great Hall. When he walked into the room it was set up with about twenty folding chairs and a lectern was at the far end.

"Welcome, comrade. Are you here for the meeting?" said a voice behind him. He turned and saw a seemingly cadaverous man with a cigarette hanging out of his mouth. He had a hunched-over bird-like frame and was wearing clothes that were too big for him and were in need of a clean. He couldn't have been much older than Tom but looked middle-aged. Tom couldn't guess his age as his looks were very deceiving.

"Hello, I'm Tom Pearson. Yes, I'm here for the meeting. What's the subject and who is giving it?"

"I'm Frederick Thomas and I'm the erstwhile chairman of this group. The subject tonight is 'The Labour Party's Failure to Properly Represent the Working Man'." And with this statement he almost collapsed in a fit of coughing. When he had got his breath back he finished what he was about to say: "The speaker is Tony Cox, deputy secretary of the Durham Miners' Association."

Just then a group of students came in and Tom introduced himself to them. By the time the speaker arrived the room was surprisingly full with a number of people standing around. The speaker was very critical of the Labour Party as he saw them not providing a feasible opposition to the government in Parliament. He was particularly acerbic about their lack of support for the unemployed and the nonexistence of good contracts for the failing companies in the north of England and the lack of proper working conditions, particularly in the coal mines.

Much of what the speaker said Tom could relate to because of his experiences in Jarrow. At question time, Tom put his hand up and asked: "I'm Tom Pearson from Jarrow. Isn't the solution to our country's problems eventually going to be to follow the Russian model?"

"Ideally, yes, but that may be wishful thinking as it couldn't happen here. The establishment is too entrenched unlike the chaos that was in Russia in 1916 and 1917. What we need to do is use our strike-power because it's the only lever we have to force change. I know of the problem you have in Jarrow with the shipyard closing and I believe the only recourse against this Tory government is to demonstrate and march on Whitehall."

After the meeting Tom was invited to join a group of the students for drinks in a local pub. There they carried on the discussion from the meeting. Several of them said they were going to a meeting of the BUF to heckle the speakers at the Miners' Welfare Hall in Deaf Hill, a village in County Durham. The featured speaker was to be, none other than, Sir Oswald Mosley, the BUF leader. They said that there would be a bus leaving the university early in the morning on the day of his speech for the eighty-mile journey. Tom declined to join the group because the day of the meeting was a Monday and he had classes and work to do for Dr. Young. He asked them to keep him in the loop for other demonstrations. However, he wondered why they skipped classes on a weekday and how they got away with it.

The next time Tom saw them at the next monthly meeting, several of the men had bruised faces and one had an arm in a sling. Apparently they had been prevented from attending the meeting by some uniformed BUF marshals and were beaten up for their trouble. They seemed very dejected and generally felt sorry for themselves. They passed a motion at the meeting deploring treatment in the exercise of their rights. Tom thought this was a waste of time. It was then he realised what a sham this society was and it was not for him. He didn't attend any more meetings.

Towards the end of the university year in June, Tom was walking towards the physics building when he saw Jane Harcourt, the arts lecturer he had met at a dinner with Dr. Young and his wife. He had seen her occasionally at the Socialist Society meetings but had never talked to her.

"Hello, Tom, I haven't seen you around recently at the Socialist Society meetings. Where have you been hiding?" she asked pleasantly.

"I got bored with their meetings and their infantile motions that mean nothing and have no practical effect. The speakers aren't revolutionary enough. They talk about just fixing the system that already exists, not radically changing it. Anyway, I got more involved in my studies and haven't got the time for their nonsense."

This was the first time Tom had actually spoken to Jane one on one and the first time he had really looked at her. She was petite with long black hair which that day was done up in a bun on the back of her head. She was wearing a light-brown dress. As he stared at her, admiring her beauty, he became embarrassed and looked down. Jane, seeing his embarrassment, smiled and lightly touched his arm. At the dinner at Dr. Young's home, he had noted the intensity in her manner and her thoughts when she talked seemed to have a depth to their meaning. This fascinated him about her.

"Look, I agree with what you say, so how about if I invite you as my guest on Saturday to the Victory Hotel here in Leeds to hear some real change-makers?" she asked.

"Fine. I'd enjoy that. Who are they?"

"Harry Pollitt, the General Secretary of the Communist Party of Great Britain, and R. Palme Dutt, the party's chief theorist. I think Ellen Wilkinson, MP for Jarrow, will be there. She was one of the founders of the Communist Party of Great Britain and she's a real firebrand," said Jane admiringly.

"Meet me outside the hotel at one on Saturday afternoon and we'll listen in to the speeches. I'll see you then." And she turned tail and walked off, leaving Tom standing there with his mouth open and with a lovelorn desire to see her again.

Little did he know that thirty-year-old Jane Harcourt was a member of the Communist Party and a Russian agent. Her real name was Lady Penelope Weston, the daughter of the Marquis of Lancaster, who had broken off contact with her family because of her radical political beliefs. She had gone to Roedean, the top girls' public school, and on to the University of Oxford, where she was active in the communist society there.

After graduating from university with a first-class honours degree in English literature, she fell in with a radical set of friends in London and was recruited by the Russians. Unbeknownst to the group, they had been closely watched by MI5, the British security service, and, tipped off by a contact, she had vanished. She spent a year at the International Lenin School in Moscow, where she and other communists from around the world, who were regarded as potential leaders, studied Marxist/Leninist theory, as well as political subversion and organisation. She reappeared as Jane Harcourt in the north of England in 1935 and was tasked with spotting possible Russian agents.

Tom arrived at the Victory Hotel well in advance of the one o'clock hour. He had shaved and bathed that morning and put on his best suit. He wanted to look his best for Jane. He had become so besotted with her and would do anything for her, just to please her. As he left his digs, his landlady joshed him about his appearance and said he looked as though he was going to meet a girlfriend. She laughed at her own joke because she knew that this was unlikely.

Tom stood at entrance to the hotel and waited. It was five minutes past the hour before Jane appeared and not from the street but from the hotel. With his heart racing, he joined her in the hotel reception area and she introduced him to a number of other people who had gathered for the meeting. They took their seats in the ballroom of the hotel and the chairwoman, Ellen Wilkinson MP, gave a few remarks then introduced the speakers, Harry Pollitt and R. Palme Dutt. During this time, Jane watched out of the corner of her eye Tom's reaction to the speeches and was pleased with what she saw. After the presentations they went to a number of small group meetings and Tom asked a number of insightful questions of the speakers, so much so that he was sought after by a few of the audience who were interested in his thoughts.

As they left the hotel after five that evening he was excited about meeting so many interesting people and was rambling on about this to Jane, and he did not notice where they were going.

"Tom, stop!" cried Jane with her hand up.

"I'm sorry to be such a bore. Thank you for inviting me today."

Jane smiled: "Would you like to come to dinner at my flat and we can talk further about the day?"

"Oh, yes. I would be delighted."

They walked to her home on Woodhouse Lane, which was a flat on the second floor in an Edwardian terraced house. She opened the front door to the flat and they hung their coats up in the hall.

She told Tom she needed help in the kitchen and put him to work peeling potatoes. Once she had put a whole chicken in the oven she opened a bottle of Burgundy wine and they went into the living room and began talking about the day.

As Tom drank the wine, he became more animated and his shyness melted away. Jane had become more mellow and relaxed as well. They enjoyed their dinner and another bottle of fine wine. Jane offered Tom a brandy, which he accepted. She disappeared into her bedroom and reappeared wearing just a silk dressing gown.

"Would you like to stay the night, Tom?" she asked him as she sat next to him on the sofa and stroked his thigh.

"What do you mean?"

"Oh, Tom, what do you think?"

She stood up and dropped her dressing gown on the floor, then sat back down, and he stared at her naked body.

"Have you ever done this before?" she asked as she undid the buttons on his fly.

"No."

"Well, I'll teach you."

6

The next morning, Jane watched through her living-room window as Tom walked down the stone steps from her front door and along the garden path to the front gate. She thought he seemed on top of the world and had a spring in his step as he nonchalantly opened the gate and started to skip down the road. His blasé behaviour was totally out of character from that of just yesterday.

For his part, Tom thought Jane must have been satisfied with their intimacy because of the way she had reacted to their lovemaking after his clumsiness and mistakes at first. She was a good and patient teacher. For him, the night was magnificent and he was ecstatic about learning how please a woman, particularly someone as sophisticated and experienced as Jane.

But this was Jane's modus operandi. Somehow, she had this need to totally control the people she recruited before she handed them on to her contacts at the Russian Embassy in London, and sex completed this domination. To her it didn't matter if her recruits were male or female; she had to have complete power over them before she was ready to release them to others.

Of course at the time Tom didn't know or suspect this and, naively, he felt extremely satisfied and madly in love as he walked down the road towards his digs. He was almost singing with joy as he opened his front door and started to climb the stairs to his flat. As he began to climb up the stairs, Mrs. Price emerged from her rooms on the ground floor.

"And where have you been, young Tom?" she asked with a grin on her face.

"You'll be surprised," he responded.

"Well, I hope she's good to you," she said, and giggled as she went back into her flat.

Tom blushed at this and hurried up to his room.

The university ended its academic year on July 1st and the buildings were oddly silent again. The hustle and bustle of students going to lectures, to the refectory or to society meetings in the evenings was gone until October, when the new academic year started. All that was left were empty buildings and a few academic staff. Some of them had disappeared on trips to do research in their respective fields or they had simply taken a holiday.

Tom continued to work for Dr. Young and was seeing Jane in the evenings. They would go for picnics on the grounds of Kirkstall Abbey and he even tried his hand at rowing on the River Aire which flowed past the city of Leeds. He was deeply in love with Jane and thought she was in love with him. She never said so but the fact that she gave herself to him was proof enough, he thought in his naiveté.

One day at the physics laboratory, Dr. Young introduced Tom to Stewart Franklin, a graduate student who had become part of the professor's team. He had come from the University of Edinburgh and was starting his PhD studies in the upcoming academic year. Stewart was a small, bespectacled, owlish man standing at just over five feet tall. Everything about him was small. His hands were tiny and well-manicured. He was immaculately dressed in a three-piece tweed suit, with highly polished brown shoes on his small feet.

Stewart's home was in the Sottish border town of Peebles where his father owned a small clothing store and his mother worked as a secretary to the managing director for one of the town's woollen mills. With traditional Scottish frugality, his parents scrimped and saved and were able to send him to Fettes College in Edinburgh, which was and is a leading boys' private boarding school. From there he had gone on to the University of Edinburgh and had graduated with a degree in physics.

Despite his outward, stuffy appearance, he was extremely funny with a wicked sense of humour and he had a very infectious laugh. As Tom grew to know him, he enjoyed his companionship and they became inseparable after their days spent in the laboratory. At work, they would get into deep discussions about the experiments they were doing that often boiled over into arguments, which Dr. Young had to adjudicate. To an outsider, their behaviour was like two brothers who wouldn't let the other win an argument. But their work for Dr. Young produced results and he was happy that his hunch about putting them together had worked out.

In the talks Stewart and Tom had in the pubs of an evening, it became evident that he was a socialist by nature and had voted for the Labour Party in recent elections. But he was disillusioned by the party and its policies and was thinking about switching his vote to the Independent Labour Party, which was a more radical and left-wing and had broken away from the Labour Party in 1932.

Stewart was interested to hear Tom's description of life in Jarrow and the unending unemployment that workers had suffered there for years. Tom took him one weekend to his old hometown and Stewart was amazed at the poverty he saw and the depressing conversations he had with a number of Tom's acquaintances.

As they sat down in a pub the evening before they left Jarrow, Stewart began to vociferously talk about what he had seen. "My eyes have been truly opened for the first time to the real plight of working people. I suppose I'm what you'd call an intellectual socialist. I've only been to meetings, read books and newspaper articles, but I have never been exposed to the harsh reality of life on the margins such as that I have seen in Jarrow."

"But you know, Stewart, Jarrow is just one town of many in northern England that is suffering," added Tom.

On the way back to Leeds from Jarrow on the train, Stewart sat silently looking out of the window thinking about what he had seen.

"Penny for your thoughts," Tom said.

"Sorry for being a bore, but I can't get over what I saw in Jarrow. There has to be radical change to these people's lives. We can't go on like this and pretend it never happened and close our minds to their suffering. But I don't know what the answer is. The Labour Party is not suggesting any solutions that would work. It's a real puzzle."

"I was reading recently about how the Russians have turned around their country after the 1917 revolution," Tom said. "Workers there are now in charge of their own destinies. Maybe we should do the same here."

"A revolution? Would it work in this country?"

"I think so. What have we got to lose?"

They both fell silent for the rest of the journey. When they reached Leeds they parted, with Stewart returning to his flat and Tom setting off to meet Jane at her home. As he turned the corner into her street he was unaware of the surprise he was in for.

Tom walked up the path to her building, opened the front door and knocked on her flat door. There was no answer, so he knocked again. The sound of his knocking seemed to echo around the flat. Now he became concerned and took out the key Jane had given him for emergencies and opened the door. As he swung the door open, he got the surprise of his life. The flat was bereft of all her furniture and her belongings. He looked around. Everything was gone. She had just disappeared. Why? What had he done?

Tom saw two other residents of the building and asked them whether they knew where she was. They told him that a moving van loaded her things the day before, but that's all they knew.

Distraught, Tom went to see Dr. Young, who also had no idea

that she had gone. He reassured Tom that he would look into her disappearance the following day. Tom eventually returned to his own flat and lay on his bed thinking back to whether there had been any indication of her having a problem with him. They had never had an argument. None came to mind and he sobbed.

The next day was agonising for Tom. Dr. Young did as he promised and checked with the university's administration. She had sent a letter of resignation but had left no forwarding address, so no one knew how to get in touch with her.

Shortly afterwards, Tom was riding a local bus in Leeds on his way to a bookshop for Dr. Young, when he thought he had spotted Jane walking on the pavement. He got off the bus quickly and he was able to catch up with the figure he had seen, but when he called her name she didn't respond. When he caught up with her and she turned, he saw it wasn't Jane. He apologised to the woman and explained his mistake.

Tom spent many restless nights after that, and Dr. Young and Stewart tried to talk to him and help him get over the sudden breakup with his first real love. His work suffered and in the end Dr. Young suggested he take time off to help him get over his loss.

Tom spent the time walking around Leeds and the countryside deep in thought, trying to rationalise his breakup with Jane. How could she just up sticks and leave with no explanation? It was obvious that she didn't love him the same way he loved her. Their relationship had been a mirage that had suddenly vanished and he was left to pick up the pieces of his crushed feeling of self-worth.

This had been his first love and a more mature person would get annoyed, yes, but then move on and write the loss down to experience. But behind all this he felt that he had been let down badly a second time in his life by someone who he thought loved him. First there was his stepfather, who Tom thought was his biological father, and now Jane. Despondency came over him again and he began to feel extremely sorry for himself and even suicidal. Many questions fermented in his mind. Why did this happen to him? Didn't other people go through this and then move on? Why couldn't he? How do you do that? Then something deep down in his psyche finally welled up and, angrily, he resolved that this would never happen to him again. He had too many things to do with his life and from now on he would focus all his attention on them.

The next day he went back to work at the laboratory and he apologised to everyone. After that not a word was spoken again about Jane.

Towards the end of September an important event in north-eastern England happened which opened Tom's eyes to what was occurring in many European countries.

It came about when he knocked on Mrs. Price's door to give her his rent cheque one Saturday morning. When she opened the door he could see she had been crying and that her eyes were puffed up.

"What's the matter, Mrs. Price?"

"Those bastards are coming to Leeds," she said venomously. He had never seen her so angry.

"What are you talking about?"

"Mosley's Blackshirts, that's who! Come in, Tom, and I'll tell you all about it while we have a cup of tea."

The Blackshirt movement in Great Britain was started by Sir Oswald Mosley in 1932, an erstwhile Member of Parliament. Officially called the British Union of Fascists, the movement was an extreme right-wing political group fashioned after Hitler's Brownshirts in Germany and Mussolini's Blackshirts in Italy. Whilst they never achieved control of the country as the others did, they caused a number of riots as they tried to recruit the disaffected people who were the casualties of the economic depression of the early 1930s. They held large rallies in London at the Albert Hall and the Olympia Grand Hall. They drew thousands to these events. They were opposed by the left-wing organisations such as the Communist Party and the Independent Labour Party. In addition, they held many smaller meetings around the country to drum up support and recruitment.

By 1935 and 1936, they began to focus their activities in the north of England, where poverty and hopelessness were fertile recruiting grounds. However, they met significant opposition from far-left parties and trade unions, whose members disrupted many of their meetings.

Tom followed Mrs. Price into her kitchen and sat at the kitchen table. Mrs. Price busied herself with filling the kettle with water. She stopped, looked out of the window for a few seconds, as if gathering her thoughts, then continued filling the kettle and put it on her stove to boil. She then sat down at the table and looked directly at Tom.

"These Blackshirts have to be stopped and I will do all in my power to see that they are," she said angrily. "After what they did to my sister's husband these animals need to be wiped from the face of the Earth!"

"What happened to your brother-in law?"

"My sister and her husband, Brian, live in Hammersmith, which is in the west of London. He was a bus driver for London Transport and an active member of the Communist Party. He and his fellow communists were involved in a number of scuffles at previous Blackshirt meetings. In 1934, they managed to get into the massive meeting at Olympia that had an audience of over twelve thousand people and among these were some five hundred protesters. They began to heckle the speakers and were set upon by over a thousand or so Blackshirt stewards. Brian was so severely injured that he spent weeks in hospital and was eventually allowed home. But he was paralysed from the neck down and my sister has to look after all his needs."

"I'm very sorry to hear this, Mrs. Price, but what has got you upset today?"

"Well, I saw this news piece in our local paper announcing that Mosley will be speaking at one of his rallies on Holbeck

Moor, which is about two miles south of here. I can't believe the authorities would allow him to come here and spew his hate speech, especially against the Jews. At least they stopped them from marching through the heavily Jewish area of the Leylands."

"When is the rally taking place?" Tom asked.

"Tomorrow in the early afternoon. I know a lot of people are going to the rally to demonstrate and try and disrupt their meeting. I'll be there with others."

Just then the kettle whistled, announcing that the water had boiled. Mrs. Price got up and made the tea.

When she had sat back down again, Tom told her he would join her on Sunday. Mrs. Price smiled and said how grateful she was for his support. They made plans to leave in the early morning so they could get a good position near the front of the speaker's dais.

The next day, Mrs. Price and Tom set off for Holbeck Moor. They were astonished, but very pleased, to see so many people heading in the same direction as themselves. Everyone they saw was angry about the fascists and said they were determined to stop their rally at all costs. When they reached Holbeck Moor, they saw that a podium had been set up for the speakers and that surrounding it was about a thousand fascist supporters looking nervous when they saw thousands of demonstrators (some newspapers estimated thirty thousand) lined up against them.

The Blackshirts began their march from Calverley Street in Leeds, reaching Holbeck Moor about an hour later. It was very clear that they were surprised and uneasy about the number of demonstrators that had turned up. As soon as Sir Oswald Mosley began to speak the demonstrators began to sing the socialist anthem 'The Red Flag', which drowned out what he was saying.

Then stones were being thrown at the fascists. Before the rally a group of demonstrators had collect rocks and stones and located them strategically around the rally site. This barrage was unsettling to the fascists, who started throwing them back. Sir Oswald

Mosley was hit at least once on the head. He decided that there was no point in continuing with the rally and started to march his Blackshirts back towards Leeds.

A melee ensued, with both sides fighting. Tom had enthusiastically joined the fray and was soon throwing stones. The pro-fascists spectators were beating a hasty retreat but fighting back. Then everything, for Tom, went dark.

He woke up in hospital later that evening and when he opened his eyes Mrs. Price was there fussing over him. He had a searing headache and, when he touched his head with a hand, he found it was bandaged up.

"Oh, Tom, how do you feel?"

"I'm not sure. What happened?" he asked weakly.

"One of those fascist pigs hit you with a stone and began kicking you as you lay on the ground. One of our lads tore him off you and with the help of another man brought you here to the hospital."

Two days later Tom was released from hospital still feeling very sore and bruised. He was elated, though, at the success they had had at what was known as the Battle of Holbeck Moor. This would go down in local history as how Leeds helped stop the spread of fascism in north-eastern England.

7

University of Leeds, September 29th, 1936

The university's academic year had begun, and once again there was the hustle and bustle of the previous year on the campus. Tom was now in his third year at the university and found himself busy with his classes and working with Stewart Franklin for Dr. Young. Also, he continued his Saturday night gig playing at the Crucible pub. As a result of his growing reputation as a jazz pianist, he was offered a second gig at the Black Cat nightclub on Sundays.

Getting home late one evening, Tom found a newspaper clipping from the *Yorkshire Evening Post* attached to a note from Mrs. Price: "I thought you'd be interested in this."

He picked up the clipping and sat down in a chair to read it. What he saw, he couldn't believe his eyes. The newspaper announced that there was to be a march of some three hundred miles to London by two hundred unemployed men from his hometown of Jarrow. The march was to be started on October 5th and would be passing through Leeds. The march, called the Jarrow Crusade, was organised by Miss Ellen Wilkinson, the Member of Parliament for the town, and the marchers would take with them the Jarrow Petition signed by about twelve thousand residents calling on the government to provide industrial investment and jobs in the town.

The organisers had spent many hours gaining support for the marchers in twenty-two towns and cities they would pass through to reach London on their month-long march. This included providing feeding and sleeping quarters for the men, field kitchens and medical support from the inter-hospital Socialist Society medical students.

There had been many hunger marches to London before from other parts of Britain and most of these were organised by the National Unemployed Workers' Movement, a communist organisation, and as such was loathed by national politicians and the newspapers.

However, the Jarrow Crusade was to be non-political and, as such, garnered support from many local political parties of all stripes, businessmen and the general public. The Labour Party nationally, however, urged its members to boycott the march and the Trades Union Council sent a message to its member unions stressing that they didn't expect their members to support the men from Jarrow. These admonishments were ignored.

The March organisers adopted strict rules for the men, many of whom had been in the army. There was a dress code of suits or jackets and ties. The marchers got up at six thirty in the morning, shaved, ate breakfast and were on parade by eight forty-five ready to leave at nine o'clock. They marched like a column of soldiers, four abreast.

Tom read that the marchers would arrive in Leeds on October 13th and he was determined to volunteer to do something to support them. First, he had to find out who was organising the marchers' stay in Leeds. So the next morning he left for the city's town hall to begin his enquiries.

He arrived at the Leeds Town Hall and the receptionist in the hall's atrium told him that some of the reception committee organisers were in what was called the crypt, which was part of the hall's large basement. She said that they were organising a get-together for the marchers when they arrived in Leeds and were planning to feed them there.

Following the directions Tom had been given by the receptionist, he found his way through a maze of passages and he eventually found the crypt. In the open space of the room were several tables set up and in one corner was a woman working on a typewriter. As Tom approached, she looked up and inspected him, with professional proficiency, with her piercing grey eyes. She must have been in her forties and a bit heavy set. She was dressed in light-green tweed suit and was wearing heavy black-framed glasses. Her greying hair was fixed tightly in a bun on the back of her head and on her hands were several rings.

Miss Gertrude Riley resented her lot in life. Her fiancé had been killed in the trenches in World War One and this bitter experience had scarred her for life. Some one million men lost their lives in the war and so there was a glut of women of marriageable age in the country. Many women after this tragic war were to remain unmarried or widows throughout their lives, resigned to their situation. But few were as bitter as Miss Riley, who made everyone she came in contact with dislike and resent her. However, one thing she was good at was efficiently running an office and the one person she respected above all others was her boss. She was the secretary to Mr. Reginald C. Davies, a leading solicitor, a city alderman and Conservative Party leader in the city council, and the main organiser of Leeds's welcome to the marchers. This had given her some social status, which she guarded fiercely.

"Yes!" demanded Miss Riley.

"I'm Tom Pearson and I would like to volunteer to help with the Jarrow Crusade when it comes here. I'm from Jarrow and I'm at university here," he said, smiling his best smile, which he hoped would melt the frosty reception he had received so far.

"We already have too many volunteers," was the response.

"Well, many of the men are probably friends of mine who I've known since childhood."

"Mr. Blackshaw is in charge of the volunteers. He'll be here in half an hour so you can talk to him then. You can sit on the chair over there and wait for him," she said, pointing to the chair furthest away from her, and she carried on typing, ignoring him.

Almost on the half hour, Mr. Blackshaw walked in. He was a tall man, smartly dressed in a well-pressed charcoal-coloured three-piece suit, which had a gold fob chain hanging from the waistcoat. He was clean-shaven apart from a small military moustache, and his grey hair was short and well groomed. Sixty-three-year-old Mr. Blackshaw had been a sergeant major in the Coldstream Guards and was well suited to his organisational role.

"Mr. Blackshaw, you have a visitor," said Miss Riley, pointing at Tom.

"How can I help you, son?" said Mr. Blackshaw in a kindly voice.

"I would like to volunteer to help you when the men from Jarrow come to Leeds. You see, I'm from Jarrow and I will know some of the men."

"Why aren't you marching? You look like a fit man."

"I'm at university here."

"What are you studying?"

"Physics."

Mr. Blackshaw's question was typical of him. He liked to know the background of the people he was dealing with.

"Well, it turns out that we could use some help doing various things like waiting at tables when we feed them and generally running around doing various tasks. Are you up to it?"

"You bet," Tom said enthusiastically.

"Right. They arrive here tomorrow. I want you to meet them at the Meanwood Baths where we are laying on washing facilities for them. They are expected there at about three, so you be there at two at the latest. Then with the other volunteers you are to bring them here, where we will lay on tea and sandwiches. They are spending the night at the Harehills Labour Club, where they'll be fed. They will have breakfast in the morning in the canteen at Montague Burton, the clothes manufacturer and retailer. And they are to leave us at about noon tomorrow. That's the plan in a nutshell. Have you got transport?"

"I have a bike and I can use that."

"Fine. I'll see you tomorrow."

The next day Tom was at the Meanwood Baths in Alwoodley, a suburb on the outskirts of Leeds, waiting in anticipation for the men from Jarrow to appear. At about three he could hear them coming without actually seeing them because of the mouth-organ music they played as they marched along. Then they rounded a corner in the road and there they were marching to the music and carrying aloft a banner that read 'Jarrow Crusade'.

The men were smartly dressed in their best clothes and each of them wore a soft, flat peaked cap. Over each man's left shoulder was their waterproof capes, neatly folded with military precision.

Among the crowd of onlookers who cheered the men on was a mother and her son and daughter. "Oh, look, Mum, they've got a dog." Among the men was a dog proudly marching with his new friends.

As the men filed past, Tom recognised David Lambert, who had helped chase away the bailiffs and move Edith Cooper back to her parents' home. David waved and came over to him when they stopped.

"Well, you're a sight for sore eyes, Tom. How have you been?"

"Getting by. What's the news from Jarrow?"

"Things are really bad. I haven't worked for over a year and for some of the lads it's a lot longer. There is nothing going on in the town. Promises of a new shipbuilding company never materialised and now there's talk of a steelworks at the Palmer site. We had to do something to get the government to help us, so it was decided we'd do this march."

"What's with the dog?" asked Tom as he made a fuss of him.

"He sort of adopted us. He's called Paddy and had joined us earlier just outside Jarrow as we started the march and had followed us for miles. He was so determined to be with us that we adopted him as our mascot and the Royal Society for the Prevention of Cruelty to Animals bought him a dog licence."

Just then several of David's friends who knew Tom came over to join them and among them was John Baker, a forty-year-old carpenter who had worked at the shipyards. Tom was appalled by their stories of how they made do with a pittance that the dole gave them to feed their families. John was the luckiest of the group, as he was a bachelor and hadn't any family responsibilities.

Once the men had washed themselves at Meanwood Baths, they formed up and marched to the Leeds Town Hall and were greeted with a rapturous welcome by people who lined the streets to see them. After the reception by town councillors in the crypt, the men marched on to the Harehills Labour Club to spend the night.

Tom left the men about nine thirty that night and he was determined to join them the next day on part of their march. He went to Dr. Young's house and asked permission to miss classes.

"Frankly, Tom, I don't like you doing this, as we are getting into the real nitty-gritty of the course and you will miss some core lectures," Dr. Young said, concerned that his star student would be held back on his coursework.

"I only plan to be gone for three days, sir," pleaded Tom.

"I know this is important to you, so what I'll do is set you texts for you to read so you will be up to date when we have our first test next Monday."

The next morning, Tom left early, equipped with a rucksack full of textbooks, a heavy raincoat and a cap to keep out the rain. He met the marchers in the canteen at Montague Burton Ltd. They were eating a large breakfast which was cooked for them by the staff of the company, and after resting in the morning, the march left Leeds about noon for their nine-mile journey to Wakefield.

The men usually marched for fifty minutes to an hour and then rested for ten minutes. The march organisers decided that this would be the routine, as all of the participants were undernourished and they worried that any longer march time would be too physically stressful for them. Ironically, as time went on, the men became physically fitter because they were more well-fed on the march than they would have been at home and they had a daily exercise regimen.

They arrived at Wakefield about four in the afternoon and were greeted by residents of the town. They were welcomed by the mayor at the town hall and fed before they were taken to Playhouse cinema to watch a feature film. They were put up for the night at the Salem Chapel.

Tom spent an uncomfortable and restless night on one of the pews in the chapel. There were no mattresses, although they were given blankets. He was glad when morning came and he could stretch his tired muscles, which weren't used to such a hard surface at night.

After breakfast, they were on the road again at nine for their ten-mile trek to Barnsley. On the way there, John Baker began to limp and, at one of the stops, Tom took a look at his ankle, which was very swollen. His boots were so worn out that he had been walking with part of the sole missing, but he was so determined to complete the trek to London that he just put up with the pain. The medical students put him in the back of the support lorry and they worked hard on his ankle. When the march reached Barnsley, Tom took him to a shoe shop and selected a pair of new boots for him. When he came to pay, the shop's owner wouldn't take any payment. What a wonderful show of solidarity for the men of Jarrow!

The next stop on their journey was Sheffield and it was there that Tom planned to leave them and travel back to Leeds. After a tea in a schoolroom at the Brunswick Methodist Chapel laid on by the Sheffield Corporation, he took his leave of his friends and wished them all the very best of luck in London.

The Jarrow Crusade reached London at the end of October and, despite the overwhelming support they had received from villages, towns and cities on their route, their reception by the politicians in London was icy. Although Jarrow's petition was presented to Parliament and a hearing before Members of Parliament from all parties, who listened intently to the town's mayor, nothing, in the long run, was done to help the distressed town.

Tom eventually arrived back at his digs in Leeds at about nine that evening. He was very tired and was looking forward to a hot bath. When he opened the door to his rooms there was an envelope that had been put under his door. It was a letter from Dr. Young dated two days previously telling him that his friend Stewart Franklin had been found badly beaten in one the streets in the old part of town and was in a coma at the Leeds General Infirmary. Tom put his bag down and left in a hurry for the hospital.

He eventually found the ward Stewart was on and sat by his bedside, staring at his friend and wondering when he would recover. The kindly ward sister allowed him to stay, although it was past visiting hours. He fell asleep during his vigil and was woken by the ward sister as she gently touched his shoulder.

"I have a nice pot of tea in my office if you would like a cup," she said with a smile.

"That would be great, sister."

When he reached her small office at the side of the ward he asked: "Has he said anything about what happened to him?"

"Not really. He has been mumbling a lot about someone he calls 'bloody Rod' and 'pack horses', but that's all. He keeps on repeating this over and over again."

Tom knew immediately what he was saying. He had been attacked by Rodney Garfield and his friends, probably outside the Pack Horse pub. But why was he found a half mile or so away?

Maybe he had tried to walk home but, in his state, had gone in the wrong direction and eventually collapsed.

Tom got up to leave and asked the sister what the prospects of him recovering were. "It's very difficult to say. It's early days yet. But he took a bad beating, so we won't know what his prognosis is for some days or until he comes out of his coma. His parents are coming down from Scotland tomorrow, so we'll see what happens to him after that."

It was a very heavy heart that Tom left the hospital that night at midnight. He was extremely angry at Rodney Garfield and his friends, and what they had done to Stewart. He planned to seek a terrible revenge on them somehow. He would do something to them that they would remember for the rest of their lives.

A week later Stewart died and had never recovered consciousness. Tom bit his lip hard until it bled and vowed revenge.

8

Tom was giving a lecture about magnetism during the first in a series of lectures on the subject to a freshman physics class. It was unusual for a third-year student to give this lecture which was usually given by a graduate student, but as Stewart Franklin had died the task was given to him. Dr. Young was present and had introduced him. Giving him the lecture had been a mark of Dr. Young's confidence in his ability.

As Tom scanned the faces of the students, he noticed her almost at once. She was sitting in the second row of the tiered lecture hall. He noticed her because she was the only woman in the class of thirty or so students.

Megan Rafferty was a redhead and she had a short boyish haircut which made her look impish. She was short but had a well-proportioned body that attracted a number of her freshman colleagues like bees around a honeypot. She had liked the attention at first but was bored by their immature behaviour which had begun to annoy her.

She had won a scholarship to the university from the famous Blue Coat School, a leading secondary school in Wavertree, a part of the city of Liverpool. Her family was Irish and her father was a stevedore in the city's docks. She had three brothers who were older than her and who also worked at the Liverpool docks. Although she was the apple of her father's eye, he was very reluctant to let her go away to university because he believed a woman's place was in the home and that she should help her mother out with chores. However, her mother and Megan had lobbied him to let her go and they had recruited her brothers to their cause. Eventually her reluctant father gave way.

Megan was a rarity in that she was one of the first women selected on a scholarship to study physics at the university. At this time the field was entirely male. She was placed first in the science entrance exams at the university and, after much discussion and argument among the science faculty, she was offered a place.

Tom spent time showing the class on the overhead projector the advances in magnetism that had been developed and the applications that were being used by industry. Megan thought he was adorable and was spellbound by his explanations. She saw that he was very enthusiastic about his subject and it was no wonder Dr. Young rated him so highly. Once she smiled at him, which flummoxed him and he went as red as a beetroot, much to her amusement. It took him a few seconds to get back to his talk.

At the end of the lecture, Megan hung back as the rest of the class filed out. Dr. Young was going over some points with Tom so she hid in the shadows of the lecture hall. When Dr. Young left and Tom was breaking down one of the experiments she walked up to him.

"Can I help you?" she asked.

"Oh, thank you," he replied. He was surprised but pleased and embarrassed to see her.

"I enjoyed your lecture. Where did you get all that knowledge about electronics?" She asked while she put away the projector in its box and started dismantling one of the experiments he had demonstrated.

"I was a ham radio operator when I was still at school and experimented a lot on my own."

They talked a long time about each other's upbringing and he was fascinated to hear about her close family and the happy times she had had growing up compared to his lack of family closeness. As they walked from the physics building, Tom asked her where she was staying.

"College Hall, and our warden there, Miss Holgate, is very strict. She runs a tight ship as far as boys are concerned. In fact, we are having a social this Saturday evening, would you like to come?"

"That would be nice. Thank you, I would," he said, smiling broadly.

"You know, you have a beautiful smile."

He reddened: "So do you, Megan."

That Saturday evening, Tom arrived at College Hall at six thirty and went to the common room where there were several women talking in a group and no men in sight. Embarrassed, he turned to leave when Megan bounded up and welcomed him and introduced him to her friends. Just then several men arrived and the gathering broke up into little groups around the room. Someone turned on a gramophone and couples began to dance.

Sitting in the corner sternly watching the proceedings was an elderly woman who Tom assumed was Miss Holgate, warden of the hall of residence and guardian of her wards' virtues. She was thin, weedy woman in her late fifties who was also a lecturer in the education department at the university.

Megan and Tom were deep in conversation when in walked Rodney Garfield and his cronies, Roger Jackson and Simon Owen. Miss Holgate bolted out of her chair and met them as they crossed the room. The music stopped and everyone looked at the three troublemakers.

"You're not welcome here. Kindly go before I call the porters," she said in a shrill, squeaky voice.

"Why? The room is full of delicious fillies who we would enjoy meeting and giving them a canter," said Rodney with a leering smile on his face.

"This social is by invitation only. Who invited you?"

"Everyone, right, girls? They know they will have a fabulous time. I see some ugly moron invited Tom Pearson so they must be desperate for real men. We've come to liven the party which I am sure needs it."

"Who are you calling a moron!" demanded Megan as she stepped forward to face the intruders with her hands on her hips. "Why don't you find your own party to go to instead of ruining ours?"

Tom then stepped forward flushed with anger. "Rodney, don't you get the message? We don't want you and your hangers-on here so why don't you just be a good boy and leave? I know it's very difficult for you to understand because you're thick in the head, but you are not wanted here."

"Who are you to tell me what to do? I'll beat the living daylights out of you, you mark my words," he replied venomously.

"Just like you did with Stewart? The police are still looking into his death. Everyone here is a witness. If something happens to me the police will know where to look. Now just go, there's a good fellow."

"Yes!" shouted the other women in the room. "Go! Go!" they cried.

For once a reddened Rodney didn't know what to say. Tom had hit a nerve mentioning Stewart and then he knew about his suspicion of him. That made him pause and decide that withdrawal was the best policy, but he couldn't resist a last jab at Tom.

As Rodney and his friends turned to go, he grabbed Megan and kissed her on her lips and laughed. Megan slapped him very hard on the face, which took him totally by surprise, and blood from his nose started to trickle down his face. He moved to hit her back, but Tom moved between them.

"You'll regret that, you bitch!" he said, wiping his face with the back of his hand as he walked out of the room to the cheers of everyone there.

The music was put back on and conversations began anew.

Tom was incredulous at Megan's action against Rodney Garfield: "Where did you learn to hit like that?"

"It helps to have three brothers who taught me how to look after myself," Megan said with a grin.

"I'd be careful of Garfield, though, he doesn't like people laughing at him."

Tom then told her about his run-in with Rodney and his suspicions about who beat up his friend Stewart.

As the weeks passed, their relationship grew and Megan would spend weekends in Tom's room. They were always together during lunch breaks and in the evening. They began to learn more about each other and found that both were interested in many of the same things. Megan was interested in socialism, which had been part of her growing up in a union family, and she told Tom that her brothers were Marxists. This intrigued him and he wanted to meet them. He told her about his grandfather and his fight for the workers at the shipyard which came to nothing in the end.

One evening, after visiting a jazz club in the city, Tom and Megan decided that it was time to consummate their love. They had discussed this many times and Megan had insisted that he should wear a condom, which she, to his amusement, called a 'Johnny'. Seeing him laugh, she explained she knew about this when she had overheard her older brothers talking one day.

They reached Tom's digs and, when the door to his room was closed, they began to kiss. Soon they were both naked looking at each other and smiling. Gently, he led Megan to his bed and they laid down and began their lovemaking.

Tom's relationship with Jane Harcourt had taught him to be a caring and sensitive lover. However, he was somewhat surprised to find that Megan was still a virgin and he hesitated.

"Are you sure you want to do this?"

"Yes."

He gently eased himself into her and she let out a little yelp.

Eventually they slowly reached an orgasm together. Megan was lost in the pure satisfaction of the moment and she sighed with pleasure when the climax had passed.

As they lay naked on the bed afterwards Megan turned to him: "That was the most wonderful experience I have ever had. Can we do it again?" And they did.

After lectures the next day Dr. Young asked to see Tom, who knocked on the professor's door and walked in when he heard the loud "Come" in response.

"Ah, Tom, come on in and sit down. As you know the university's year ends next week and I've been asked to give a talk at a conference being held at Imperial College in London the week after. I was wondering whether you might like to come as my guest. You will be meeting many leading scientists and it would be good time for you to decide what you are going to do after your final year next year."

"I would very much like to do this. Thank you for asking me."

After they talked about the arrangements, Tom hurried off to meet Megan at a local café to tell her his good news. When he got there she wasn't there and nor was she at their usual pub.

"Lost somebody, asshole?" asked Rodney Garfield, who was walking past him in the street carrying a suitcase.

"No!"

"If you're looking for your ugly girlfriend I saw her getting on a train with another man," he said with glee as he watched Tom's face turn into a frown and a look of concern.

"Why do you like to lie all the time, Rodney? You haven't seen her. You're just saying that to yank my chain."

"True, I could be, but I've just come back from my parents and I saw her at the station when I got off the train."

Tom dashed off to the station and found out that the train for Liverpool had left fifteen minutes before. He walked back to his digs in a depressed mood. Why had she suddenly left without saying where she was going? It didn't make sense.

When he got to his room, he found a note from Megan telling him that her mother was very sick and she had to go and take care of her. She was going home with one of her brothers and would write and let him know what was going on. Her last paragraph was ominous: "Take care of yourself, my darling. I will always remember the good times we had together. All my Love, Megan."

Was this a letter ending their affair? What had she meant by remembering the good times? Tom would never see Megan again.

9

London, September 30th, 1936

This was Tom's first visit to London and he was overawed by the sights and sounds when he arrived at the busy St. Pancras train terminal. He had caught the two twenty-four train from Leeds, which got into London at about seven thirty. Even at that time, the station was full of people shouting and jostling each other in the pursuit of porters or taxis. He couldn't believe how rude and obnoxious many of the people were compared those in Leeds or Jarrow. It was a totally different experience for him and he didn't like it.

Dr. Young, who had gone to London the day before to stay with friends, had given him written instructions of how to get to Imperial College in South Kensington. He was booked into a room at the university's Beit Hall of residence in the Student Union Building. To get there he had to catch the Piccadilly Underground line to South Kensington. He started to look around for a sign for the Underground and saw it across the station concourse. Getting there was easier said than done because he had to cross a stream people walking parallel to the Underground entrance. He waited for a break in the stream and dived for the gap and made it to the entrance hitting a few people with his case as he went.

It was then, as he was gathering his breath, he felt something in his back pocket. He turned around and quickly caught a small boy as he was about to run off with his wallet.

The little street urchin was badly dressed in a filthy jacket, short trousers and shirt, all of which didn't fit him. That was all he was wearing despite the cold blast of autumn. He wore no socks but had on ill-fitting leather shoes which probably had been passed down from an older brother. His brown hair was greasy and was in a tangled mess underneath an equally filthy cap. His hands and face were grimy and clearly he had never had a bath in his life.

"Now what do you think you're doing?" Tom said as he held on to the boy's collar. "Just give my wallet back to me."

The boy handed his wallet and made a move to run away but Tom's grip was too firm.

"Let me go!" screamed the boy.

"Not until you tell me your name and why you're stealing from me."

"Me name's Arffer. That's all I'm going to tell you, mate. Now let me go."

Arthur began to struggle and kick Tom on his shins. Then he landed a knee in Tom's crotch which forced him to let go. The boy had learned to fight in the rough streets of Bethnal Green and he wasn't going to let this hick from the country beat him. Unfortunately for Arthur, when he broke away from Tom and blindly ran, he collided with a police sergeant who was coming over to see what the kafuffle was about. The sergeant grabbed Arthur by the scruff of his neck.

"Are you alright, sir?" he asked Tom as he was still getting his breath back.

"Yes, sergeant. Thank you."

"I saw him try and steal your wallet and assault you. Do you want to press charges?"

"No, there's no need, although I'm interested to know what drives these children to such lengths."

The policeman let Arthur go and he ran off out of the station.

Then the sergeant answered Tom's question: "Poverty, pure and simple. There's no work for their parents, who are destitute, and the only way they survive is to steal and scavenge what they can. Apart from stealing, the women beg for money around stations like this with a small child in their arms. The younger ones prostitute themselves at night so their families can get by. They always have a hard-luck story, so never believe what they say because it's probably a lie. But they have to survive somehow."

Tom thanked the sergeant again and made his way to the Underground ticket office. He then took a lift which descended some ninety feet to the Piccadilly Line train platform. This experience was very disconcerting for him as this was his first ride in one. The lift seemed to drop precipitously and a number of other passengers were amused at his reaction, which was shown all over his terrified face.

"Never mind, dear," said an old lady standing next Tom. "The first time is always the worst."

Tom stood on the platform and waited for a westbound train. He was fascinated by the large advertising posters for things like Bovril, beers and clothes. Then he heard a distant rumble which came from the tunnel and this grew louder as a train approached. It suddenly burst out of the tunnel and stopped at the platform and the doors opened. When he got off the train at South Kensington station he ascended in another lift some sixty feet up to the street level. This time he was not as nervous as he knew what to expect, but the lift juddered as it came to a stop at ground level.

After getting directions from a newspaper seller outside the station, Tom found his way to Imperial College and entered the Beit Quadrangle from Queen's Gate and reported to the porter's lodge at Beit Hall. He found his room on the third floor and sat at a desk reviewing the conference materials that had been left there.

As he lay awake on his bed that night, he couldn't help thinking about scruffy Arthur and his family and what chance they had of bettering their lives. The national government at the time was not doing enough to help this underclass of people who had no hope. He took out the letter from his grandpa, which he always kept in his wallet, and reread it. Something must be done to help these people, and it seemed from all he had read that the Russian governing experiment was improving the lot of the worker and the poor in that country. Perhaps this was the answer.

The next morning Tom was at breakfast by himself in the dining hall when a student about his age sat down next to him and introduced himself as Jacob Levine. It turned out that he was a physics major so they had a long conversation about the many trends in the field, particularly the work that was being done on high frequency radio signals propagation. Tom explained he was going to a conference at the university and was looking forward to hearing later that afternoon a presentation by Mr. Arnold Wilkins of the Radio Research Station.

"That's great. We can both go together. We students are supposed to sit at the back of the auditorium and let the great and not-so-great scientists sit in the front," said Jacob.

"Tell me about Imperial College, Jacob. I'm thinking about doing post-graduate work here. What's it like being here?"

"It's very challenging because there are so many bright students here that makes the environment extremely competitive and driven. But that's a good thing because it keeps everyone on their toes."

"What's going on apart from academics?"

"A lot of political activism. For example, there's a big push to get students to go to the East End of London where the pro-Nazi Blackshirts plan to have a march through a heavily Jewish area. We Jews are determined to stop them," he said. "The stupid government have decided not to ban the march and as a result there will be major riot. Apart from various Jewish organisations who will demonstrate, there are all sorts of other groups that also want to stop them, like the communists, anarchists, trade unionists and members of the Independent Labour Party."

"I remember when the Blackshirts tried to hold a rally last year near Leeds on Holbeck Moor, many of us students and many others stopped them," Tom remarked with a smile of satisfaction. "There was a big fight but eventually they ran away. The trouble was I spent several days in hospital as a result of being hit by a stone but it was worth it to know that we had stopped them."

"Crikey, that must have taken a lot of guts. Do you want to join us this Sunday?"

"I'd like to but I have nowhere to stay."

"We can go and stay in my parents' house in Hampstead. They're away, but our housekeeper Mrs. Jacobs will look after us, I'm sure."

"That would be great. I can catch the late train to Leeds on Sunday evening so I can be in class on Monday."

Tom looked at his watch: "We'd better go to the conference."

At lunchtime, Dr. Young briefly joined Jacob and Tom at the university's refectory. He had been able to wangle, as he put it, a ticket for Tom to attend the rector's cocktail party that evening so he could meet several professors from different universities. Dr. Young told him he should only stay for half an hour, but it would be helpful to get to know some of them.

The afternoon's programme included Mr. Arnold Wilkins who, with Dr. Robert Watson-Watt, was developing a new technology called a radio direction finder, which was later called radar. The technology had been developed originally by a German scientist in 1903, but its range was very limited and it was used to avoid ship collisions at night or in bad weather. Mr. Wilkins' talk was going to be an update on the developments of this new technology and Tom was looking forward to hearing him. The talk was to be couched in general terms because a lot of the advancements his team were making were top secret.

The radio direction finder system used radio beams that would bounce off incoming aircraft. An oscilloscope would pick up the beam returns and be used to calculate their distance, thus giving early warning of an impending attack. The team of scientists had designed a large transmitter that could beam a pulse at hundred kilowatts at twenty-two-megahertz frequency, which at that time was extremely powerful.

The team had, by 1935, successfully demonstrated the equipment's abilities to pick up an aircraft at about sixty miles at a height of seventeen thousand feet. With the threat of German aggression, the British Air Ministry had approved the building of a network of stations and transmitter towers along the eastern and southern seaboards of Britain, which were to be completed in 1938.

Tom was enthralled by Mr. Wilkins' presentation and looked forward to meeting him at the cocktail party, although he thought the great scientist wouldn't bother to talk to him, a mere undergraduate student.

Tom met Dr. Young at the entrance to the City and Guilds building on Exhibition Road and they both entered a very large room after showing their invitations to a porter dressed in a red morning coat. The room was full of scientists busy talking and many made cursory acknowledgement of Tom when he was introduced to them and then carried on talking among themselves.

Tom was introduced to Professor George Thomson, the head of Imperial College's physics department.

"I understand from Dr. Young here that you want study for your master's degree at Imperial. In what field of physics would you be interested?"

"I think radio frequencies and their application to worldwide communications. Better frequency modulation, for example, would help in such areas as RDF or the signal-to-noise ratios in radio transmissions."

"What makes you think we would accept you for our master's course?"

"First, my academic record and a favourable recommendation from Dr. Young, who has been my mentor. Second, my abiding interest in doing research into electronics with all its possibilities in the future. I believe Imperial College would give me the best chance of achieving my research goals."

"Hmm. We'll see once we get your application, young man," said the unusually somewhat impressed professor.

Just then, Mr. Wilkins joined them and was very interested to hear about Tom's academic career so far from Dr. Young.

"How did you enjoy my talk this afternoon, young man?" he asked.

"I was intrigued by how you'd increased the power of the radio beam. It is something I was interested in when I was in school and read up on Huelsmeyer's Telemobiloskop. I know it had limited range with one kilowatt of power, but how did you increase it to find aircraft farther off?"

"That, dear Tom, is a state secret. When you have your master's degree let's talk. Here's my card. Now I must circulate. It was nice meeting you." And with that he turned and started talking to another group of men.

Tom left the cocktail party buoyed by the contacts he had made and picked up his raincoat and cap from the cloakroom. He wanted dinner but the university refectory was closed so he headed off to a pub that had been recommended by his new friend, Jacob. He studied the rough map Jacob had given him and put his collar up and started to walk. When he left the building, the lack of any streetlights made the night pitch black and it was raining steadily. There weren't many people around and at times it seemed he was the only person on the street. Following Jacob's map, he walked down Queen's Gate to a quiet side street called Queen's Gate Terrace and headed to Gloucester Road where the Gloucester Arms was located.

As Tom was halfway down Queen's Gate Terrace, he was suddenly aware of someone's footsteps behind him. He turned to look if he could see anyone through the darkness and rain, but the street was empty and, as he continued on, he heard the footsteps again. Was he being paranoid? Was someone following him? But why? He could only think that he was about to be robbed. He picked up his walking speed and finally reached the pub.

It was a quiet evening in the warm, inviting pub that had just a few regular customers drinking and talking. Tom ordered a pint of bitter and a porkpie from the landlord. He found a table by the fire and began to eat the porkpie. As he did this, a man in a grey raincoat and trilby hat came in and sat at the bar. Tom didn't take much notice of him and thought he was another 'regular' and carried on eating.

Dimitri Smirnov was a small man in his late forties who owned a small antiques shop on Gloucester Road. He was well known by the landlord and other customers, who greeted him when he came in. He was always meticulously dressed and always sported a gregarious tie to match his mood. Tonight it was a bright yellow one with black polka dots. He spoke English with a guttural accent and he let everyone know he was from Poland, although he was Russian. What did they know, these stupid bourgeoisie British? He had lived in London for about ten years. What was remarkable about him was not his thin face, his short grey hair or his large beak-like nose, but his piercing black eyes that seemed to focus with laser-like precision on anyone he was displeased with. This stare disconcerted the most determined person and made them look away in fear. They knew then not to cross him.

But Dimitri had a secret. He was known to his masters in Moscow as an 'illegal'. This was a member of the Russian secret service, or any foreign secret service for that matter, who had no diplomatic cover should he be caught. This afforded him a lot of flexibility without being noticed by the authorities. He had nothing to do with the Russian Embassy in London because he knew it was well covered by MI5, the British internal security service. He had survived these last ten years by keeping the NKVD agents at the embassy at arm's length and only contacting them by pay phone or dead letter drops. His main mission was to recruit British citizens to spy for Russia and he was good at it. That's why he had been given this young man's name who was sitting there by the fire unaware of what was going to happen to him.

Dimitri picked up his Scotch whisky from the bar and went over to the fireplace and put it on a shelf above the fire. He then started to warm himself in front of their fire. As he did so he struck up a conversation with Tom. They were out of earshot of the men at the bar, although he spoke softly in case he was overheard.

"What a miserable night. The damp really gets to you," he said to Tom.

"It certainly does, but it's more penetrating where I come from," replied Tom.

"Where's that then?"

"Jarrow. It's in the north of England."

"I've never been there. What's it like?"

"Pretty bad with unemployed men from the shipyards and the unrelenting poverty."

"How did you get to London then?"

"My father is a schoolteacher, so we were better off than most people. Now I'm a student at Leeds University and I'm down here for a seminar at Imperial College. And where are you from?"

"I'm Polish and I have been an antiques dealer here in London for the past ten years. What's your field of study?"

"Physics."

"I was never any good at science. My teachers in Kraków used to despair of me. Now history and art are my fortes," he said with a laugh. And Tom responded with a laugh.

Dimitri sat down on a chair across the table from Tom. They talked for over an hour about the political situation in Britain and Tom warmed to this friendly stranger. Dimitri bought two rounds of drinks, which Tom realised afterwards was to loosen his tongue and thoughts.

Finally, Tom felt that he could speak candidly to this charming, good listener: "I wish I could do something to alleviate the stresses on the poor from my town or anywhere else for that matter. From what I read, the Russian experiment seems to be working well and we should do something like it here. My grandad was a proud union organiser and a communist who believed it could work here. I would like to see his wish fulfilled."

"But communism has a bad reputation here. It wouldn't fly in Britain," tested Dimitri.

"The reason why it hasn't been accepted is because the powers that be, who control the government and the newspapers, don't want any change in the status quo. They have control over our society and are frightened of losing power to the workers. Even the working class are frightened of change, so introducing a communist system is going to be a slow, hard process that will take years to happen."

"I suppose there could be revolution as there was in Russia," suggested Dimitri.

"I doubt that would ever happen. Russia was in a real mess and Lenin and his colleagues were able to capitalise on it. But they had their problems with the White Russians and the civil war, although they prevailed. No, the only way we'd see a communist government here is by getting more members voted into office on town councils and eventually Parliament itself. I suppose I'm a socialist by birth and nature." Tom laughed.

"What's the difference between socialism and communism?" Dimitri questioned.

"I suppose socialists believe in democracy and achieving their policies by force of their arguments. Communists believe in autocracy by a small clique of people and in central control of everything in people's lives from manufacturing, farming and government."

"What do you want to do after your studies, Tom?" asked Dimitri, changing the subject.

This was the first time Dimitri had used his name and Tom was puzzled about why he knew it because he had never introduced himself.

"How do you know my name?" he demanded.

Dimitri blushed. Such a stupid mistake.

"Well, I was asked to look you up when you were in London."

"By whom?"

"Jane Harcourt."

"Jane! Where is she?"

"Abroad. America, I think."

"So it was you following me then?"

"I'm afraid so. Jane told me she thought you might work for us in the long term."

"Who is us?"

"Please, I am going to tell you something in total confidence that is not to be divulged to anyone. Will you promise me at least that?"

"Alright, but it doesn't commit me to anything," Tom replied as his curiosity was aroused and he thought it wouldn't hurt to listen.

"My name is Dimitri Smirnov. Both Jane and I work for the Russian government and we want you to join us."

"You mean you want me to spy for you!"

"Well, yes. You said you wanted to do something to help the poor and workers. Here's your opportunity to ensure that we lead the vanguard of social progress in Europe."

"What you're saying is you want me to betray my country."

"No. What I'm saying is I want you to help us rescue Russia from the quagmire it was in when we took over. We need technology to help us survive. We can't do it without help. We have Germany flexing its muscles again and I suspect the right-wing Nazi party there will want to stop our development."

"But I have no information I can give you."

"Not now, Tom. But maybe in the future. All I'm saying is

that you must keep a low profile politically and follow your career where you want it to go. If you want, we will be touch with you several years from now. What'd you say?"

"I need time to think this through," he said cautiously.

"That's fine and it is as it should be. You can help our cause greatly as time goes on, so keep an open mind on how you can do this," he said warmly. "Now I must go. Please give my proposal a lot of thought as together we can make society better for everyone and not just for a few."

With a loud "goodnight" to everyone, Dimitri Smirnov left the pub. That was the last time Tom would ever see him.

On Saturday afternoon Jacob and Tom left for Jacob's parents' house in Hampstead in north London. They caught the London Underground to Hampstead and walked to nearby Redington Road. They walked up to a large Victorian house and Jacob let them in with a key. They were greeted by Mrs. Jacob, the family's housekeeper, and later that evening they had a wonderful dinner.

The march by the Blackshirts the next day was to start at two o'clock in the afternoon and two to three thousand of Mosley's Blackshirts would gather in Royal Mint Street ready for the march east on Cable Street, a heavily Jewish neighbourhood at that time. Some estimates put the number of anti-fascist demonstrators at twenty thousand. Despite a petition with over one hundred thousand signatures, the British Home Office granted permission for the march and provided about six thousand policemen to keep the sides apart.

Jacob and Tom arrived at Cable Street at about ten in the morning and were put to work building barricades and collecting bricks, stones, sticks, chair and table legs to use as missiles to be thrown at the police and fascists. About one thirty the police began to clear the street so the march could take place. Some of the policemen were on horses and charged the demonstrators, who fought back fiercely.

Jacob and Tom had been stationed behind a barricade of

upturned produce barrows and tables. The police began to easily demolish the barricade and it was then that fights broke out between them and the demonstrators. Tom joined in, but as he dragged a policeman off his horse, he was hit from behind by police truncheon. He staggered down a side street reeling from a bloody wound on his head. As he passed a door to a bread shop it suddenly opened and strong hands grabbed him and dragged him inside.

Gus Cohen, the baker, and his wife, Evie, had seen from their living room on the first floor what had transpired and rushed down their stairs to the front door in time to grab Tom before the police arrested him. Gus at sixty-six had wanted to join the demonstrators because he was so angry at the authorities for letting the fascists march through their neighbourhood. For once in his life he listened to Evie and his son Mark, who urged him to sit out this demonstration.

Gus and Evie sat Tom down in their living room and began to clean his wound. Tom remembered very little about what had happened to him, but he had a raging headache and a deep six-inch cut on his head.

"There, there, son, just relax and we'll clean you up," cooed Evie as she worked on his wound.

Suddenly from the street there was loud cheers and hollering. Gus went out to see what the rumpus was all about and ran back into the shop shouting with glee at the top of voice: "They ran away like the rats they are. Mosley cancelled the march when he saw the crowd of demonstrators lined up against him. Whoopee!"

"Well, I never," was the only response from Evie. "We need to have this young man seen by a doctor because he needs stitches. We can't take him to see Dr. Segar otherwise he will be arrested. He will have to come here."

Gus went off in search of Dr. Segar in a good mood and was not his crotchety self at all. Evie smiled. Well, today's events were just the fillip he needed, she thought to herself. He had become very restless and bad-tempered in the last couple of years or so and it was great to see him smile and be happy again. She wondered how long this mood would last, but she had decided she would enjoy it while it lasted.

Tom slowly started to recover from his dazed state as he lay on their settee and tried to sit up but his dizziness returned.

"Now take it slowly, luv. You've had a bad whack to the head and me husband has gone for the doctor. How about a nice cup of tea? By the way, my name's Evie and Gus is my husband."

"Thank you so much for helping me. I'm Tom and I don't want to put you in any danger from the police."

"There's no fear of that. Things will now calm down and return to normal and we can go about our business. Now how about that tea?"

When the kettle boiled and the tea was properly steeped in the teapot, Evie brought Tom a hot mug of sweetened tea. He swallowed the hot drink with enthusiasm and began to feel much better.

About an hour later Gus returned not with Dr. Segar but a nurse. The doctor, Gus said, was busy with a number of casualties at his surgery and sent Nurse Berry to take a look at Tom.

Nurse Berry cleaned Tom's wound with antiseptic and stitched him up without using an anaesthetic. His head was still very numb and he didn't feel a thing. She then wrapped the wound with disinfected gauge and bound his head with a bandage. She gave him some drugs to help his headache and left in a hurry to go back to the surgery.

Tom began to feel much better and after an hour decided he'd better return to Hampstead and pick up his suitcase so he could catch a train which left St. Pancras Station at nine that evening. Gus said he would walk with him to the nearest Underground station, which was Tower Hill.

Jacob was very relieved to see Tom when he arrived at his home in Hampstead.

"Where have you been? And just look at you covered in blood," he said, concerned about his friend. "I lost you in the melee."

"As you can see, I had a bit of spot and bother. I ran into this policeman's truncheon," Tom said, smiling. "What happened to you?"

"When the police horses charged I got stuck under a barrow which fell on top of me. I was helped out by a couple of the lads and we beat a hasty retreat into someone's house until the police left."

"I've got to catch a train at nine back to Leeds. So I have to leave you. It has been nice getting to know you and I hope we can work together at Imperial College."

"You're not going anywhere before you change your bloodied shirt and coat. I'll lend you one of my shirts and a coat. Wait there I'll get them. And the other thing, I'll phone for a taxi to take you to the station."

Tom arrived at St. Pancras Station at about eight thirty and made his way to the waiting room. As he walked towards it, he passed a bar where many people were drinking and singing raucous songs. They all seemed well inebriated, but what he saw made him stop in his tracks. There, in the midst of the crowd and still in the Blackshirt uniforms, were Rodney Garfield, Roger Jackson and Simon Owen.

Tom backtracked so they would not see him and went into a café for a cup of tea and a piece of cake. He supposed they were planning to catch the same train that he intended to and this was the last thing he wanted. He decided to catch the overnight train that left at midnight, which was known as the 'milk train' because it stopped at every station on the line to deliver or pick up milk as well as newspapers and mail.

Tom bought some magazines and a newspaper and settled down to wait for three hours. He eventually reached Leeds at about six in the morning having slept a little. After a bath and a change of clothes he was ready for the day ahead.

However, he didn't know that unexpectedly a person from his past would appear needing help and that this fateful meeting would eventually enable him to wreak his revenge on Rodney Garfield and company.

10

Just as Megan Rafferty had promised, a letter from her arrived two weeks after Tom had returned from London. He feverishly opened it to read the two-page letter, which was in her recognisably neat and precise writing. When he had finished, he read it again and again.

Megan said that her mother had died and the responsibility of looking after her father and brothers fell to her as the only daughter. As a result, she couldn't return to university to continue her education as she had to keep house for her family. As far as her relationship with Tom was concerned, she expressed her love for him but the duty to her family came first and so she would no longer be able to see him. She asked that he not contact her as her family situation had changed their relationship irreparably.

Tom couldn't believe that she wouldn't be coming back to the university. He didn't know what to do. There was no address on the letter so he didn't know where in the big city of Liverpool she lived. He'd have to talk to Dr. Young and get his advice. He was the only person Tom could trust with this type of personal problem. He was due to go to a dinner at Dr. Young's house the following day and he decided to get there early so he could talk to him.

The next evening, Tom knocked on the front door of Dr. Young's house and he opened the door.

"You're a bit early, Tom, but come in."

"I know, Professor, but I need to talk to you about something personal."

Dr. Young looked puzzled and a little concerned: "You better go into my study and we can talk there in private. I'll just go and tell Susan where I'll be. Take a seat, I won't be a moment."

Tom sat down on a comfortable chair and Dr. Young returned.

"Now tell me what's on your mind."

Tom told him about his affair with Megan and showed him the letter he had received.

"The question is what should I do? Should I try and find her?"

"I'm afraid you'll reach a dead end there even if you found her. She and I had a long conversation about her situation because she was one of my most promising first-year students and I did not want to lose her. As she sees it, she has no choice. Her family are forcing her to make the right decision as far as they are concerned. If she doesn't comply they will never speak to her again and she would be ostracised for ever. If she was a boy it wouldn't matter but because she is the only girl in the family that's her lot in life as far as the family see it.

"Old fashioned thinking, maybe, but it's a reality. It is unfair, but that's how many families are run by their parents and it is about time this was changed. We are getting more women now at university than ever before but there are still parents who don't believe in higher education for their daughters."

"So what should I do?" Tom asked.

"Nothing. You can't change the situation and you would only make it worse for her if her family were to find out about you. Just have fond memories of her and of your short relationship then move on. It's tough, but if you love her, you will help her more by leaving her alone and not making her life more unbearable. Of course it's up to you what you do, but I would recommend you leave her alone."

"I never thought of that," Tom said morosely. "Thank you for not pulling any punches. I'll have to think about what you said."

"Now let's join the other guests," said Dr. Young.

In the days that followed his talk with Dr. Young, Tom fell into a deep depression, so much so he was again getting failing grades on his degree course. His concerned professor suggested he take a week off to recover; although he insisted on carrying on, things became worse. Finally, Dr. Young ordered him to take two weeks off.

Tom was angry and bitterness overwhelmed him yet again. As far as he was concerned his life had been a waste. His parent, who turned out not to be, had spurned him, his two love affairs had ended suddenly. His world was on a downward spiral and he believed that no one cared a 'tinker's cuss' about him. In his mind's eye, he was alone now and in his thoughts he grew angrier. His mind was in a whirl of different thoughts, which had triggered only the dark side of his personality. Outwardly he would be the same friendly Tom Pearson, but underneath all of this would be the desire for revenge on his perceived enemies wherever he saw them.

And then there was the dream. It was the same one night after night. There was a party in his stepfather's house in Jarrow with his new wife, his nemeses, Rodney Garfield, Roger Jackson and Simon Owen, and his girlfriends, Jane Harcourt and Megan Rafferty. They were all talking about him in derogatory terms and laughing at their jokes at his expense. In the end, his stepfather raised his glass and made a toast to Tom and they all laughed. At this point he awoke, and he was sweating and angry.

Tom finally came out of his depression more determined than ever to succeed in his career, but the dark side of his personality remained and he was quick to take offence. Music, though, was his panacea and it calmed his troubled mind. He had given up playing at the Crucible pub because he wanted to focus on his studies and two evenings at weekends was too much. He now only played on

Saturday nights at the Black Cat nightclub, where he was totally absorbed in his music and forgot his troubles or perceived troubles.

After one performance, Tom was leaving the club at about one o'clock in the morning and was walking up Woodhouse Lane when he was approached by a tramp who was asking for money. He got some loose change from one of his pockets and was about to give the man the money when he recognised the face that looked up to him.

"My goodness, John Baker," he exclaimed when he recognised his friend from Jarrow and the Jarrow Crusade.

"Hello, Tom. I'm afraid you caught me at a bad moment." He laughed at his own joke.

"I'll tell you what, I know an all-night café nearby. Let's buy you some dinner and a cup of tea and talk."

They reached the café and sat down. John attacked his meal ravenously and it was obvious he hadn't eaten for days. Tom let him eat his food before he started asking any questions. When John finished and began to drink his tea, Tom asked him what happened to him.

"When we got back from the Jarrow Crusade the town was full of appreciation for what we did and I worked for a plumber for a while. Business dropped off after a couple of months and he had to let me go. I did some odd jobs but there was nothing permanent. I became permanently unemployed and got a few shillings a week from the Labour Exchange mainly because of my soldiering in the war.

"About two months ago I decided to try and find work in Leeds, but I struck out here. I need to find work doing something," he cried as he broke down in tears.

Tom let him regain his composure before he said: "Here's what we will do. First, you can come and stay with me and then on Monday we'll start searching for a job for you. Now drink up and let's go back to my place."

John Baker slept on the sofa in Tom's flat and was still fast asleep at midday. Tom was able to do some homework on two papers that were due the following week when his friend finally stumbled out of his bed. After a breakfast, laid on by Mrs. Price, who had been told of his presence, John had a bath and a shave. He put on some of Tom's clean clothes and Mrs. Price gave him a haircut.

When Monday morning came around, John registered at the Labour Exchange so that he could get his 'dole' and see whether there any jobs open that would suit him. One job he saw was for a plumber for a local building contractor. John filled in the necessary papers and set up a time when he would be interviewed by the company's managing director the next day.

John and Tom then paid a visit to the Salvation Army Barracks on Ackroyd Street and rummaged through their collection of second-hand clothes that John could wear. Tom paid a donation to the Salvation Army and they left with a suitcase full of clothes and shoes.

The following day, John Baker left for his interview with the construction contractors armed with his certificates of competences and a reference from his former employer in Jarrow. He got back in the early afternoon looking very depressed and dejected.

"They had already filled the job when I got there. I guess someone had an inside track and was offered the job."

Tom tried to remain positive, saying that it was only the first interview John had been to and he should not feel so discouraged. However, he thought with so many people out of work the chances of an out-of-towner landing a job was remote. He had to help his friend but the question was just how?

Tom was in the university's refectory one lunchtime when he spotted a clerk from the treasurer's office, Percy Tremaine. That department was responsible for non-academic hiring such as administration or facilities staff. Tom sat down next to him and began chatting about the new buildings that were going up on the campus.

"Any new jobs being posted?" Tom asked, taking the bull by the horns.

"Not really. There's a job we're posting next week for a maintenance man to work with Jack Holiday, the head of the university's maintenance department. One of his men is retiring and we need to fill the post. Why, are you interested in the job?"

"No, but a very good friend of mine would be. Can I get a form from you to have him fill it in? It would save the university time and advertising money if he's the right man."

Tom followed Percy back to his office and picked up the personnel form and a copy of the job description. As he was leaving, he met Malcolm Gillespie, who was an assistant treasurer and someone he had met several times at dinner parties at Dr. Young's house.

"Hello, Tom. What are you doing here?"

Tom then explained why he had come to the treasurer's office and told Malcolm about John Baker and his need for a job. Malcolm had been one of the volunteers who helped out when the Jarrow Crusade had passed through Leeds and remembered meeting John at the time. He was shocked to hear his story.

"Leave it with me and I'll see what can be done. Give the personnel form to me when he's filled it out."

A few days later John Baker was told he had an interview with Jack Holiday, head of the university's maintenance department.

Tom briefed John about Jack Holiday: "Some say that he is crusty and mean but he has seen many students pass through the halls of residence over the ten years he'd been head of maintenance and has heard all the excuses for damages and all the complaints about the upkeep of the university's buildings. There was nothing he hasn't heard before. This gives him a patronising attitude towards everyone, including professors. Don't be overawed by that because he is good at his job."

The next day John returned from his interview with Jack Holiday with mixed feelings of how it went.

"Thanks for the warning about his attitude. He really is an old curmudgeon but I liked him. I hope he liked me," he said, worried about whether he would get the job. Two days later he found out the job was his and started work the following Monday.

Now that John was employed, he found a small flat to rent on Gill Street and began his new career. He was ever grateful to Tom and gradually paid him back the money he had spent on him. Tom was reluctant to take it but John insisted, because to him it was about getting his pride back. At work, he was liked, particularly by Jack Holiday and two months later he was invited to Christmas lunch at Holiday's house.

* * *

As winter turned to spring, Tom was busy with exams in his final year at the University of Leeds. In the middle of May, he had received a letter from Imperial College in London offering him a place to study for his master's degree.

His euphoria crashed to the ground when he heard about John Baker's murder from Mrs. Price, who had read about it in the newspaper. He had seen little of John but sometimes he had run into him on campus. Apparently, his body had been found in an alley off George Street near to a pub he used to frequent. According to the newspaper account, he was attacked from behind with a blunt instrument which had smashed his skull in with a single blow.

As he ate his breakfast, Tom read the newspaper account. He couldn't believe what he was reading, particularly the part where it said drugs were found on the body. It didn't make any sense because his friend was not a drug user. He realised that he would have to arrange a funeral because John was all alone in the world with no next of kin. He had to go down to the city morgue and claim the body and make arrangements.

As he was putting on his coat to leave for the physics laboratory, there was a loud knock on the front door. When he opened it there were two men standing on the stoop.

"Tom Pearson?" asked the older man.

"Yes."

"I'm Detective Inspector Roberts from Leeds CID and this is Sergeant Reynolds. We are looking into the murder two nights ago of a John Baker. I believe he was a friend of yours?"

"Yes, that's right. I read about his death this morning in the paper. Look, John has no next of kin so it falls to me to arrange a funeral for him. When can the funeral directors take his body?"

"We're here on more urgent business. We'd like you to accompany us to the station to answer a few questions and make a statement," said an irritated inspector.

"Why? Am I under arrest?"

"Not yet. Do you want us to arrest you?" he replied ominously.

"Sergeant Reynolds will stay here and search your room. Is that alright?"

"Do you have a search warrant?"

"No. But we can get one."

"Then you'll have to get one," said an irritated Tom Pearson.

Tom didn't like the inspector's demands and supercilious tone, which grated with him. He was determined not to let them intimidate him and wanted to make sure they did everything by the book. He had this strange feeling that he might be in trouble and, although he wanted to be seen as cooperating, he needed to be cautious. This was an important position to take because he didn't know what was going to happen and it was important to let them know with whom they were dealing. Their interrogation tactics would be different if they knew he wasn't going to be browbeaten.

Once in the interview room at the old Victorian police station, he was left alone in dank room that smelt strongly of disinfectant. The walls were a lime green colour and the room was windowless. There was a single light that hung down from the ceiling in the middle of the room over a table and four chairs. He sat in one.

Half an hour passed before Inspector Roberts reappeared carrying a green folder. Sergeant Reynolds was at his side. The inspector was a man in his late fifties and had that tired look of someone who had been passed over for promotion many times. He had a very condescending demeanour that probably drove his superiors mad, but he was a good detective and his case solvability rate was higher than average. He wore a rumbled suit that fit uneasily on his heavy-set frame and one word described his dress style, 'scruffy'.

Sergeant Reynolds, on the other hand, was thirty-two, was well dressed as a man about town and obviously spent a lot of time and money on his appearance. He was the inspector's third sergeant in the last eighteen months, as the inspector was a hard taskmaster and didn't suffer fools gladly.

"Now what's this all about?" Tom asked when the two men had sat down opposite him.

Ignoring the question, the inspector asked: "How did you know John Baker?"

"From my hometown of Jarrow." He then explained John's background and how he had fallen on hard times after the Jarrow Crusade and how he had found him a job.

"When did you last see him?"

"I don't know. Maybe a couple of weeks ago when I was walking to a lecture across the quadrangle. We hadn't been in contact much. He had his life and I had mine."

"You mean to say after all you did for him you had little contact with him after you found him a job?"

"That's correct."

"I don't believe you!" barked the inspector aggressively.

Tom was taken aback by the sudden outburst but didn't show it. He realised it was part of this man's interrogation technique to cower people into telling him the truth or what he wanted to hear. Tom wasn't going to play his game.

Tom smiled and appeared unruffled and told the inspector: "I frankly don't care what you believe, but that's how it was between us."

"Did you know your friend was a druggie?"

"No, because he wasn't."

"We found heroin in one of his jacket pockets. How do you account for that?"

"I can't. Tell me, were there any syringe marks on his arms?"

The detectives looked at each other.

"I thought not. Has a sample of his blood sent for testing to see whether there are traces of other drugs in his system?"

"That's our business, not yours," Sergeant Reynolds exclaimed defensively.

"That's fine. Have you ever thought that the heroin was put in his pocket to distract you from the real reason he was killed? This ploy by the murderer seems to have worked successfully."

Tom was surprised at himself. He was now an intelligent and confident man. Gone was the nervous kid of the past. He supposed his recent problems had made him more confident in his abilities and his determination to see that no one would run rough shod over him ever again. He was his own mature person from now on and it showed.

"Where were you last night between ten and eleven?" demanded the inspector.

"Studying for my finals in my room."

"Can anyone vouch for this?"

"My landlady, Mrs. Price, brought me a cup of cocoa at about ten or so, I think. You'll have to check with her about the time because I was so focussed on my work I don't know precisely."

Then the inspector brought out a small beige envelope from the file and emptied its contents on the table.

"Have you ever seen this jacket button before?"

"No. It looks like an expensive blazer button to me. Why?"

"Are you sure it's not one of yours?"

"I don't own a blazer. I couldn't afford one."

"Alright, I want you to write down for me a statement outlining your relationship with Baker and then you can go. However, don't leave Leeds without telling us." He pushed some sheets of paper at Tom and got up and left. Sergeant Reynolds remained.

That evening Tom called into the Pack Horse pub for a pint before heading home. Perched in their usual place near the bar were Rodney Garfield and his two friends.

"I hear the police interviewed you about your murdered friend," shouted Rodney so that the whole pub would hear. There was a deathly hush as everyone waited for his response.

"That's right. They have a witness and a lot of useful clues which will help them track down the killer. It seems whoever it was made many mistakes so it will be only a matter of time before he's caught."

Tom was handed his pint of beer by the landlord and sat at the bar and began to drink. The people in the pub started to talk amongst themselves again now that the show was over. It wasn't long before a flushed Rodney sidled up to him and conspiratorially asked what clues the police had found.

"I have no idea. They wouldn't tell me." This was all Tom would say and he made no mention to Rodney about the button. He wondered to himself why Rodney was so interested in knowing about the clues.

The next morning Tom went to see Jack Holiday. He found him in his workshop and when he saw him he seemed relieved. While Jack made some tea for them, Tom asked: "Have you any thoughts on who would do this to him?"

"Not a clue. He worked hard and everyone seemed to like the man. I'm flabbergasted. I just don't really understand why someone would do this."

"What was he working on the day he was killed?"

Jack went and got his logbook and studied it.

"Ah yes, in the morning he was over at refectory repairing one of the sinks and in the early afternoon he went and fixed a radiator that wasn't working in room number twenty-six Devonshire Hall and then later he was at the chemistry building. They were having a problem with their lighting. That's it."

Tom knew immediately who roomed at twenty-six Devonshire Hall. No wonder Rodney Garfield had tried to get information on police evidence from him the previous night. Now Tom suspected that he was involved in the killing of John Baker and probably that of Stewart Franklin the previous year. But Tom needed more than a hunch. He needed clear evidence and he knew how he was going to get it.

At the weekend, Rodney and his friends were going to be in Manchester for a British Union of Fascists rally and training. Tom knew they wouldn't be back until Sunday night so he decided to look around Rodney's room very early on Sunday morning. After his gig finished at the nightclub at about midnight, he walked towards the university's campus and to Devonshire Hall.

There was a party going on in the hall and the noise was his friend so that he could slip in and out without being noticed. The porter was not at his desk by the front entrance so Tom was able to find the spare key he wanted on its hook on the key rack. He climbed the stairs to the first floor and went up to room number twenty-six. He put on a pair of leather gloves he had brought with him and knocked on the door in case someone was there. Getting no answer, he unlocked the door and stepped in, locking it behind him.

Tom switched on the light and started to look around. He felt his heart pounding, although he felt also a sort of elation about what he was doing. He first looked in the wardrobe where suits and jackets hung. He soon found the blazer with a button missing, which also had a spattering of what looked like blood. He then moved to the radiator which was between the two beds under a window. Behind the radiator was a brown paper bag with several ampules of a liquid. Also in the bag was a small leather case with a syringe and needles in it.

Just as he was preparing to leave, Tom heard a commotion coming from the stairway to the first floor. People were cheering and calling out Rodney's name. Damn, they've got back early, he cursed to himself. As they were on the stairs there was no way he could leave the room. He had to find a hiding place in the room and quickly. The wardrobe was no good because Rodney might decide to change his clothes, and he couldn't escape through the window because there was no ledge outside to stand on. There was nothing to it but to dive under the bed nearest the window.

It was tight squeeze but somehow he got underneath just as he heard a key unlock the door. Two men came in and one of them threw a suitcase on the bed under which Tom was hiding. Tom let out a stifled gasp as the suitcase laded with a thud.

"I think I'll change," said Rodney.

"I'll wait for you downstairs, Rod. There's a young filly I saw as we came in I want to chat up," said Roger Jackson, one of Rodney's acolytes and his roommate.

"I won't be long, Rog. See if she has a friend, right." And they laughed.

The door to the room closed and Rodney began to undress. He got some trousers from the wardrobe and then stopped. He could tell that someone had been in the room because the hangers with his clothes on were in disarray and not neatly aligned as he usually left them. He noticed the cupboard where he kept his shirts, socks and underwear was partly open. Panicked, he rushed over to the radiator and was relieved to see his drugs were still there.

Thankful, Rodney sat on the bed by the window under which Tom was silently gasping for air.

"I think you need a little treat," he said to himself out loud. He then filled the syringe with heroin from his stash. He wrapped a rubber band around his upper arm and, when his vein was sufficiently enlarged, he injected himself. He released the band and let out a satisfied sigh.

Rodney sat on the bed for at least thirty minutes enjoying the high. He eventually got up and unsteadily staggered to the other bed. He crashed onto it and fell asleep.

Tom waited until Rodney began to snore before he peaked out from his hiding place. Just before he started to get out from under the bed, he heard footsteps and he retreated back into his hiding place. The door opened and in walked Roger Jackson.

"For goodness' sake, Rod, did you have to do this now!" he said with disgust, looking at his prostrate friend. He put the drug paraphernalia away and threw a blanket over his friend. He then left the room.

Tom clambered out of his hiding place some five minutes later. He quietly opened the door and peeked out, making sure no one was coming. He quickly ran up to the second floor as he heard people coming up the stairs from the front hall. He hid in a broom closet while someone passed by. How was he going to get out of this place? He was in a panic but after a while he calmed down. He remembered from the time he was a hall resident that there was a back staircase with windows that overlooked a garage. If he could go back down to the first floor he could open the window and drop down on the garage roof and escape that way.

When he heard no other movement, he cautiously emerged from the broom closet and went down the back stairs to the first floor. He unlocked the window and tried to open it. It wouldn't budge. Finally it began to move and he eventually pried it open. He climbed out and closed the window behind him, then walked across the garage roof and climbed down its drainpipe to the ground. He went around to the front of the hall and quickly left the spare key on the porter's desk.

The next morning, Tom bought a newspaper and took it to his room. Wearing gloves he pulled a sheet of typewriter paper from the middle of a pile on his desk and started to compose an anonymous letter to the police by cutting words and letters from the newspaper and sticking them down with paste. He told the police to search room twenty-six because they would find evidence of John Baker's murder and the drugs that were hidden behind the radiator. He told them that maybe the occupants know something about Stewart Franklin's murder as well.

Tom again selected an envelope from the middle of the stack so that his fingerprints weren't on it. He addressed the envelope to the police in capital letters to disguise his writing and placed the letter in the envelope and sealed it. He carefully put the envelope in his jacket pocket and walked down to the centre of Leeds to the main post office. Using a handkerchief, he posted the letter in the post box.

Tom expected the police to leap into action immediately after receiving his letter but he waited impatiently for something to happen. It was a week before the police executed a search warrant and made their discoveries, including a cricket bat which, after tests, they determined was the murder weapon. Rodney Garfield was charged with murder of both John Baker and Stewart Franklin, and his friends, who tried to alibi him, were charged as his accomplices, with obstructing the police and providing false evidence.

By the time their trial came around a year later, Tom was in London at Imperial College and read about it in a newspaper. Both Roger Jackson and Simon Owen pled guilty after the more serious charge was dropped and testified against Rodney. In his arrogance and thinking he could get away with the crimes despite the evidence to the contrary, Rodney pled not guilty, although his parents begged him to admit to his crimes so he would avoid the death penalty. At trial Rodney Garfield was found guilty and sentenced to death. At a separate trial, Roger and Simon were sentenced to five years each for obstruction and providing false evidence.

Rodney Garfield's execution date drew nearer a year after his conviction and all his appeals had failed. He went to the gallows blaming everyone else, including Tom, for his crimes and showed no remorse as he made his final walk to his execution. When Tom read about his death he didn't feel any compassion for the man who had killed his friends. He had no regrets about his role in his downfall. His revenge was now complete.

11

London, January 1939

Tom was in his final year of his master's degree course at Imperial College. The course and research work had been really challenging and he was only one amongst a group of the leading graduates, but he was not the best in his class as he had been at the University of Leeds.

Tom had become a firm friend of Jacob Levine, who he had met two years previously, and they had decided that, because of the intensity and pressure they were under pursuing their degrees, they would spend one Sunday a month doing something other than their work. What started out as just the two of them spending a relaxing few hours soon grew into a group of at least six fellow students.

These getaways were often to pubs, football matches or to dinner at the Lyons Corner House in the Strand. There they spent many happy hours discussing world affairs, the state of the British economy, girls and football. It became clear to Tom that most of his friends had socialist leanings and one actually confided that he had joined the communist party. Tom didn't realise it then, but this information about his friends would help him later in his work for the Russians.

Like many acolytes of communism who never lived under its dictates in a police state, Tom and his friends believed in the theory of humanism and social equality where everyone shared in the country's wealth and successes. Little did they realise that this was only shared by a small fraction of party elites in Russia. They believed in the dogma that was propagandised by communist leaders, particularly when they compared it to Western countries' laissez-faire societies where government control over every aspect of people's lives was abhorred.

At the beginning of 1939, people in Britain were growing very concerned with the threat of Nazism and were trying to come to terms with it. The Nazis were conquering more and more territory in Europe. First it was Austria in March 1938 and then in September that same year the negotiated deal with Britain and France over the annexation of parts of Czechoslovakia, which gave most of that country to the Nazis.

What had incensed everyone, apart from the flagrant country grabs, was the weak leadership shown by Britain and France in the face of blatant aggression by Germany. The farce of the so-called 'Peace for our time' treaty reached in 1938 with Germany by Britain's Prime Minister, Neville Chamberlain, was a case in point. The Nazis agreed that any disputes with Britain would be negotiated and peacefully settled. Although this at the time had popular support, there were many in government, academia, the diplomatic corps and society in general who saw it as a hoax perpetrated on the British government by a master of deceiver, Adolf Hitler.

The world situation had skewed Tom and his friends into thinking about what they would like to do after graduation. They all felt they wanted to work in industry or government research departments to further Britain's scientific strengths against Germany.

* * *

One afternoon in late January, Tom was heading back to his bedsitter in Clapham to finish a paper he was writing when a complete stranger greeted him as he was leaving the Clapham Common Underground station.

"Do I know you?" Tom asked suspiciously.

"No, but Dimitri Smirnov sends his regards."

"Where is he?"

"He was recalled to Moscow last month and I have been asked to work with you in his place. My name is Alexei Dorokhin." And they shook hands.

Tom's new contact was completely different from the dapper Dimitri Smirnov. He reminded Tom of one of the weasels in *The Wind in the Willows*, a children's book he had read when he was younger. Alexei was an emaciated-looking man with ill-fitting clothes. His face was pointed and prominent on it was a large nose that had clearly been broken at some time. Under his nose was a small blond and scrawny moustache, and when he smiled his teeth had a brown/black tinge to them, showing that he was badly in need of urgent dental work. He had tobacco stains on his right forefingers from his ever-present cigarettes. He was wearing a grey raincoat which had a worn and creasy collar, and an old, scraggy fedora that looked like it had come from a second-hand shop in a very poor neighbourhood. Under his hat was his prematurely grey hair, which was long, unwashed and oily.

In fact, thirty-one-year-old Alexei was on his first assignment overseas for the NKVD and he was another one of its illegals (agents who did not have diplomatic cover if caught) operating in the Great Britain. He had been an English translator for the spy agency in Moscow, but Joseph Stalin's Great Terror campaign had eliminated hundreds of NKVD agents, including Dimitri Smirnov, so there was a shortage of experienced agents. Alexei was suddenly put in the NKVD's international department, which was responsible for all foreign operations, and he was sent to London.

"Let's take a walk on the common so we can't be overheard," suggested Alexei.

They walked towards Clapham Common on a street called The Pavement and crossed over to the open expanse of the common. They walked along a footpath towards Holy Trinity Church and finally sat down on a bench near the church.

"Tom, are you still interested in helping us fight the fascists?"

"Maybe," he responded guardedly. Was this man the best the Russians could do as a contact? he thought sceptically.

"What are you worried about?" asked Alexei, sensing caution in Tom's voice.

"I've read in the newspapers that there are show trials at the moment in Moscow where many are accused and, after an appearance in court, are executed. This seems like how the fascists operate to me."

"I wouldn't believe everything you read in British newspapers. They are only the propaganda arm of the British government. Look who owns them: people like Lord Beaverbrook and Lord Northcliffe, who are just lackeys of the government. Even the much-feted BBC has as its director general Sir John Reith, another friend of the government. No, it's prejudicial reporting to stir up hatred of Russia, no more than that. There are maybe one or two people from the old regime being tried for their corruption, but that is all.

"Now tell me, Tom, what are your views of the world situation?" probed Alexei, changing the subject.

"I believe that the world would be a better place if everyone was equal and had opportunities to better themselves despite their upbringing or status in society. The British government believes in the status quo and the fascists believe in giving power to the few and crushing all opposition. It seems that communism offers a good alternative in theory and I am willing to give it a try as an alternative."

"What about your Labour Party, don't they provide an egalitarian system you want?"

"No. They're not much different from the Tories. They are run by the labour unions who really want everything to remain the same except with them in charge. Their ideas are moribund and not radical enough to create real change in this country. They talk about nationalising this and that industry but they have no sweeping plans to develop them. Now in Russia there is a sweeping new system that has a few teething problems but everyone there knows the plan.

"Also, we should start by getting rid of the Royal Family and its hangers-on. We have to clear out all these lords and courtiers who are all parasites. We should take away their land and put it to better use so the working men and women can prosper, just like they did in your revolution and in the French Revolution."

Tom's frank views clearly surprised Alexei and it was obvious that he was naive about the true facts on the ground in Russia. Alexei knew a number of the people in the NKVD who had disappeared, never to be seen again, and he was glad to get out of Moscow. Even so, he was frightened for his own safety and was determined to make a success of his new assignment, although he would never know when he might be recalled. This foolish Englishman was an important recruit and he wasn't going to mess this up.

Alexei continued: "We need you to help us grow this sweeping new system, as you call it, but we can't do that if we can't expand our position, say, in technology. War is likely between Russia and Germany, so we need a lot of help, because when the communist party took over our industries and military, we found out that we were sadly lacking in modern systems and technologies. This is where you can make a real difference."

Tom didn't answer right away as he was thinking about Alexei's proposal. They walked to a nearby mobile café for some tea and sat down again on some benches to drink it.

"You look concerned, Tom. What is it?"

"You're asking me to betray my country? Why would I do that?"

"Think about my proposal this way. You want to introduce communism into Britain as a way of improving the lot of the working man and his family. The only way we can do this is to show the world that our ideals work and should be adopted worldwide. Without that we can't succeed and our cause will be lost. You are not betraying your country but saving it from disaster. Do you want to see another great depression like 1929 and 1930 from which Western nations are only just recovering? We have a cause worth fighting for!"

"Maybe I can help you. But I wouldn't know where to start," Tom said eventually.

"Well, here's my plan," said a clearly relieved Alexei, who probably thought the conversation was heading into negative territory. "First, we need you not to attract attention to yourself from the authorities, such as being active in the British Communist Party or speaking out publicly about your views. In other words, keep your thoughts under cover. Second, find a job working for a government department. You'll be finishing your degree this summer so now's the time to plan your career. We want you to work some time before you could be of use to us, so you won't hear from us again for maybe a year or so. Don't be concerned because we will not forget about you."

They talked for another half an hour and Alexei answered most of his many questions satisfactorily.

"There is one final thing before we go our separate ways," said Alexei. "We want you to visit one of our safe houses in France this summer so we can give a more thorough briefing and teach you some basic espionage techniques. Have you got a passport?"

"No."

"You'll have to get one. I'll be in touch with you about the travel plans and details later on. Thank you for your help."

And with that, Alexei walked off and was soon lost in the mill of people shopping.

Tom remained seated on the bench and gave his conversation

with Alexei a lot of thought. At least, he rationalised naively, he could always back out of the arrangement if he didn't agree with what he was asked to do.

The next day Tom visited the post office in Clapham and picked up a passport application form. Reading it through on the Underground on his way to the university, he was surprised at the documents the passport office wanted. He had no birth certificate or letters of recommendation from a prominent person such as a vicar, bank manager or doctor as the form required. He wrote to Dr. Young at the University of Leeds asking for a letter of recommendation and went to see his bank manager with the same request. When these arrived, he spent the better part of a day at Somerset House in the Strand so he could get a copy of his birth certificate. Somerset House was the depository of all birth, marriage and death certificates for England and Wales at this time.

Armed with the documents and pictures, which had been taken in one of the many photographic shops at Charing Cross, Tom sent off his application. Two months later a brand-new passport arrived.

With his university career coming to an end when he graduated that June, Tom wrote to Arnold Wilkinson. He hoped Mr. Wilkinson would remember him after their brief meeting two years previously. A few weeks later, he received a letter calling him in for an interview.

Precisely five minutes before his interview, Tom walked into the Air Ministry building at Aldwych and Kingsway in central London. He was shown into a large waiting room where there were several other young men about his age waiting. He recognised two of them from seminars he had been to over the years. He went up and introduced himself again to them. Despite his friendly greeting, they were both sullen and quiet and didn't want to talk. He realised that all the other interviewees seemed to be very nervous, although he wasn't and he didn't know why. His confidence in his own abilities had grown over the years and it wasn't arrogance. He had not been shy about asking questions or putting forward his own ideas either at the university or at social settings.

Tom sat down and took a book out of his briefcase and began to read. The first candidate was called and so began a long wait as each person went in and exited out of another door so he and the rest of the interviewees couldn't get any idea what the interview panel was asking. But what he did notice was that he was the only interviewee carrying a briefcase in which was six copies of his thesis he had written as part of his master's degree course.

Two hours later Tom's name was called and he was ushered into a large room. At one end there was a large table with three men seated behind it. There was a lone chair in front of it to which he was directed and was asked to sit by the escort who had called his name. He recognised Arnold Wilkinson but not the other two men. A gruff Scotsman, who was the chairman, introduced himself and his two colleagues. He was Robert Watson-Watt, scientific advisor on telecommunications to the Ministry of Aircraft Production and the pioneer and developer of radar. He was sitting on the panel with Dr. Edward Bowen and Arnold Wilkinson, who were his two main collaborators in the development of radar.

"Mr. Pearson, why do you think we would take you on as a member of our research team?" demanded Watson-Watt immediately when Tom sat down.

Tom looked at him for a few seconds. He decided to take the 'bull by the horns' and not be intimidated by the man because this was what was expected.

"Because I'm first class at what I do and radio spectrum of frequencies is my abiding interest, as you will see from my thesis."

Tom opened his briefcase and took out three copies of his thesis and handed each surprised man a copy.

"Thank you, Mr. Pearson. Could you briefly talk about its main findings?" commanded Dr. Watson-Watt.

Tom spent the next half hour presenting his findings and taking questions from the panel, which were at times very aggressive as they were testing him and his views. He enjoyed the experience and thought he gave as good as he got. Finally it was over and he was dismissed.

In April, Tom received a letter from Arnold Wilkinson informing him that he had been accepted to work on radio frequency research. He was to report the Bawdsey Manor in August. He had to look up where this was at the local library and found it was in Suffolk on the east coast of England facing the North Sea.

12

Alexei Dorokhin contacted Tom again at the beginning of May. As they walked towards the bandstand on Clapham Common, Tom told him about being accepted to work on radar research. Alexei was delighted at the news and congratulated him on his success.

"We've arranged for you to visit a place in France for two weeks at the beginning of July. We want you to cross the Channel from Dover to Calais on July 5th and you will be met by one of our people. He or she will take you by train to Paris and put you on another train to Mâcon, where you will be met again and taken to our safe house. Here's some money to buy your tickets."

Alexei handed him an envelope with money and journey details. They talked further for a few minutes. Alexei wished him good luck and left him as he headed to the Underground station.

Tom decided to take the train from Charing Cross in London on July 4th so he could catch the early ferry the next day to Calais. When he got off at the Dover Priory station, he walked down to the seafront and found a small hotel. The next morning he caught a ferry across the Channel to Calais arriving at about nine in the morning. His instructions said that he was to sit on a bench by the port exit. He did so and began reading a book to pass the time as he waited.

About half an hour later, as he was deeply engrossed in his book, he was aware of someone standing next to him. He looked up into the most beautiful eyes he had ever seen. The woman smiled and extended her hand to shake his.

"Tom, I'm Madelaine and I have been asked to take you to Paris. Do you speak French?"

"No."

"I didn't think so. Most Englishmen do not," she teased, and smiled. Her English was very good, although she spoke with an accent.

Tom reckoned that Madelaine was probably in her mid-twenties. She was about five feet tall and had short dark hair under a French beret. She was dressed in workman's clothes of dark blue trousers, a grey jacket and French clogs. Underneath the jacket he could see a blue striped shirt and what intrigued him was that she didn't seem to be wearing a bra. Her well-proportion breasts were free to roam wherever they liked as she moved about. The rest of her body was muscular and he thought that she had the body shape of one of those beautiful female statues in the Victoria and Albert Museum. He was entranced by her.

They walked together into the centre of Calais and caught a train for Gare-du-Nord in Paris. The train was so full that he sat very close to Madelaine and they talked about university life. Madelaine was a graduate of the Université de Strasbourg, where she had been studying economics and was working as a waitress part-time in a Paris restaurant. She came from a family of doctors in Strasbourg, both her parents worked in private practice and her brother was at the same university studying medicine.

Tom was very attracted to this effervescent French woman. He told her all about life in Jarrow and his growing concerns about British workers. She said she had the same views despite her wealthy upbringing and had joined the Parti Communiste Français or PCF. She showed a great deal of interest in his background and pummelled him with questions. She managed to find out about his love of jazz and the fact he often played piano in small clubs in his spare time.

An hour before they arrived in Paris, Madelaine had fallen asleep on Tom's shoulder and he had put an arm around her. They took the Paris Metro to Gare-de-Lyon, where Madelaine put him on a train that went to Mâcon. As she said goodbye, she kissed him on his cheek and waved as the train left the station.

By the time Tom arrived in Mâcon it was about one in the morning and he had been instructed to spend the night in Hotel Renard on the Rue Bigonnet, which was opposite the train station. He was due to be picked up from there at seven the next morning. As he left the station he easily found the hotel, which was a small pension with only fifteen rooms. As he entered the hotel, he saw the night porter fast asleep with his head resting on the reception counter. He coughed loudly and the man woke with a jolt. He handed him the card Madelaine had given him which said who he was and that he had a pre-paid room booked.

Tom found his room at the top of the building. To call it a room was a bit of an exaggeration, as he banged his head several times on the low hanging and sloping ceiling. It was more like a closet, but it had a bed, which he was glad to collapse onto after his tiring journey. Although the mattress on the bed was very lumpy, he was able to find a comfortable spot and was soon dreaming of Madelaine.

The next morning Tom was extremely stiff from the uncomfortable mattress, but he was able to wash and shave in the bathroom on the floor below. He went down to the restaurant on the ground floor, where there were a number of people including some men who were probably locals who had stopped by for their breakfast on their way to work. They were known to the middle-aged waitress, who clucked around them like a mother hen. There was a man sitting by himself in a suit, who was probably a salesman who had spent the night at the hotel before he moved on to customers in another town. Also, there were two old ladies who were likely permanent hotel residents.

Breakfast of coffee, rolls, cheeses and various cold meats was welcome as Tom was very hungry, having not eaten the day before. As he was finishing his second cup of coffee, a man came into the restaurant and asked in French whether he was Tom Pearson. He nodded.

"My name is Marcel Durand and I'm to take you to Sergy," he said, again in French.

Marcel was a big man, standing at least six feet five inches, and was in his late fifties. Tom thought he would be a useful bouncer at a nightclub and guessed he had been a wrestler in his youth because of his two cauliflower ears and a broken nose. His hands were the size of large pineapples and just as knurled. He wore an ill-fitting jacket and a waistcoat that didn't match his trousers. Tom noticed a bulge under his left armpit and, when he moved, a butt of a revolver was clearly visible. But Marcel was a gentle giant who had a kind nature as he stood in front of Tom with his cap in hand. Tom smiled and offered him some coffee and a seat at the table.

They left the hotel and Marcel opened the back door of a Citroën Traction Avant saloon car and they started their three-hour journey to Sergy.

Sergy was a small village of some 260 people at that time in the south-eastern tip of France, very close to the Swiss border. It was nestled in a large woodland and mountainous park, which was some ten miles as the crow flies from Geneva, Switzerland. The NKVD had chosen this quiet village so that if they got word of a raid by the Deuxième Bureau, the French spy agency, from their agent in Paris they could quickly and easily escape to Geneva.

The Citroën drove through the village of Sergy to a large manor house about a mile outside it. The car entered the property through a guarded gate which was opened by a severe-looking man with a shotgun over his shoulder. The house was on the side of the hill and overlooked a valley of vineyards.

As the car drew up to the front of the building, the front door opened and out stepped a stooped old man who looked to Tom to be in his eighties. He had grey hair and a beard and was wearing a traditional kosovorotka Russian shirt, black trousers and Cossack boots. He was walking with the aid of a walking stick. Despite his outward rickety appearance he had piercing grey eyes that studied Tom meticulously as he put out his knurled hand to shake hands.

"Welcome. I'm Victor Borgan and I am your host for the next two weeks," he said in excellent English and in a firm, authoritative voice. "Before we go in, I ask that you use David Suskin as your name with other students and our staff. Only I and our driver know your real name. Also, don't give away any personal information such as your hometown or university. We do this for security reasons to protect you once you return to England."

Tom thought this was a strange request but agreed to abide by Victor Borgan's rules.

Victor Borgan was by definition a survivor. He was a language teacher from Rybinsk in western Russia and joined the Cheka, the first Russian internal security agency before the NKVD, just after the October Revolution in Russia in 1917, which brought Lenin and the communists to power. Although he was considered too old for operational responsibilities at fifty-eight, he helped Felix Dzerzhinsky, the first director of the Cheka, to organise the rag-tag agency behind the scenes. It became a formidable secret police force and enabled Lenin and his successors to maintain power.

In 1925, he had retired and was living in Leningrad (now St. Petersburg). He was regarded as an 'Old Bolshevik' and these men had been targeted in the Great Terror led by Nikolai Yezhov, head of the NKVD between 1936 and 1938. Although he had been called in for interview and questioned, he was let go and was regarded as not a threat to the Russian People because he evidently had always kept a low profile when he retired. He managed to survive the questioning and its consequences mainly because of the contacts he still had in the NKVD, many of whom were eventually summarily executed.

By 1939, he was brought out of retirement and set the task of training foreign agents, as the Great Terror had decimated the ranks of the NKVD and there was no one of any rank or experience left to fulfil the task. He had cobbled together his training staff from less experienced personnel. He knew his team was not perfect, but he had to make the best of the people he had.

Tom picked up his suitcase and followed Victor Borgan into the house.

"This is Anna, and she will show you to your room," instructed Victor Borgan. "We are about have lunch so if you could just put your case in your room and come downstairs I will do the introductions to your fellow students."

When Tom entered the lounge, he was introduced to everyone, including the trainers. There were five other students, all young men about his age – two from Italy, a German, a Dutchman and a Spaniard. They were told that training would be in English as this was spoken by everyone. The first session began after lunch and was given by a political commissar on the Russian revolution, its goals and how these would be achieved.

Political Commissar Vitaly Abramovich droned on for two hours and his students were heavy-eyed at the end. But they got their own back on him by peppering him with a number of pointed questions. It was obvious to everyone that he wasn't used to being questioned closely and critically by his students, and this only motivated them to carry out their pursuit of him by questioning him further. He became angry and started shouting at them and then he beat a hasty retreat from the classroom, much to the amusement of everyone, including Victor Borgan. He had heard the noise from his office and looked into the room to see what was going on. Victor had been forced to include this lecture by his bosses in Moscow, but he knew how Europeans would react to it; after all, they were not docile Russians and were used to questioning everything.

The lecture was all the talk and laughter at dinner stimulated by the good French wine supplied by a local vineyard. Everyone had been cautious of each other at first, but Victor saw that they began to gel as a group led by Tom and one of the Italians. They were all interested to hear from the Spanish student, Felipe Gomez, talk about the Spanish Civil War, which had come to a bloody end that April with Franco's fascist forces finally winning. Felipe told the group that there were too many warring factions on the Republican side. For example, the Trotskyists were always at loggerheads with Leninists or Marxists and vice versa, and they all hated the anarchists, who they tried to eliminate them with summary executions. According to Felipe, towards the end there was chaos in the Republican ranks and no military cohesion because of these factions.

The next two weeks were covered with talks on such issues as network recruitment and organising covert meetings. They were taught and practised the basics of surveillance and how to avoid it, as well as how to use drop boxes. They were given rudimentary lessons in secret writing, which included the enciphering and encoding of messages to be sent, as well as deciphering and decoding incoming messages. They learnt how to use one-time pads for sending covert messages and the latest Russian advances in photography.

Victor Borgan was pleased by the progress his students had made. He was concerned, though, about Tom, who seemed to be very critical of the progress Russia was making and he had seemed extremely cynical in his views. Victor had seen Tom's file and realised that the work he was starting back in England would be extremely valuable to the Russians in the long term, so he decided to guarantee the Englishman's cooperation if he should decide to abandon his role. He made a call to Moscow and discussed his concerns about Tom with his bosses in the NKVD. They agreed his plan of action.

At the end of the two-week training period, Victor Borgan

threw a lavish end-of-course party where they all became very drunk. By the end of the evening, Tom was introduced to a newcomer who said he was part of the staff. Tom felt very woozy and struggled to find his room and, with the help of this new man, he collapsed on his bed.

The next morning, Tom woke up naked on his bed feeling the after-effects of the liquor, or so he thought. He remembered nothing about the night before except for bright flashes before he fell asleep. He thought it must have been the effects of the vodka Victor had brought to liven up the party. He had the hangover of all hangovers and his throat was dry. Years later he was to find out what had really happened.

Tom stumbled out of bed, dressed quickly and went down to breakfast. He was in desperate need of coffee but when he reached the dining room there was no one there. Everyone had gone – his fellow students, trainers and even the kitchen staff. It was then that he looked at his watch for the first time and saw it was two in the afternoon.

Just then he heard a car driving up to the house. He ran to the front door and was relieved to see the Citroën pull up with big Marcel Durand in the driver's seat. Tom rushed upstairs and packed his bag quickly. When he looked back at the manor house as he was driven away, he thought his experience of the last two weeks had been surreal and he was glad to see the back of the place. He still didn't know whether he wanted to become a Russian agent.

Tom slept on the train from Mâcon to Paris and only woke up when the train came to a juddering halt in the Gare-de-Lyon and porters were shouting, "C'est Paris," at the top of their lungs. He was one of the last passengers to leave the train as he still felt very fragile from the night before and, as he handed his ticket to the collector at the barrier, he saw Madelaine.

"Hello there, Tom. My God, you look awful!" she exclaimed as she kissed him on the cheek.

"That, Madelaine, is a long story. I could do with some coffee."

They went to the station buffet and he drank two cups of coffee and ate a croissant.

"I'm supposed to take you to Calais but by the time we get there tonight there won't be any ferries so we'll go in the morning. You can stay with me tonight and we can have dinner at a small bistro I know."

"I'm in your hands. But first I need to tidy up."

They took the Paris Metro underground train to Saint Marcel and walked to Madelaine's flat on Rue Jeanne d'Arc. The flat was on the sixth floor and the building had no lift so they had to walk up. It was a small one-bedroom flat that had a small kitchen and bathroom. Tom ran the bath and got in. He was feeling a lot better now, particularly after seeing Madelaine again, and his head had stopped pounding. The bathroom door suddenly swung open and Madelaine came in with two glasses of wine and sat on the edge of the bath. At first he was embarrassed, and then he relaxed and they talked as he washed himself. She handed him a towel as he stepped out of the bath.

After dinner at Le Chat et La Lune bistro, they went to a small club to dance. Madelaine seemed to be known by most people, including the owner, Henri.

"I've got a surprise for you and I hope you won't be angry," Madelaine purred in his ear as they were dancing. "I asked Henri whether you could play some jazz during the band's intermission and he said yes."

Tom didn't know whether to be annoyed or not. But how could he be mad with such a beautiful woman?

"I don't know. I'm very rusty."

"Go on. Please, for me."

"I'll see what I can do."

When the intermission came, Henri came up to their table and asked Tom to play for them. He sat down at the piano and started to play 'Embraceable You', 'Mood Indigo', 'Blue Moon' and some traditional jazz favourites. Everyone in the audience stopped talking, the people at the bar went quiet and the musicians who were on break came back to listen. Soon the bass player started to improvise, followed by the saxophonist and then so did the drummer until all the members of the little band joined Tom. The session lasted about thirty minutes and when it had finished the audience were on their feet applauding and cheering.

Madelaine was overjoyed by Tom's playing. She had never seen or heard a performance like it. People were buying them drinks and asking him to play again. By the time they left the club it was one in the morning.

As they entered Madelaine's small flat, they began to undress each other and were soon lost in passionate lovemaking.

As Tom's ferry pulled away from the quay in Calais the next day, he could see Madelaine waving to him and blowing kisses. He stayed on deck until Calais disappeared from view and he was just left with the circling seagulls.

Part Two

A Spycatcher Emerges

"You will never be able to tell your friends or family what you really do for a living. You will never be the celebrated hero, rather always the unsung protector in the shadows watching over those who need the sacrifice of you and your colleagues."

Maxwell Knight, MI5 Spymaster during
World War Two and author of *How to Become a Spy*

13

Moscow, Russia, February 16th, 1938

When Robert Johnson looked back at what unfolded in the late 1930s, he realised that both he and Tom Pearson had one thing in common: they both were real novices on different ends of the espionage spectrum. They were both to learn their trade without much guidance from their superiors. They were both thrown into the proverbial deep end to see if they survived, and they did.

While Tom was busy in his final year of his physics master's degree course at Imperial College in London, Robert Johnson had reached a stage in his career when he had to make choices. His career as major in the Royal Marines was coming to an end and at forty-eight he had been approached by a friend of a friend to join the British intelligence services because of his language skills, an eye for detail, which is vital for a successful spycatcher, and a sceptical mind-set that had paid him dividends over the years. He liked being a prosecutor of recalcitrant lawbreakers so he had accepted a position to work for MI5 and MI6.

Robert found himself in Moscow at a critical time when relations between Britain and Russia were at a low ebb. His official title or cover was an assistant military attaché at the British Embassy and he was the embassy's head of security. In truth, he was undercover and none of his colleagues or even the ambassador himself knew of his real role, which was to search for information from Russian citizens about the machinations of the very secretive Russian government and confront any Russian moles in British groups in the country.

The powers that be in the security services had him appointed because the British ambassador, the Viscount Chilston, had refused to have a passport control officer appointed to the embassy despite the current cauldron of fear, anxiety, deception and plots by vying political factions in Russia.

The title of passport control officer was a euphemism and cover for British intelligence officers in all countries. But the British ambassador wouldn't have one. An experienced operative in that position could ferret out critical information and help prevent security breaches. And so the task fell to Robert, unofficially. No one knew why the ambassador wouldn't have anyone there from the intelligence services in the embassy. Perhaps he had had a bad experience in one of his other postings, or was it the financial scandals in the mid-1930s at the British embassies in Poland and the Netherlands that had involved passport control officers?

Anyway, as far as everyone else was concerned, Robert was part of the military attaché's staff and he reported secretly to a Foreign Office contact in London.

Robert, after a year in his post, was bored with his assignment. He was not one for the social round of embassy life because you had to be good at small talk and gossip, which often had no practical meaning or use. He thought that some of the diplomats he knew could happily make small talk to a rock if they had to. Anyway, he was a pragmatic man who didn't like the nonsensical round of embassy receptions and avoided them whenever possible. Thus, he was not well known among the diplomatic community or among the Russian hosts and he liked that arrangement.

His boss at the embassy was army Colonel Roy C. Firebrace, who was the head of the British Military Mission in Moscow. Reporting to the colonel also was an RAF group captain and a navy captain. The problem was that the Russians were not very forthcoming with information of any use to these attachés, so in his junior role Major Johnson was not called on to interface with his Russian counterparts very often. This freed him up to concentrate on embassy security and other matters.

Major Robert Johnson was six feet two inches tall and slender and was fastidiously dressed at all times. He had a small, waxed moustache on his upper lip which he cultivated every day, as he did his greying and thinning hair. He was a no-nonsense man, with a dry wit, and was obsessed about keeping himself fit. He had a punishing exercise routine carried out in the basement gym at the embassy first thing every morning, followed by a cold bath. He never married, although he had several opportunities over the years but could not settle on any one woman or they couldn't settle on him. Maybe he was too fussy and even his mother had given up trying to find him an acceptable wife.

He was a graduate of Manchester Grammar School and the University of London, where he studied mathematics. Wanting a change from academic life, and much to his parents' annoyance, he became a midshipman at the Royal Naval College in Dartmouth. He transferred at the college to the Royal Marines officer training and graduated in 1908.

Robert saw action in World War One as a captain in the Royal Marines Light Infantry. He had been wounded in 1916 at the Battle of the Somme when, as a company commander, he was leading his marines on an assault north of the River Ancre. He was hit by shrapnel in the left eye and spent months recovering, first at an army hospital in France and then he was transferred to the Royal Naval Hospital Stonehouse in Devonport in Britain. The doctors replaced his eye with a glass one and he spent a month getting used to it.

Following his rehabilitation, he was promoted to major and became a staff member of the Royal Naval College, Greenwich, which provided advanced training for senior naval officers. Because of his highly developed analytical skills, he was transferred to naval intelligence under Vice-Admiral Maurice Fitzmaurice in 1923. His success there led to his appointment to the post in Moscow in 1936.

Apart from his intellectual and military skills, he had a natural ear for foreign languages. Six months before he left for Moscow, he had immersed himself in the Russian language and read avidly Russian newspapers and literature.

From his office window at the embassy, Robert could see the Kremlin across the other side of the Moscow River. The Russians always worked late into the night because the lights on the Kremlin were ablaze well past midnight and you couldn't get hold of anybody at the various commissariats (ministries) before midday. It was not that he wanted to. The Russians he dealt with in his military capacity were a boorish lot who only came alight after a few glasses of vodka late into a boozy night and then it was to insult you or your country.

He had come to the conclusion early on that Moscow and other cities he had been allowed to visit in Russia were desolate and forbidding places. It was worse in winter, when blankets of snow constantly fell and getting around was a major challenge. There was no street lighting that helped him walk to his flat in a five-storey building a quarter of a mile from the embassy. It got dark in the winter at five in the afternoon and the sun didn't rise until eight thirty the next morning, but you never saw it because of the permanent overcast clouds which gave the city a depressing, sombre appearance.

In addition, there were bands of criminals that roamed the streets at night who attacked and robbed unsuspecting victims. It was a lawless place outside the confines of the Kremlin, as people were fighting to survive. In general, the populous had become extremely jaded about the 1917 revolution and the utopian promises that were made by its leaders. Now only a few benefited, but they lived in constant dread of who was informing on them and whether they would be arrested.

Joseph Stalin, who was the authoritarian leader of this third-world country, ruled by fear, and leading Russians lived under the constant threat of arrest, torture and execution or banishment to the gulags for real or perceived crimes. Since 1936, the country had been consumed and terrorised by what was called the Great Terror, which lasted until the spring of 1938. There had already been two show trials of top-level leaders who had, as expected, been found guilty and executed. These men were mostly old Bolsheviks who had been leading revolutionaries in 1917 and were men who Stalin regarded as serious competitors. They had stood zombie-like in the dock and made false confessions after being forced to do so by their torturers. There was a rumour going around that there was to be a third show trial that coming March.

But these show trials were just the tip of the terror nightmare because there were many summary arrests all over the country and executions of many lower-level people in the NKVD (the Russian intelligence service) or GRU (Russian military intelligence), generals and admirals and lower ranks in the military, commissars, intelligentsia, artists, poets and peasantry. Some estimates put the number of people who died at one and a half million, and many more were sent to the Russian slave labour camps in places like Siberia.

The tension in the air was palpable, as if everyone was waiting for the shoe to drop on them with a loud knock on the door in the middle of the night. Hardly any work was done by the British embassy staff with their contacts in the government and Robert didn't know from one meeting until the next who his opposite number was going to be. The officers he knew had a habit of disappearing and never being heard of again. The purges had decimated the ranks of the NKVD and other security services.

Agents were being recalled from all parts of the world and most were tortured and executed on little or no evidence of guilt by kangaroo-like courts.

Robert was obsessed about security at the embassy and his strict military training had given him an eye for detail that would have escaped others. He knew full well that the Russians were determined to infiltrate the embassy to learn British secrets. When he first arrived, he tightened up on access to the building and was fastidious about logging in all visitors, however important or unimportant they were. In addition, he discharged some of the Russian workers the embassy employed who were probably NKVD or GRU plants and restricted the others to certain areas. This had made him many enemies among some of the embassy staff but he had the backing of the ambassador. His standing in the embassy was raised when he found crude listening bugs in the many of the rooms and offices used by diplomats as well as in the 'holy of holies', the safe room where extremely confidential meetings were held.

As he sat in his office at the embassy going over a report that he was about to send to London, his telephone on his desk rang. The voice on the other end told him that Viscount Chilston wanted to see him immediately.

Viscount Chilston was a career diplomat educated at Eton and had been an army officer before joining the diplomatic corps. He had been appointed British ambassador to Russia in 1933 and was due to retire in December 1939 after nearly forty years in the diplomatic corps. His years of experience had moulded him into a shrewd and sardonic man who was an accomplished linguist, something rare among senior British diplomats.

The ambassador's office was the size of a small ballroom at an English country house with shelves of books and a number of paintings of past kings and queens. At the far end sat the ambassador behind a large oak desk. It took Robert several seconds to march across the room to reach Viscount Chilston, who waved him to sit down as he finished signing some papers which he then handed to a male secretary.

When the secretary had left, the ambassador looked up.

"Robert, it seems we have a major leak from this embassy. Apparently, the Secret Intelligence Service have been interrogating a NKVD defector in Switzerland who told them, among other things, that the Russians were getting copies of our cables to and from London," said the irritated ambassador.

Robert wondered why he hadn't been informed about this through his back channels: "How long has this been going on, sir?"

"They didn't say. I want you to do a thorough investigation right away starting with the cipher clerks, as one of them is more likely to be the culprit, and then work your way up the ranks of staff."

"The only thing I ask, sir, is that the knowledge of these leaks be kept between the two of us. I don't want the perpetrator to be warned so he could cover his tracks."

"Of course. That sounds like a sensible idea. And Robert, I want you to report to me each day at five on the progress you've made."

Robert sat in his office and reviewed in his mind the approach he would take to find the traitor in the embassy. He was uneasy about immediately pinning the blame on the cipher clerks, who were low-paid and were often treated with distain by diplomatic staff. But he had to start somewhere and the cipher clerks had to be his first avenue of investigation.

He knew the weakness in the code system at most embassies was the interface with humans, be they cipher clerks and other staff from each department who would see the messages before they were encrypted for transmission or vice versa when they were received. There were five clerks at the embassy who had responsibility for encrypting and decrypting messages given to them by the diplomatic staff for cables that were to be sent or received. They used a twenty-four-volume code book to prepare the outgoing messages and to read the incoming ones. Each word had a numerical code and the task was laborious but essential for security.

The NKVD or the GRU knew about this weak link and exploited it so that they could read the embassy's coded messages. There had been several instances in the past at other embassies where cipher clerks were caught providing information to foreign intelligence agencies for money or because they were being blackmailed. SIS wasn't averse to putting pressure on cipher clerks in other countries' embassies and had 'turned' clerks in the same way to gain information about British adversaries.

There was a procedure each evening when that day's decoded messages were destroyed. This was supposed to be supervised by a junior diplomat, usually a third secretary, who was supposed to watch a janitor put that day's messages in the embassy's boiler to incinerate them. This task was seen as very menial by the attachés, who would often leave it to the cipher clerks to supervise the task. The compromised clerk could just keep any important messages to pass on to his contact.

Robert read the personnel files of each of the cipher clerks that evening and nothing stood out. Each of them had really high grades and were given highest level of security clearance. Each man was married and three of them had been accompanied by their wives. He decided to interview each one with the excuse that London had asked him to regularly screen everyone working at the embassy.

It wasn't until the last interview a few days later that matters started to take shape. Randell Wilkins was a man in his late fifties and had experience working for British embassies in many parts of the world. He was about to retire the following year and was happy and unafraid to speak his mind. When Robert asked him what he would like to see changed in procedures, he suggested that documents should be shredded by using a hand-cranked machine that looked like a pasta maker.

He said he saw one demonstrated in Germany in 1935 when he was in the Berlin embassy by an Adolf Ehinger who made the machines: "That would stop little 'Lord Fauntleroy' giving us a hard time when we incinerate the day's documents. We could destroy them as we go along during the day instead of having to wait until later. It'd be more efficient."

"Who is little 'Lord Fauntleroy'?" Robert asked, amused by the comment.

"James bloody Bollinger, that's who. He's the only attaché that supervises our destruction of messages each day. The others leave it for us to do. He goes through each document before we put them in the boiler. When he spots one he wants to keep he'll put it into his leather folder. He's always in the department looking over our shoulders and seems to regard document destruction as his bailiwick. I asked him once why he did that and he told me to mind my own business. Well, he's the boss, so I don't think about it anymore.

"You know, Major, I'm glad I'm retiring because if the service has people like him around, I'm well out of it. I've seen some lousy diplomats in my time, but he takes the biscuit! I'm sorry to be going on so, sir, but he gives me the creeps."

Robert reviewed Honourable James P. Bollinger's personnel file. He had been in Moscow a year. He was the youngest son of Lord Ellsworth, a law lord who had spent many years as a judge in Britain and had retired from the bench five years previously. James was the youngest of four siblings who included two girls. He was educated at Eton and the University of Cambridge, where he read philosophy and gained a second-class honours degree in the subject. He joined the Foreign Office in 1932 and had been posted to the embassy in Cairo, Egypt, in 1935.

The Honourable James's yearly reviews were not very impressive and he had been admonished on one occasion for behaviour unbecoming a British diplomat. No other details were given about the offence of which he had been found guilty. He had been given a warning that his continuing service would be terminated should the offence occur again. Robert's attention was piqued at this and he was determined to find out more information.

Robert didn't really know James Bollinger well, but his experience in the Royal Marines meant that he was very adept at judging people and he was rarely wrong. Their paths had crossed mainly in meetings and he didn't really like the aggressive, know-it-all diplomat who seemed to be hiding something by the bluster he projected. Maybe he was really shallow because he was always making crude jokes heavily laced with innuendos that seemed like a cover for something. He had been one of the diplomats who had made a big fuss over the security measures Robert had introduced.

The weekly diplomatic bag was due to leave that evening and Robert wrote a note to his contact at the Foreign Office asking for more details of James's offence in Egypt and he asked him to reply through the diplomatic bag only.

Robert decided he'd have to follow James Bollinger to see whether he was the quarry he was looking for. He didn't understand why the man was collecting discarded messages unless it was for nefarious reasons. He knew at that time Britain and France were trying to entice Russia to join them in peace talks with Adolf Hitler so there had been a lot of cables back and forth with London on this subject which would be of interest to the Russians.

14

Robert left the embassy at six that evening and walked to the building where his flat was. His usual NKVD tail was there and followed him as he walked along trying not to fall on the ice and snow. The pavement hadn't been shovelled so he had to climb over snowbanks. He reached his building and waved to his tail and shouted goodnight. He felt sorry for the man who was always there when he went anywhere such as the ballet, concerts or to embassy receptions.

The living accommodations in one of the wings of the embassy were appalling and those at Hodgson House, the former embassy building which was still used, were just as bad. The embassy was extremely draughty and the coal-fired boiler was always breaking down. Robert decided after his first year in Moscow that he would find his own accommodation. He had a small private income left to him by his parents and a housing allowance from the British government so he rented a flat. He had spent many hours updating and repairing it. It wasn't perfect but it was better than what was on offer at the embassy.

Robert climbed up the stairs to his fifth-floor flat. All Russian buildings had no lifts and because they were badly built there was often problems with plumbing or electrical. It took weeks for anyone to come and fix whatever was wrong. In the end, he often did his own repairs.

When he reached his flat, he turned on the light and went to the window to close the curtains and, as he did so, he saw his tail trying to keep warm.

In his bedroom a transformation occurred. He changed into Russian workman's clothes and boots which he had collected from an outside market in the summer in case he needed to go incognito at any time. He then put on a false beard and dark make-up to hide his light-skinned hands and face. And his 'piece de resistance' was his Russian glasses with plain lenses. He also had a second-hand overcoat, warm hat, a scarf and mittens.

He then pulled out of its hiding place his Leica camera which had a fast film in it for night shooting. He put the camera in the inside pocket of his overcoat with his skeleton keys in case he needed them. He picked up an old hawthorn walking stick which had a one-foot knife hidden in its hilt. And now the metamorphous from a dapper military attaché to a tramp was complete. As he left the flat, he put a bottle of very cheap vodka in one of his overcoat pockets.

The tramp left his apartment block by a back door, which was used by the janitor. He placed a piece of tape across the latch so that door would open easily when he returned. He walked down a small alleyway which came out on a side road and this led to Sofiyskavn, the road running past the British Embassy. He leaned against the parapet that overlooked the Moscow River and waited.

At about seven James Bollinger emerged from the embassy after supervising the destruction of confidential papers and was carrying a large brown envelope. The tramp snapped a photograph of him holding the envelope. He turned left outside the embassy and walked along Sofiyskavn with the tramp following. He caught a tram on the corner of Serfimovich Ulitsa and the tramp had to run to catch the tram. The tramp sat at the back with other Muscovites and watched. The tram reached Gorky Park and many of the passengers got off, including James Bollinger. But the tramp couldn't see him. Panicked, he looked around and, after a few unnerving seconds, he caught sight of him entering a restaurant, one of several near the park entrance.

Gorky Park was opened ten years previously and, even in the dead of winter, it was the playground for Muscovites with its exhibition halls, fairground, formal gardens and woodland all in about three hundred acres of land in the middle of Moscow. It was officially called the Central Park of Culture and Leisure and was named in 1932 after a famous Russian writer, Maxim Gorky.

The restaurant was in a pedestrian walkway which led to the fairground and the large Ferris wheel, which was a central attraction. As the tramp passed the restaurant he could see through the large picture window James Bollinger seated at a table with two men and one of them had the envelope. There were picnic benches on the other side of the path across from the restaurant so the tramp sat on one of the benches. He took photographs of the men surreptitiously, but all the time he looked around to make sure he wasn't being observed.

After an hour, James Bollinger and the men left the restaurant. The one carrying the envelope went off by himself and James and his companion walked to small bar on Krimsky Val. The tramp sat on a bench nearby and took photos. He got out his bottle of vodka and pretended to drink from it and play the part of a drunken vagrant.

Two cold and damp hours later, the two men left the bar and caught a tram which was headed across the Moscow River. The tramp didn't follow because he had enough photographs and had seen all he wanted. It was time to head back to his flat.

On the way there the tramp passed some other vagrants around a brazier keeping warm and he decided to stop and warm himself before his long walk home. This was a mistake.

"That will cost you a rouble. Pay up!" said the drunken leader of the group as the tramp approached.

"I haven't got any money, but I can give you my bottle of

vodka." And he offered the bottle to the man, who snatched it from him and took a swig.

"You don't sound Russian to me. Where you from?"

The tramp had to think quickly: "Estonia. I was in the Russian army and was demobbed here in Moscow."

The tramp turned to leave, thinking he'd better go before things got out of hand. He had walked a few yards when he heard someone coming after him. He turned to see three of the group coming towards him and their leader had drawn a knife.

"Now we want your wallet, you bastard!" he screamed, and lunged at the tramp, who was able to parry the thrust with his arm. The two other vagrants closed in and the tramp was able to draw his knife from his walking stick and plunged it into the chest of the leader. The man fell to the ground clutching his chest and his compatriots stopped dead in their tracks and watched him writhing on the ground.

With their attention momentarily elsewhere, the tramp took off running and soon there was a hue and cry after him. But he was fit, unlike the alcoholics chasing him, and he soon outpaced them. He took off down side streets and alleys because he was worried that the noise and kerfuffle would attracted the attention of the police. Sure enough, he heard klaxons and saw two police cars racing towards the scene. He took off his glasses and beard in case someone might give the police a description and threw them into a rubbish bin in one of the alleys.

Finally, the tramp made it back to his building and let himself into his flat. The first thing he did was pour himself a large scotch and sat down to relax. What an evening, he thought, but he was glad to get the evidence he needed. He looked down at his arm and saw blood. Damn!

Robert stripped off his jacket and saw a large knife wound on his arm. He cleaned it off in the bathroom and put some of his scotch on it to cleanse it. Then he tore up an old shirt and used it as a bandage.

He spent the next two hours developing the film from the camera in his bathroom. He hung up the wet prints to dry overnight and went to bed.

The next morning, Robert went to work as usual. He had wrapped his tramp's clothes in a brown paper parcel and put the walking stick down one of his trouser legs. The photographic prints were safely in his briefcase. His tail was there outside his building and he wished him, as usual, a good morning. When he reached the embassy, he went to the boiler room and threw in the clothes and the walking stick, saving the dagger to use as a letter opener.

Robert then made arrangements to meet with Viscount Chilston. They had a long conversation and the ambassador telephoned the Foreign Office in London on the scrambled phone in the embassy's 'safe room'. This black telephone with its bright green handset was introduced into the embassy in 1937 and was used only when top-secret discussions were to take place and there was a need to encrypt the line.

At three that afternoon Viscount Chilston summoned James Bollinger to his office. Robert sat in a chair to the ambassador's right. As he entered the office, James Bollinger was surprised to see him and became clearly nervous as he sat down in front of the ambassador's desk.

"Mr. Bollinger, it has come to our attention that you have been supplying the NKVD with confidential communications between this embassy and London," said the ambassador starchily.

"Ambassador, that's not true at all. I suppose Robert here made up a story. He's never liked me, you know," he said superciliously.

"We have witnesses who saw you take certain papers from those to be destroyed. What have you done with them?"

"Ah, the odious and hateful men in the cipher room. I took those documents out because they were not supposed to be destroyed and I filed them away in our registry."

"Major," said the ambassador.

As Robert got up he spoke for the first time: "Thank you, sir.

How long have you known Vladimir Kuznetsor?"

"I've never met the man," James Bollinger said tartly.

"That's funny, you met him last night."

"No I didn't!" he barked angrily.

"If you are going to lie, do it properly." With a sigh, Robert handed him the photograph that he took of the men in the restaurant. James Bollinger blanched.

"Did you know that he was a NKVD operative?"

"Absolutely not. He was a friend of mine who I met at some party or other. His name to me is Olaf Vasiliev."

"Who's the other effeminate-looking man?"

James flushed: "He's a very close friend called Vasily Mikhailov."

"Is he your lover?"

"Well, actually…" And his voice trailed off.

"Is he!" Robert demanded in a raised voice.

"Steady on, Major," remonstrated the ambassador. "A chap is allowed to keep some things private."

"No, sir, not if he's leaking secrets to the Russians. Are you being blackmailed because of certain pictures they've got of you with your boyfriend? Have they threatened to reveal your secret if you don't hand over what they need?"

"No, that never happened!" cried James and he began to cry.

"Oh, no! This picture is of you leaving the embassy last night with an envelope which has some writing on it. And this photograph is of Vladimir Kuznetsor, your NKVD contact, saying goodbye to you and your lover outside the restaurant. But look, he's carrying the same envelope with the same writing. What a coincidence."

James Bollinger began to cry uncontrollably. Robert sat back down again and waited for him to stop blubbering.

When he stopped, he started to get control of himself and then asked a question: "Was Vasily in on the blackmail plot?"

"Very likely. They needed to keep you sweet on him to get what they wanted."

This answer brought another round of crying and wailing.

After a few minutes the ambassador spoke up: "Get a grip on yourself, man, and listen. A British delegation from the Foreign Office is due to fly in tomorrow for two days of talks with ministers of the Russian Government. With them will be two Special Branch policemen who will take custody of you. After the talks, you will accompany the delegation back to London. The authorities will then decide what to do with you."

"They'll hang me!" cried James.

"Probably. That depends on any useful information you could give them," Robert said, keeping the pressure on James Bollinger.

"In the meantime," continued the ambassador, "you will be locked in the storeroom in the basement. We've put a camp bed in there for you and we will feed you. Take him away, Major."

15

Tsaritsyno, Russia, August 13th, 1938

The reign of terror in Russia was beginning to ebb. The last show trial in Moscow had been in March and, whilst there were some further trials in the regions, much of the bloodletting had dissipated. What was left of the Russian hierarchy was nothing short of disastrous. The leadership ranks of the NKVD had been virtually annihilated, as well as those of local government officials throughout the country. The officer ranks of the Red Army and Navy had been decimated so much they were in a tragically weakened state and far from able to defend the country. What was still left was fear. You could sense it in people you were in contact with, and the only friendly contacts you had were other diplomats from other embassies.

Elsewhere in Europe the situation was very tense. The Germans had marched into Austria in March without a shot being fired and Hitler was talking about rescuing Germans in the Sudetenland in Czechoslovakia.

This day Robert was sitting in the early evening on the veranda of an old dacha in Tsaritsyno, just south of Moscow, and he was enjoying a cool breeze after temperatures had reached the mid-seventies during the day. The embassy had rented this small cottage from the Russian government and senior embassy staff took it in turns to spend weekends there. It was delightful to sit there with a book and look out at the rolling hills and wheat fields below. For this short time, Robert was able forget the turmoil of life in Moscow and the growing war clouds on the horizon in the rest of Europe.

Robert was expecting a new friend of his to join him for dinner and a game of chess. They had often done this late into the night, drinking Robert's hoarded Scotch or his friend's Schnapps when he was the host. They enjoyed these evenings as they chewed over the latest political happenings in this god-forsaken country they found themselves in.

His friend was forty-seven-year-old Klaus von Dannhäusser, a second secretary at the German Embassy. Klaus was from a small town in Bavaria where his family were noted beer brewers and he had been educated at Harrow and then the University of Oxford. But like all young men at that time, he was caught up in the tragedy of World War One when he served as an artillery officer. After being demobbed from the German army, he joined the Auswärtiges Amt, the German foreign ministry, and was first based in Washington and then London before being sent to Moscow.

Robert and his German friend had a passion for chess. In Robert's case, being a mathematician by training, the game had always appealed to him because of the tactical puzzles it presents and the need for fast problem-solving as it challenged the brain. Robert was in the right country to indulge his infatuation. Russia was viewed as the epicentre of chess. Just about everyone played it in clubs dotted around that vast country. It had become a national pastime when the Russian government, after the 1917 revolution, set up chess schools and ran tournaments. There were chess clubs at trade unions halls, the military had clubs and so did cities and towns; even the NKVD had a club in Moscow.

Klaus and Robert met one cold January night at the Central Moscow Chess Club in the Ministry of Justice building on Llyinka Street. Robert had just finished a game when this rather imposing figure stood over him and asked, in bad Russian, whether he would like a game. He had noticed him watching him play and he was curious about who he was. He was too well-dressed for a Russian citizen and had a definite positive and somewhat overconfident air about him. He must have stood at least six feet four or five and his blond hair was cut short in a military style.

They played three games that night and each was a draw. Robert found out that he was from the German Embassy and he realised that he needed to cultivate him as a potential contact for the British government. But he was under no illusion that the German saw him as a useful British contact.

Truth was that Robert liked this bear of a man, his ready sense of humour and his no-nonsense approach to life. He was very sharp and insightful in current events and about the Russian government's eccentricities. They played every week from then on. Sometimes they played at each other's flat and got totally wasted as the night wore on with either whisky or schnapps. They both enjoyed giving their minders from the NKVD the slip each time they met. In fact, they had quite a game going on to see who could be more creative in losing them.

Both their embassies rented dachas near to each other, so on summer evenings they played chess after dinner. They both knew that the dachas were wired with NKVD listening devices, so they didn't say anything important inside. There were no devices for some reason on the verandas, so they went there in order to talk in confidence and sometimes they went walking.

Robert saw Klaus coming down a path towards him and he waved to him to join him. When Robert reached him, he saw that he was in a sombre mood, but he brightened when they shook hands.

"I wanted to get out of range of their listening devices to ask whether you heard that you are about to get a new ambassador. Viscount Chilston is retiring and Sir William Seeds is taking his place in January," Klaus announced.

This caught Robert totally by surprise and it must have shown on his face. Klaus gave one of his loud guffaws.

"How did you know that?" Robert asked incredulously.

"A little bird from London let foreign minister von Ribbentrop know last night and he sent our ambassador, von der Schulenburg, a cable."

"Klaus, this is all news to me. Do you think the Russians know?"

"Probably. They have tentacles all over the place including in the corridors of Whitehall. The decision was made in April and has been a closely guarded secret. Apparently your Foreign Office is going to make the announcement next week."

Robert could see that his lack of knowledge of this news amused Klaus, as he was chortling as they went up the path to the dacha.

After dinner of trout, which was accompanied by a dry white Burgundy wine, they settled down to play chess on the veranda. Robert poured them both a large scotch and they began to play. Two hours later they had almost finished the bottle of Talisker single malt Scotch whisky and they sat there enjoying its peaty taste. Then that sombre look came over Klaus again that Robert had seen when he first arrived that evening.

"Robert, we've been friends for many months now and I know you will hold in confidence what I tell you," Klaus slurred, as he had obviously drunk too much and had let his guard down. Suddenly, he had become an emotional and confused man, a side Robert had never seen before.

"I need to talk to someone about the situation which a number of us in the Foreign Service feel about Germany's foreign policy at the moment. Frankly, we don't relish the future of Germany under the Nazis. At least von Neurath, our last foreign minister, was one of us in that he lent an aura of respectability to their expansionist foreign policy plans. But now we have the Champaign salesman, von Ribbentrop, who has been hoisted on us. Frankly he knows nothing about foreign affairs and is a complete playboy. The man has no morals and he has mistresses in many cities. Just ask your Duchess of Windsor!"

"What do you mean?" Robert asked sceptically. "She's not 'ours' but we are grateful the Duke met her and abdicated. Was she his mistress?"

"Yes, when he was German Ambassador in London."

"Well, I never." Robert laughed.

"Well, to get back to what I was saying," Klaus said, slightly irritated that he had got off the subject of what he wanted to say. "We can only see disaster rearing its ugly head and we can't have that again. You must warn your government somehow. It seems that our Chancellor is not satisfied with conquering Austria, as he is now making moves against Czechoslovakia under the pretext of rescuing German nationals there. It's only time before he moves against other countries. Your Prime Minister Chamberlain is a weak man in dealing with Hitler and so is France's Édouard Daladier."

"I agree. I thought Germany had made great strides in recovering economically from the austerity of the Versailles Treaty, but I must admit the world is concerned with Hitler's expansionist policies."

"Well, it seems that Hitler is also thinking about courting the Russians. My guess is that he wants to transfer some of his military divisions to the west of Europe. He's already tasked Karl Schnurre from the economics department of the Foreign Ministry to start negotiations in the beginning of the New Year for a new trade agreement with the Russians. So you see, we are heading for Armageddon once again after all the work that was put in to revitalising Germany! It's all been a waste!"

"How do you know all this?"

"I've been told to help Herr Schnurre when he comes here to Moscow. I've seen all the papers that our ambassador has. And from the way he briefed me, I suspect something else is afoot, but I don't know what. This is terrible for Germany. We can't fight a war all over again!"

Klaus started to softly cry and eventually he fell asleep in his chair. He was obviously so distraught and Robert wondered how many other diplomats felt the same way. He had seen the carnage of World War One first-hand and could not contemplate a repeat of the apocalypse, with so many lives lost or devastated. It was certain he was suffering mentally from what he had seen and, when he was with Robert, he was putting on a performance of the happy-go-lucky Bavarian he wanted to be.

In addition, he said that there had been an increase in so-called 'diplomats' at the German embassy who were either Gestapo officers or members of the Abwehr, the German intelligence service. Klaus had been more cautious recently about their meetings because he was particularly fearful of stirring up any interest by them in himself.

Robert helped him with great difficulty to navigate the corridor in the dacha that led to the small second bedroom. He put him to bed and went to bed himself in the other room. He lay there thinking about what he had heard and trying to decide how he was going to report his findings to the Foreign Office.

That Monday morning Robert wrote a report and sent it to his London contact via the embassy's diplomatic bag. He never mentioned anything to anyone at the embassy about the change in ambassador. Viscount Chilston was in London for talks at the Foreign Office and was probably briefing Sir William Seeds, his successor.

Robert didn't see Klaus again for over three months. One evening he suddenly turned up at the Central Moscow Chess Club, and during one of their games he whispered that he had been away in Berlin working with Herr Schnurre, the German trade negotiator with the Russians, to prepare for a series of meetings in May 1939.

That night was the start of regular updates from Klaus on the secret trade negotiations between Russia and Germany. The Germans offered a credit line of two hundred million Reichsmarks for the much-needed capital goods Russia needed in return for the export of materials such as oil to Germany. As Klaus's reports grew in number, Robert wondered whether there was a more secret agreement in the offing and Klaus confirmed that this was the case.

Robert reported all this to the new British ambassador, Sir William Seeds, who seemed unconcerned about these negotiations and his suspicions of a sub-plot. Because of his reaction, Robert also sent reports and concerns to his MI6 contact in London.

Sir William was negotiating an anti-Nazi alliance between Britain, France and Russia, which the Russians had proposed in April 1939, whereby the Russians would station some 120 infantry divisions supported by tanks and artillery on Russia's western border. If the Nazis attacked Europe these forces would cross Poland in support of Britain and France. The only problem was that Poland would not agree to this and was adamantly opposed to having Russian forces on its territory.

British Admiral Sir Reginald Drax, head of the British and French delegation, eventually visited Moscow to start negotiations on August 14th with Marshal Kliment Voroshilov. The British and French delegation had irritated the Russian government by showing no urgency in arriving in Moscow. Admiral Drax and French general Joseph Doumenc arrived after a long and laborious trip on board the freighter *City of Exeter* and then by train from Leningrad to Moscow. This circuitous journey indicated to the Russians a lack of urgency compared with the German trade delegation, which had flown in from Berlin.

The British and French governments, because of the intransigence of Poland, did not confirm the deal. Instead they had instructed their negotiators to keep talking but never to come to any agreement. This stalemate in negotiations frustrated the Russians and so they began talking to Germany about a non-aggression treaty between the two countries. This came to be known as the Molotov-Ribbentrop Pact, named after the foreign ministers of Russia and Germany.

Robert found out from Klaus about the non-aggression negotiations between Germany and Russia and the fact that von Ribbentrop himself was coming to Moscow to sign the agreement on August 23rd, which was in several days' time. They were sitting one evening in a small bar they used to frequent after their chess game when Klaus announced this news. Robert left immediately for the embassy to warn the ambassador of this impending crisis.

As Robert briskly approached the embassy on foot, a car pulled up next to him and two large men got out. He took off running but he was overtaken by the car which mounted the pavement and trapped him against the embankment wall. The two thugs grabbed him and a third man produced a syringe and injected something in his arm. He must have lost conscious immediately because he didn't remember the ride in the car.

Robert didn't recall much from the days that followed because he was in and out of consciousness. He knew he was in a cell of some sort and all around he heard cries, sobs, groans, people wailing, and interrogators cursing in Russian and shouting at inmates.

In his semi-conscious state he knew he was on an iron bed and he was wearing a straitjacket. When he tried to call out no sound would come out of his mouth. Every so often someone would come into his cell and he would feel another the jab of a syringe and he would fall asleep again.

Robert had no idea how long he was in this comatose state. Eventually, he remembered being manhandled again into a car. When he began to wake up again from his stupor, he found himself in the British Embassy infirmary. He was very thirsty and had an almighty headache. As he began to look around, the embassy's doctor came in and began examining him.

"What happened to me?" he asked incredulously.

"Robert, it looks like you have been drugged. There are at least six or seven puncture wounds on your arms. Do you remember anything at all?"

"Not really."

When the doctor had gone, he lay there in bed trying hard to remember what had happened. The doctor said that he had disappeared over a week before and the embassy guards had found him in the early morning at the end of the embassy driveway two days ago. At first they had thought he was some drunk sleeping it off on a warm night but then they saw who it was.

It wasn't until the next day that Robert started to recollect what had happened. He rang the small bell on his bedside table to summon the nurse. When she appeared, he demanded to see the ambassador. He tried to get out of bed but fell on the floor. Damn it, his legs weren't working.

"It's vital that I see him urgently now!" he screamed.

About two hours later, Sir William Seeds came to see him.

"Sir, I have found out that the Germans are about to sign a non-aggression pact with the Russians! That's what I was trying to warn you about before I was kidnapped," Robert said excitedly.

"We know, Robert. They signed the pact a week ago. Someone clearly wanted to stop you telling us. I'm afraid all our work has come to naught. Now I want you to rest and we will make plans to have you returned home."

When he had gone, Robert wondered what had happened to Klaus. It was only after the war that he found out that he had been interrogated in Berlin and shot.

Two weeks later Robert caught a train to Leningrad and a British ship home. His Russian adventure was over, but his career was about to take an unusual turn.

16

Royal Marines Depot, Deal, England, December 5th, 1940

When Major Robert Johnson came back from Russia in 1938, he was sent back to the Royal Marines because no one seemed to know what to do with him at the security services. He supposed he had fulfilled his assignment and the agencies at this time were very small and organisationally chaotic. He was assigned to the Royal Marines Depot in Deal, Kent, and was put in charge of recruit training, which was done there and at Eastney Barracks in Southsea near Portsmouth. This was an urgent requirement during the early part of World War Two as the Royal Marine brigades were to be raised to divisional strength and other battalions were to be added.

Robert had a good team of instructors and, after he had reorganised the running of the training, everything seemed to be moving along smoothly. And then he became bored. He realised that there was no way the Royal Marines would activate a one-eyed, middle-aged officer into an operational battalion. So he was stuck in a training battalion. Some people would have told him that what he was doing was important, and so it was, as the country was ramping up the size of its military. Nevertheless, he felt he was not being used to his full potential and his training team could easily function without him. He was 'chaffing at the bit' to be doing something useful for his country, which was in dire straits at this time.

Britain had declared war on Germany in September 1939 and the German army, like an unstoppable juggernaut, swept through the Low Countries of Holland, Denmark and Belgium and then through France by the end of June 1940. Now Britain stood alone. Winston Churchill had become Prime Minister in May that year and he was immediately faced with the task of rescuing the British Expeditionary Force from the beaches of Dunkirk; a few weeks later the evacuation began of British troops from Norway following the invasion of that country by the Germans. So there had been nothing but defeats for the beleaguered country.

One Monday morning, Robert was sitting in his office nursing a persistent hangover from a mess dinner the night before, when the telephone rang. His secretary, a petty officer in the Women's Royal Naval Service or what was known as the Wrens, said that a Lieutenant Commander Ian Fleming was on the line. He had met Ian Fleming on several occasions at the Admiralty Building in Westminster. He was an assistant to Rear Admiral John Godfrey, Director of Naval Intelligence, and had been one of the people who had de-briefed him on his return from Russia.

"Ian, what can I do for you?"

"Are you a happy camper where you are, old chap?"

"Not really. It was a bit of a come down after my Moscow tour."

"I thought so. Look, come up to town and meet me at my club, Boodle's, on Wednesday, say, at noon. I've got someone I'd like you to meet."

Before Robert could ask him who this person was, he had rung off.

That Wednesday found Robert walking up St. James's Street in the pouring rain. He had come up to London the night before by car because of the nightly bombing the train service was unreliable. He had spent the night in the basement Naval and Military Club in Piccadilly. Staff there had set up cots for members in the building's bomb shelter. Strangely enough, there hadn't been an air raid that night because of the bad weather so they weren't disturbed.

Robert reached Boodle's on time and was ushered into the dining room by one of the hall porters. Ian Fleming was sitting with a very tall man who was well built and had a warm, welcoming smile. They both rose to greet him.

"Robert, welcome! I'd like you to meet Maxwell Knight, who you probably heard about. Max and I go back some time as we were colleagues briefly."

They shook hands.

"That's very true. I'm glad to meet you at last, sir," Robert said as he retrieved his hand from a strong grip.

Maxwell Knight was dressed in a plain, crumpled navy suit and Robert guessed he was in his early forties. He had short, combed-backed, parted-in-the-middle brown hair that was beginning to go grey at the sides. Apart from his bushy eyebrows, he had a bulbous nose and rather large ears. But he was not an ugly man and was attractive in a rumpled sort of way. He could be very charming and he often swept his female agents off their feet. His voice was low and rich, and you paid close attention to what he was saying as an automatic reflex when working with him.

He was smoking a hand-made cigarette and, as they sat down, he offered Robert one from a silver cigarette case that had a stylised 'M' embossed on it. Robert turned down his offer.

"I read your report you submitted after your return from Moscow and, I must say, it was very thorough. Now that the Russians teamed up with the Nazis, we'll have to be very watchful of their spying here, but even if they were our allies I wouldn't trust them. Tell me, what it was like dealing with them?"

The waiter appeared and took their drinks order and Robert

waited for him to leave. He then spent the next fifteen minutes giving Maxwell Knight his thoughts and he seemed to be very interested in what he had to say and peppered him with insightful questions.

During lunch they discussed the war and the political situation now that Winston Churchill was Prime Minister. Over coffee and brandies Maxwell Knight turned to Robert, looked him in the eye and said: "I would like you to come to work for me, focussing on Russia and their spy networks here. We've been able to catch a few but it needs someone to concentrate on this evil full time. Some people in the secret service see the Germans as the only target. That's wrong. What do you say, Robert?"

And that's how Robert began work again full time for MI5 in 1941. The pay was awful, but his pension from the Royal Marines and his inheritance from his parents allowed him to find a comfortable flat in Richmond, which is a town just west of the city.

He attended a four-week orientation course at the Blenheim Palace in the country near Oxford, which was the temporary war-time home of MI5 where most of the administrative staff and the agency's registry were based. Registry was the department that stored and organised all of the agency's files on subversives and other suspects. It was a vital source of information as they worked through cases.

Having completed the course he was assigned a broom closet of an office at MI5's headquarters in St. James's Street in London. The so-called office was very sparse indeed. He had a desk, a table lamp, two chairs and a safe. All officers were under strict instructions that they were not to leave any files or papers on their desks when they were not there, even if they just went to the bathroom! Every night these documents were to be put into the safe at night and only the individual officer and the director of MI5 knew the combination. Such was the strict security.

It is important to understand just how eccentric Maxwell

Knight was and that this was part of his brilliance at running agents. There has been no one like him in the security services history. His success rate in running to ground subversives has never been matched. Part of his success was the secrecy of his operations and his obsession with security, even with his interaction with colleagues in other departments in the agency. To start with, his office was away from MI5's headquarters in a new block of flats called Dolphin Square which was close to Westminster. He met his key officers there and briefed agents in seedy hotels far away from prying eyes. He just didn't trust anyone at head office. His paranoia was justified when he became the first senior officer to suspect Anthony Blunt of being a Russian mole inside MI5. Blunt was one of the Cambridge Five Russian spy network.

The other eccentric part of him was his passion for all types of wild animals. His flat on Sloane Street was a menagerie of creatures from foxes, snakes, birds and at one time a bear cub. His staff never visited him at his flat, but there were these stories from people who had. His staff would often be surprised at meetings in Dolphin Square when he would have one of these animals with him.

Robert spent his first two weeks reviewing files on communist activity. Maxwell Knight had been able to insert two agents into the organisation of the Communist Party of Great Britain (CPGB) and had secretly placed listening devices at its headquarters on King Street in Covent Garden, London. The members of the party were involved in a number of subversive activities and MI5 was able to keep a watch on these and to take action when necessary.

It was from one these recordings that Robert's first operation for MI5 began on a cold February day. The recordings had picked up a discussion among several representatives from Glasgow about the significance of getting hold of plans of an advanced torpedo design at the Royal Navy Torpedo factory in Greenock, Scotland. At this time, the Royal Navy was about to manufacture a new and very advanced torpedo, which would be of interest to the Russians.

One of the participants in the discussion assured others that they had a person in the factory that would acquire the plans so they could be photographed.

MI5 didn't want to alert anyone at the factory by carrying out an overt investigation because they needed to round up all members of the network. They didn't know at this stage who was the leader, but they knew the name of a communist sympathiser in the area so he was their first suspect. His name was Angus Cameron and according to his file he had been to Russia in 1935 as a British representative at the world congress of the Communist International, or Comintern, which was an organisation that promoted the spread of communism around the world.

Robert telephoned Superintendent Charles Watts, the head of special branch in Scotland. MI5 had no arresting powers and relied on special branch officers, who were policemen, to arrest and prosecute suspects. These officers had the task of watching and gleaning information on any suspect organisations in their region. This was often done by physical surveillance on suspects or by the use of informants.

Superintendent Charles Watts was a Glaswegian through and through, having served as a policeman in some of the toughest neighbourhoods, such as the Gorbals and Bridgeton areas of the city. He was brought up in a Gorbals tenement by a very strict mother and a drunken father. He joined the Royal Navy at the age of sixteen and, following promotions over the years, left the service as a chief petty officer in the Royal Navy police and then he joined the Glasgow Police force. He was well-respected by Maxwell Knight as a shrewd and resourceful officer, and Robert was warned not to underrate him.

"How's that old bugger Max?" the superintendent asked in a booming Scottish brogue down the telephone. "He and I did a lot of work together. Is he still chasing those commie bastards?"

"Yes, and that's why he added me to his team," Robert responded. "In fact, that's why I'm calling you. We have had word that there is a communist network at the Royal Navy Torpedo factory in Greenock."

"Hmm. I wondered when this might happen. We've been keeping an eye out on that place for any activity for some time because this is a really sensitive factory. Who do you think is behind this?"

"We know through our sources in London that Angus Cameron might be involved, but the question is who has he got in the factory to carry out his espionage work. The point is the navy is planning to start work on a new torpedo sometime in the next two weeks and it seems that the plans will be in danger of being copied at that time."

"Leave it with me, Major. I'll make some enquiries and get back to you."

Three days later Robert got a call from Superintendent Watts. "I think we've got something. Get up here and I'll have a car meet you."

Robert let Maxwell Knight know what was going on and he caught the overnight sleeper to Glasgow and arrived at seven the next morning. He was met at the station by Inspector Brian Wilcox and driven to police headquarters in St. Andrew's Square.

When he walked into Superintendent Watts' office to meet him for the first time, he was struck by the size of the man. He was six foot five inches and built like a professional wrestler. No wonder he didn't brook any nonsense in those tough areas of Glasgow. Robert thought you wouldn't want to get on his bad side, ever. He had curly red hair cut short and was wearing half-moon spectacles that hid his blue eyes. He took his glasses off and came around his desk to shake Robert's hand.

"Thanks for coming here, Major. We think we have the man you are looking for. His name is Charlie Spotswood, who is a general handyman and house painter who does work for the torpedo factory, and he's there right now painting some offices there. He is a fervent communist and lives on Newark Street in

Greenock. He does a lot of handyman work for the navy and, as such, has made friends with a number of workers at the factory. We've made a list of these men and we can interview them when the time comes."

"The latest information I have is that the copies of the plans will be made in the next week and then given to the Russians in London," Robert said.

"Right, here's what we do. Major, you and Inspector Wilcox take over the surveillance of Spotswood. I suggest that when he's seen with the plans or suspected of having them, he is followed so we can arrest his contact as well. Now, you'll be in an unmarked car with a new-fangled gadget called a car radio which Brian here can use to let me know when he's making a move."

17

Late that afternoon Inspector Wilcox and Robert set off by train to Greenock. They were picked up at the station by a young detective constable in an unmarked police car.

"Have you ever done any surveillance work, sir?" Inspector Wilcox asked.

"A little bit but not much."

"Every copper hates it because ninety per cent of the time nothing happens. Let's hope this is a ten per cent occasion."

Inspector Wilcox parked the car in a side street opposite the entrance to the factory gates and hidden from casual view. They soon saw Charlie Spotswood as he arrived to begin work that afternoon. He seemed to know many of the workers who were returning from their lunch break and was specifically friendly with a security guard at the gate who didn't even want to see his pass.

"Whew! Did you see that?" said Inspector Wilcox as he finished taking photographs with his camera. "So much for security! This place is due for a shake-up when this is finished."

The rest of the afternoon was spent with nothing much going on. Come the end of the shift at the factory, workers poured out through the gates, including Charlie Spotswood. One of the inspector's constables joined them in the car. He was dressed in workman's clothes and had been infiltrated into the factory as one of its maintenance workers.

"He's been decorating the factory manager's office where the plans are kept, sir."

"When do you think he'll make his move?"

"Well, he's about halfway through the job, so he'll still want time working there to return the plans. He has asked that he work overtime so that he can finish the job because the factory manager has been on his case to finish up. My guess is tomorrow."

Charlie headed off in his van with the police following him. About a mile later he parked and went into a pub called the Oban Bar.

"John, hop into the bar and see who he's meeting. We can't go in there because it's a working men's pub and we'd stick out like a sore thumb."

An hour later, the constable was back.

"He's meeting with Angus Cameron. It looks like their plan is going forward. I couldn't hear much because of the noise from a band, but from what snippets I heard, I heard Cameron say that it was a go then."

That night in his hotel room Robert called Maxwell Knight and briefed him on the plans for the following day. He wished him 'good hunting' and then rang off. The next day would be the culmination of Robert's first successful operation and he was eagerly looking forward to it.

The same surveillance routine was followed the next day. However, there was no sign of Charlie Spotswood when the shift workers left. Robert was concerned that he had spotted them the day before, but Inspector Wilcox cautioned him to be patient as they waited for what seemed like for ever. Sure enough, two hours later, Charlie was seen leaving with his painting equipment and what looked like a roll of papers among rolls of wallpaper. He loaded everything into his rusty van and started to drive away.

They followed him to Upper Greenock railway station where

he caught a train to Glasgow and they just made the same train. He was carrying some the rolled-up papers in his tool bag. They left the detective constable with the car and he was to report to Superintendent Watts on what was happening and to arrange for coverage in Glasgow when they and he got there. Each time the train stopped at a station they checked to see whether he had gotten off, but it seemed like Glasgow was his destination.

As they got off the train in Glasgow, two other special branch officers took up following him just in case he had spotted them. A car pulled up to meet Inspector Wilcox and Robert, and in it was Superintendent Watts. From the station Charlie took a taxi to a house on Lynedoch Crescent in the wealthy West End of Glasgow.

When they reached the house on Lynedoch Crescent, Superintendent Watts used his car radio and summoned reinforcements. Twenty minutes later, two cars pulled up with some six plainclothes police officers in them. Inspector Wilcox sent three of them around to the back and then, led by the superintendent, the rest of the officers marched up the front steps to the front door. The brass plate on the front door announced that this was the home of a Professor Peter Renwick. The superintendent knocked on the door and after a few minutes it was opened by an old butler.

"Yes?" asked the man in a supercilious tone and looking down his nose at them.

Superintendent Watts ignored him and barged past, followed by the rest of the officers.

"Police. Out of the way. Where is your master?" he demanded of the startled man.

"The professor is in the basement," cried the now-frightened butler.

As they went down the stairs to the basement, there was a crash as someone was escaping out of the back door of the house. When they reached the basement there was a startled Professor Renwick standing beside a long table with a camera on a tripod focussed on a drawing. Beside this was a stack of letter-sized documents of engineering specifications.

"Who the hell are you!" he shouted.

"Police. And you're under arrest for espionage and treason!"

"What! Where's your warrant!"

"We don't need one, Professor. The Emergency Powers Act 1939 gives us the right to enter your house if we suspect espionage is being perpetrated."

Just then a handcuffed man came tumbling down the stairs accompanied by two of the superintendent's men.

"Ah! Mr. Spotswood. I'm glad you could join us. I was just telling the professor that you and he will be charged with espionage and treason."

"Treason! That's a hanging offence, isn't it?" cried Charlie. "I didn't sign up for that!"

The professor was now as white as a ghost.

"But we weren't dealing with the Germans. It was with the Russians," he stammered, as if that was an excuse.

"In case you didn't know, Professor, the Russians and the Germans are allies and thus what you pass to them will likely end up in Nazi hands."

"I want a solicitor before you go any further," said the professor, gaining some semblance of composure.

"'Fraid not. You and Charlie here are going on a trip to London to our interrogation centre for spies near Kingston. They will decide whether you can have a solicitor or not. Take these commies away and out of my sight!"

The professor was handcuffed and bundled of the house, shouting out as he went. He and Charlie were unceremoniously forced into a black van.

Robert started to go through the professor's papers in his study. But after an hour of meticulous searching for hidden documents, he found nothing except his diary. Looking closely through it, he noticed that every three months or so there was an entry that just said 'Relativity Society' which was followed by a city name. He noticed there was one for Glasgow the previous month.

Then he had an idea. He went into the kitchen where the butler was sitting with a large glass of brandy. Poor man was still shaking.

"I see from the professor's diary there was an entry for 'Relativity Society'. Do you know what that is?" Robert asked kindly.

"Not really," said the frightened man. "As far as I know, it's a group of professors who meet every so often over a luncheon. They met here last month."

"Do you have a list of their names?"

"No. The professor always kept that to himself. All I know is that there were six people for lunch."

The next morning Robert attended the formal arraignment of Professor Renwick and Charlie Spotswood held in secret. After this, he visited the professor in his cell.

"I'm Robert Johnson of MI5. Can you tell me what the 'Relativity Society' is?"

"I don't know anything about them."

"Mm. That's strange because you have a lot of entries for them in your diary and your butler said you hosted ten of them last month."

"I have nothing to say. Now, go away!" he shouted.

"We'll see."

"What do mean?" he asked with a look of a deer in headlights. "There's a lot more of us you know. You can't stop us!"

In the meantime, Inspector Wilcox and his men rounded up Angus Cameron. They also arrested four men from the torpedo factory, which included the security guard, and charged them with misappropriation of government documents.

Robert was in his hotel room when the telephone rang. It was Superintendent Watts.

"Bad news, I'm afraid. I just got word from London. The professor has topped himself in his cell at the detention centre.

They hadn't even started to interrogate him."

Robert swore. The professor was his only lead to the 'Relativity Society'. He realised that he'd have to start all over again. At that time he didn't know his enquiries would lead to a more malicious plot by scientific subversives.

Four months later both Angus Cameron and Charlie Spotswood went on trial at the Old Bailey in London. The whole trial was 'in camera', meaning it was not open to the public or the press. Halfway through the trial both men changed their pleas to guilty and each was sentenced to ten years' hard labour.

Robert had to admire their stoicism under integration because their interrogators were able to glean very little from either of them. It seemed that they had been just hired hands so to speak, recruited by Professor Renwick at the behest of someone else who was a key player in a Russian spy network. And it was this person Robert was determined to find.

Part Three

And Then There Was Disillusionment and Entrapment

"There are some who become spies for money, or out of vanity and megalomania, or out of ambition, or out of a desire for thrills. But the malady of our time is of those who become spies out of idealism."

Max Lerner, US author, columnist in the New York Post, *April 1952.*

18

Tom Pearson joined Telecommunications Research Establishment at Bawdsey Manor in July 1939 and had immediately become very absorbed in the work. This research facility was in an old mansion close to the Suffolk coast which looked out onto the North Sea.

Tom first started work in a team who were continuing to develop the chain of radar stations that would pick up incoming German bombers. These were a number of early-warning radar stations built by the Royal Air Force that stretched along the south and east coasts of England and the east and north coasts of Scotland. At this time, there were about two thousand scientists at the research labs working in buildings adjacent to the manor house which had been purchased by the RAF in 1936.

Tom's stay at Bawdsey Manor was cut very short as the research establishment was moved to the University College at Dundee, Scotland, because of concerns about possible German bombing of its coastal site. In May 1940, they were on the road again this time to RAF Purbeck near Worth Matravers, which was in Dorset near Swanage in the south of England. Tom supposed that the powers that be in London wanted them nearby rather than over 450 miles away in Scotland.

Tom hadn't heard from his Russian contact since he had got back from France in June of 1939 and it was just as well. In August of that year, the news of the Soviet/German non-aggression pact hit the newspapers. He couldn't believe that Stalin had even contemplated such a deal. Stalin was supposed to be on the side of the proletariat and against right-wing parties such as the Nazis. Many devoted communists felt a complete betrayal of their cause, while many Nazis were equally shocked to find themselves in league with the devil, having so long opposed communism. This was the folly of appeasement and Tom wondered how Madelaine in Paris felt about the pact.

In June 1941, a momentous event revitalised British communists. The galvanising event was Hitler's surprise attack on Russia called 'Operation Barbarossa'. It's called a surprise attack, although the British, through intercepts at Bletchley Park, had warned Joseph Stalin, the Russian leader, that this would happen. In addition, his country's own agents within the British establishment had done the same thing. He chose to ignore all these warnings with dire consequences because he was distrustful of the motives of the British government and the reliability of the infamous 'Cambridge Five'. The British government didn't know at the time that these five agents had infiltrated the Foreign Office, MI5 and MI6, and their treachery wouldn't be discovered until the 1950s.

By this time, Tom's communist ardour had begun to dissipate as he believed now it was a lost cause that may have been a workable ideal. But it had been destroyed by Russia, which had become just another dictatorship. Also, word was spreading about the purges and the disillusionment spread. Tom chuckled when he heard the news of the Nazis' invasion of Russia and believed that Stalin was getting his just desserts in thinking he could have an honourable treaty with a monster such as Hitler. Of course, Tom didn't know that Stalin would become an equal or greater monster than Hitler with the number of people he had exterminated.

Tom's wish that he would be forgotten was dashed a month later when he was contacted by someone from the Russian Embassy in London. He was at a science meeting at the Ministry of Defence in London, at which he had given a presentation of the latest work of a team he now led. He was walking out of the ministry building at six in the evening when a large man in a badly fitted suit stopped and asked him where Trafalgar Square was. Tom explained. It was pitch black because of the air-raid blackout and there was no one in the street. He said thank you and told Tom to meet him in The Coal Hole pub in the Strand near Charing Cross as he had some news from his friends in Moscow.

Tom was perplexed because he thought he had escaped being called on to work for the Russians and he was determined to tell them no. On his way to the Strand, he noticed he was being followed by two men and when he entered the pub they did not follow. Sitting in the corner with two pints of beer was his new contact. He was a bald and unshaven man who looked like a nightclub bouncer. There was a large, two-inch scar down the side of his face.

"Who are you?" Tom demanded.

"I'm Viktor Gorev, but you must call me Brian Neal."

"Why?"

"Because I don't want anybody to know who I really am."

"But I do. Where's Alexei Dorokhin?"

"He's back in Moscow."

Tom laughed: "You people seem to be here today and gone tomorrow."

"Please?"

"It doesn't matter. I wonder how long you will last before you too are purged."

The man looked angry and was about to lose his temper. Tom continued: "How can I help you?"

Viktor gathered his thoughts and, as if reading from a prepared script, said: "Now that our countries are allies we need you to feed us information on the radar technologies you are working on."

"I don't think that's on," Tom said definitively.

Viktor ignored him and carried on: "We need the information to fight against our common enemy, the Nazis."

"Now that's interesting. You people were only too happy to link up with them for the past two years and now the Nazis have invaded you come crawling back asking for help. Why should I help Russia that has let down many people like me who naively thought your country was a shining example of how a communist state could work?"

Viktor Gorev was taken aback at this tirade. He saw that Tom was really angry.

"I think you have to know that not cooperating with us now is a death sentence," he threatened. "Do you realise that all your previous contacts are now dead and the killing will go on until we get what we want? Stalin and the Russia are ruthless, and we will get what we want in the end."

"Well, you'll have to do it without me," Tom said as he started to get up, but Viktor put his heavy hand on his shoulder, forcing him to sit again.

"Before you go, I want you to look at this." Viktor took out of his briefcase a large envelope and showed Tom six pictures of him cavorting and having sex with the strange man who had visited the farm in France on his last night. Then the lightbulb was turned on. That was why he felt so groggy the next morning: he had been drugged. He realised that this had been a set-up as a guarantee of his cooperation. It was a classic honey trap.

"As you see, we have some very comprising pictures of you that I am sure the police here would be very interested in. Also, a witness statement from the man in the pictures stating that the incident took place today in London. Your obscenity laws in this country are very strict. Maybe you'll get two or three years' imprisonment or hard labour. And, of course, your career would be over."

Tom was traumatised and felt demeaned. What was he going to do? He had to think fast. Part of him wanted to murder Viktor Gorev. Part of him wanted to seek retribution for his humiliation. When he was first recruited in 1939, he was quite willing to help Russia; now it seemed he had very little choice.

"I'm here in London for another day. I'll meet you here tomorrow at the same time and give you my decision."

Sensing victory, Viktor said: "That won't be necessary because you will do as you're told. I will contact you again next week at your location and we expect you to bring some documents for us to copy."

And that's how Tom reluctantly started to feed information to his Russian handlers.

It was very easy to take documents after work. Tom was billeted in the village of Swanage and he would ride his bike to and from the Purbeck RAF station. Security was tight at the main entrance as the scientists left each evening. Their bags were searched as they left so Tom devised a plan to throw his briefcase over a hidden part of the perimeter fence, go through the security check and pick up the bag once he was on the outside. He chose that part of the fence because it was hidden from the view of sentries at the main gate. He had noted that patrols around the perimeter fence were started at night, long after work was done for the day, and they were spaced apart, passing every half hour. This gave him enough time to retrieve the bag.

Once Tom recovered the bag, he would take the bag with the papers to an address in Swanage once a week, spend a couple of hours in the Black Swan Inn, and then pick up his briefcase with the papers. The next morning he would go to work, show his pass at the gate and go to his assigned hut. The security guards never searched bags on the way in.

Tom was still seething at the blackmail the Russians had perpetrated on him. Most of the documents he gave them were fairly low grade as far as security was concerned. He was still looking for an opportunity to get his revenge and then in February his chance came.

At the end of February 1942, a commando raid called Operation Biting, or the Bruneval Raid, took place. The Germans had built a very sophisticated radar installation, called Würzburg radar, on the French coast near a town of Bruneval. It was part of a chain of these installations which had been photographed by the RAF reconnaissance planes. The trouble was the British didn't know what their purpose was, but the RAF had been suffering recent heavy losses and it was thought these installations had something to do with it. It was decided to capture part of the equipment and take it to their laboratories so they could be dismantled and learn about the technology so that jamming devices could be used to incapacitate the system.

British paratroopers parachuted in and after a brief firefight they were able to capture the installation. With them was an RAF technician, who dismantled key parts of the equipment. This was taken to a designated beach and placed on a landing craft and then loaded at sea on motor torpedo boats for fast shipment to Britain. The paratroopers had also captured a German radar technician who proved invaluable in understanding the operation of this sophisticated equipment.

The Würzburg radar equipment was brought to Tom and his colleagues at the Telecommunications Research Establishment and teams of scientists began to disassemble it. He was part of one of these teams which began to analyse it and to understand its operation and capabilities. These teams were all working long hours and they never left to go to their billets. They worked in shifts sleeping in the corner of their wooden huts on mattresses for just a few hours at a time and grabbing sandwiches and tea from the canteen when they could.

After two weeks of this intense and successful work, Tom eventually returned to his billet in Swanage. As he arrived on his bicycle at about ten that night a large figure emerged from some bushes. It was one of Viktor's men.

"Get into the car," he said, pushing Tom towards a parked vehicle in one of the lanes. Inside was Viktor Gorev.

"Where have you been? We haven't been able to reach you for several weeks," Viktor Gorev demanded to know.

"We've been focussing on some important projects and I haven't been able to leave the station for that time."

"We understand that the British have captured an advanced radar system from the Germans and your laboratories are analysing it. It's an absolute priority that we get hold of the documents as soon as possible. That's your assignment."

"Fine, I'll do what I can," Tom responded in a weary voice.

"You'll do more than that, otherwise your past indiscretion will be revealed to the authorities," he shouted.

Tom was bundled out of the car, which drove off.

As he was lying in bed that night thinking about his encounter with Viktor Gorev, he was frightened. He was in a cold sweat. Since he couldn't sleep he got up and poured himself a large whisky. He took two large swigs of the drink and began to develop some ideas of how he could get out of the situation he was now in. He could doctor the data on the Würzburg radar equipment, which would take the Russians some time to trace back the errors to him, or continue sending them information and hope no one in the British security services would find out. Both choices would cause problems for him and he feared the Russians' retribution most, which had far-reaching consequences for him. They had a reputation of harsh justice to those who opposed them and this was seen in the purges they conducted in the late 1930s. Tom feared for his life if he should cross them.

* * *

One profound effect of Operation Barbarossa was Winston Churchill's unfortunate order that the security services and the code breakers at Bletchley Park were to stop any intelligence-gathering about Russia as they were now an ally against Nazi Germany. This threw a wrench into the security services' investigation of Russian spying because reading their cables was an invaluable source of information.

Despite the Prime Minister's order, the Metropolitan Police and MI6's Radio Security Service, as well as the Polish Security Service continued to pick up messages between Moscow and Russian agents in Europe. Also, MI5 still had its clandestine listening devices at the British Communist Party headquarters, which still provided useful leads.

At a routine meeting held at Maxwell Knight's office in Dolphin Square, Robert Johnson met for the first time Dr. Reginald V. Jones, MI6's principal scientific adviser and scientific officer at the Air Ministry. This brilliant scientist struck people at first as very arrogant and self-assured but once they got to know him they recognised his true genius. He was a real prodigy and at the age of thirty had the ear of Prime Minister Winston Churchill.

Dr. Jones and his team had already gained the grudging respect from government mandarins following his successful development of the jamming and distortion of enemy radio waves. This system countered the Luftwaffe's use of radio navigation systems that had given their bombers more accurate bombing of British cities.

"Dr. Jones has some concerns he wanted to share with us," said Maxwell Knight as a way of introducing his guest.

Dr. Jones began: "For some time now we have become aware that many of the development successes in radar have been leaked to the Russians. We know this because our Polish colleagues have been able to intercept communications from London and Moscow. There seems to be a mole or several moles in our scientific community. Needless to say, we are extremely upset that this is happening right under our noses and, although the Prime Minister doesn't want to upset the Russians, he does want the British traitors caught and neutralised. Can you work on this?"

"We've been concerned for some time about Russian activity," said Maxwell Knight. "I strongly believe that the Russian threat is far greater in the long term than that of the Nazis. Not everyone here at MI5 agrees with me as their prism is focussed mainly on Germany. This is fine in the short term as we have the 'Double Cross' system working well.

"The threat of invasion is very much diminished since Hitler has decided to attack the Russians and has sent many divisions to his eastern front. Since Barbarossa we've seen an influx of so-called diplomats who we know are NKVD agents. They are based at their London embassy and have diplomatic cover. We'll have to start at the other end of this conundrum by trying to trace which of our citizens is giving them information."

"I recommend you start looking at the scientists at the Telecommunications Research Establishment which is moving to Malvern College in Worcestershire in May," said Dr. Jones. "I believe the leak could come from there. If you like, I could contact Jimmy Rowe, who is the superintendent of the TRE, and ask his cooperation. You'll see he is a very intense man focussed on his projects. A spy in his midst would be anathema to him."

"I think that Robert here could take up the role of director of security. They'd have to move the present man in that position but I'm sure a promotion could be found for him somewhere."

Because the Telecommunications Research Establishment (TRE) was so important to the war effort and in danger of attack, it was decided to move the whole operation again. This time the government took over Malvern College in Worcestershire, a boys' private school. The school gave the TRE adequate room to expand its operations and its pupils were transferred to Harrow School in North West London until 1946.

Arrangements were made for Robert Johnson to work at the TRE at Malvern College as head of security. He didn't know it at the time, but this was the start of a major national security investigation which would net many leading scientists during the war and in the subsequent 'Cold War' in the 1950s.

19

Malvern, Worcestershire, May 1943

Robert Johnson caught an early-morning train from Paddington Station in London for Great Malvern. He wanted to arrive at the Telecommunications Research Establishment (TRE) at Malvern College early as he was eager to start his new assignment. His journey to Malvern would normally have been about four hours, but the trip took much longer than he had planned because of the bombing the night before in London and surrounding suburbs. The train was late leaving Paddington and progressed at a snail's pace towards the West Midlands, stopping at all the big and small stations on the way.

When Robert reached Great Malvern station at three in the afternoon, he took a taxi and arrived at the base's guardhouse, which was a temporary wooden hut at the entrance to the college. On his approach to the college, he noticed barbed wire several feet deep surrounding the grounds. He signed in, received his identification papers and was given his billet assignment, which was the Abbey Hotel in the town. Leaving his case at the guardhouse, he went in search of Dr. Rowe, the TRE's superintendent.

He found Dr. A P. 'Jimmy' Rowe's office in a beautiful, old

wood-lined classroom in the college's famous tower. He had to wait because the superintendent was in the middle of a staff meeting. Finally, half an hour and two cups of tea later from Dr. Rowe's apologising secretary, he was ushered into the man's office.

Robert had conjured up in his mind a tousled-haired, untidy scientist in his rolled-up shirt sleeves and dishevelled trousers held up by ill-fitting braces. How wrong his assumptions were. Dr. Rowe was a small, bespectacled man in his mid-forties. His neat moustache was carefully manicured and Robert expected that he spent some time each morning perfecting his appearance. Over the next few months, as he got to know him, the scientist was always immaculately dressed in a three-piece suit. Robert could never remember seeing him with his jacket off.

Dr. Rowe always had his pipe lit and was continually cleaning it and loading fresh tobacco. He never seemed happy with it. This was probably his way of contemplating issues and problems and coming up with solutions just as some people doodle on a sheet of paper or walk up and down thinking through a problem.

"Now, are you absolutely certain that the leak is coming from TRE? I just can't believe this," he clucked like a worried father whose otherwise virtuous child has been caught out committing a serious transgression.

"I'm afraid so, sir. We have a number of intercepts of Russian traffic detailing some of the projects you are working on here. For example, the information on some of your work on the Würzburg radar equipment that was captured by commandos in February has already found its way to Moscow."

Dr. Rowe was silent for a long time. He had put his pipe down and had become red-faced with anger and then, like a volcanic eruption, he barked, "I want you to find this snake in my organisation, do you hear!" He got up and looked out of the window onto the school's quadrangle with his back to Robert.

After a few seconds he calmed down, but he was still angry:

"I'm told you're good, so I hope you can track this monster down. You have my full support with anything you want."

"What's security like here, sir?"

"The army have surrounded us with barbed wire and they are on call if we need them. The RAF police provide protective services and their commander is Flight Lieutenant Wilfred Channing. As you saw from the main gate they inspect passes and check in outsiders such as suppliers."

"Sir, I plan to do a complete review of the security here and tighten it because of these leaks. First, I would like to review the personnel files on the people working on the Würzburg radar equipment that might give me a clue into the leaker. How many people are we talking about?"

"There is about twenty scientists directly involved. But I have no idea who else worked for the team. There are secretaries and clerks, I suppose, but you would have to know something about radar to be able to tell what's important to copy. There are about a thousand people here at the moment and we are busy recruiting. Let me get my secretary to dig out the files on the Würzburg team and an organisation chart so you'll know who's who. I have reserved an office for you near me so we can work together. Let me show you around."

As they walked around the college buildings, Dr. Rowe introduced Robert to his lead scientists in each area. Robert saw that every classroom, every science laboratory, even the boy's dormitories had been turned into workrooms. The school gymnasium was now a large store house and the school's beautiful library had become the drawing office. Two of the houses on college grounds had become hostels for those that could not be billeted in town. However, the canteen for feeding everyone was still in the town at the Winter Gardens and it wasn't until several months later that temporary buildings were built on the college grounds to house the canteen and a much-needed workshop.

It wasn't until eight in the evening that Robert arrived at the

Abbey Hotel. He found his room and gratefully collapsed onto the bed. The next morning he was up at five and began his fitness routine with a three-mile run around Great Malvern to get some perspective of the town. Returning to the hotel, he took a quick cold bath and went to the Winter Gardens for breakfast. There weren't many people there at that time, although he did sit down with two men who had pulled an all-nighter.

He was in his office by seven and spent the morning reviewing the personnel files of the Würzburg team. They had all signed the Official Secrets Act, which threatens them with prosecution and imprisonment if they divulged state secrets to an enemy or a potential enemy. But there was no vetting report in each file. There were letters of recommendation from university professors and even government ministers, but nothing of an official nature. Robert sighed at the discrepancy but realised that the speed with which these teams needed to be recruited was more important than the long processes of vetting each individual.

Robert walked down to the guardhouse at the main gate and asked to see Flight Lieutenant Channing. He was ushered into a small office where the flight lieutenant was on the telephone. When he saw Robert he waved him to a chair and told the person on the end of the telephone line he would call back.

"I'm pleased to meet you, Major," he said as he shook Robert's hand with a hearty gusto.

"Oh, I don't use my title, as I'm not in the military anymore. It's plain old mister these days," said Roger with a smile.

Flight Lieutenant Wilfred Channing was a middle-aged man of rotund build and stood at about six feet tall. He was partly bald with a mournful face and baggy eyes. He reminded Robert of a faithful but alert Labrador dog. Despite his size, he was smartly dressed in his blue RAF uniform and Robert noticed two medal ribbons on his uniform for the Meritorious Service Medal for distinguished service and British War Medal given to all those that served in World War One. In fact, Wilfred Channing had joined the Royal Flying Corps in 1916 as a mechanic and then transferred to the RAF police when it was formed in 1918. He rose in rank because of his dedication to his responsibilities and a keen eye for detail which enabled him to solve important cases.

Despite his outgoing bonhomie, Flight Lieutenant Wilfred Channing was a bitter man. He regarded his assignment to the TRE as a slap in the face and a punishment for his challenges to authority and past transgressions. Now, here was this major from the security services here to tell him how to run security at this god-forsaken base. Well, he was going to show this man that he wasn't going to be pushed around.

"How can I help the great and mighty MI5?" he asked with an insincere smile on his face.

Ignoring the remark, Robert told him of the leak of secrets that had been traced to the TRE and his job was to discover the culprit. He said: "What they do here is so important to our success in the war that we have to pull out all stops to plug these leaks as soon as possible. In order to do this we have to first tighten security here. I have the full backing of Dr. Rowe and the Air Ministry to initiate this. For example, from now on everyone's briefcases or packages will be searched – and I mean everyone, whoever they are – as they leave or enter the base. We will conduct random searches of individuals and their workstations. We will no longer just check passes. All vehicles will likewise be searched. There will be stepped-up patrols around the perimeter to make sure our leaker has not found another way to pass his contraband to someone outside. And that's just the start."

"But I haven't got the manpower to do all this."

"How many more men do you need?"

"At least thirty for round-the-clock shifts."

"I thought so. I came up with the same figure when I reviewed the security system here. I have arranged for this number of reinforcements to be sent here. The Air Ministry told me they would be here either tomorrow or the next day. In the meantime, you will have to make do with the men you have. The new system is going to cause chaos at first but eventually people will get used to it."

Flight Lieutenant Channing was stunned at the sheer audacity of the plan and marvelled at Robert's grip on the situation. A respect began to emerge for the man from MI5. This plan would be difficult to execute, but he was determined to make it work. This man clearly had the ear of people in the Air Ministry and working well with him would help the flight lieutenant's career.

Robert then went back to Dr. Rowe's office for a senior staff meeting. He arrived just as everyone was gathering and was introduced to the group by Dr. Rowe. He outlined his security plan to the group of free-wheeling scientists who were aghast at the restrictions that were being put on them and their people. The TRE had operated like a university campus with very few restrictions and Robert's proposal faced a lot of consternation and push-back.

Finally Dr. Rowe spoke up. "Gentlemen, the question is do you want your work to be given to our country's enemies as we now are getting the upper hand in this war? There have been indications that they have been focussing on our work here and that's why we left Swanage. We've got to make sure they can't get our secrets, and that is why Mr. Johnson has been brought in to make sure this never happens. I'm sure there's no one here who would like to see this."

There was a mumble of agreement, but still the group was not happy. The general consensus was the grudging acceptance of the tighter security plan.

Robert then spent the next three days interviewing the Würzburg team members. He didn't discover anything abnormal in these interviews, although he was intrigued by one man who seemed very nervous. As Robert asked his questions the young man broke into a sweat and was unnecessarily evasive in his answers to simple questions. The others in the team had been impatient to get the interview over so that they could get back to their work benches. According to his personnel file that Robert had on his desk, Tom Pearson grew up in an impoverished town in the north-east of England and had gained scholarships for his university education. There was nothing strange in this, as many of these brilliant scientists who had come from poor backgrounds had succeeded in the same way. It was their pure academic brilliance that had got them where they were today. Also, Robert knew that some people were totally useless at interviews when they were questioned by a senior security officer. He found the man's behaviour unusual, though, and decided to look further into his background. He made a call to London.

Tom Pearson was extremely agitated after his interview with Robert Johnson. He thought that the authorities were now on to him and he didn't know what to do. This new security man was dangerous. He had increased the number of RAF police officers who stopped everyone at the gates and searched them. They clearly had been tipped off about Tom's activities for the Russians. What was he going to do? The only good thing was that Viktor Gorev had not contacted him since he'd been in Malvern and he had no way of reaching them, not that he wanted to. Maybe he's gone back to Moscow, he thought, but that didn't make sense because he would just be replaced by another thug.

Tom couldn't concentrate on his work when he got back from the interview and snapped at his colleagues, who began to avoid him. He was relieved when his shift ended. He climbed onto his bicycle, stopped at the front gate to be searched and then rode about a mile and a half to the Blue Bell Inn, where he was billeted with three other scientists.

The Blue Bell Inn was the unofficial watering hole for a group of twelve or so scientists who spent their downtime arguing about and discussing the work they were doing.

Although Tom enjoyed the group, he just went to his room that evening and lay on his bed trying to decide what to do. About ten minutes later, there was a loud knock on his door which startled him. Had they come for him? He carefully opened it to see the pub's young barmaid standing there. She smiled and handed him a folded piece of paper. He said nothing as he took the paper and closed his room door. The girl looked at the closed door, puzzled by Tom's behaviour because he had always been friendly and polite. She shrugged. Perhaps he was not as cute as she thought.

Tom unfolded the paper and read pencilled instruction which said, 'Car park now.' Oh God, his whole world was falling apart. The Russians had found him! He thought about ignoring the order but he realised they would catch him. He could pour his heart out to Robert Johnson and take his chances with the wrath of the British authorities. He decided on the coward's way out and went down to the bar and out of a side door.

In the shadows of an oak tree near the car park was Viktor Gorev.

"Get in!" he ordered, indicating his car.

He got in the back of the car next to Tom.

"Why haven't you let us know where you were?"

"How am I going to do that? I'm hardly going to telephone your embassy. Calls there and mail are probably intercepted by MI5. What do you suggest?" said Tom sarcastically, which was probably lost on Viktor. He'd just about had it with this bully.

"The information you gave us on the Würzburg radar was useful. But now you are developing a ground scanning radar for bombers at night. We want any plans you have of this system."

"How do you know about that?"

"We have contacts in London that know about these things. Anyway, I've arranged a house where you can take these plans and they can be copied for our use."

"I don't know whether I can do this. We have a new security officer who has increased searches and guard patrols. They know something is going on and so have tightened security. It is not like Swanage where things were much looser."

Viktor smiled and produced from his pocket a very small Minox miniature camera. The camera was only three inches long and one inch wide. Tom had seen one demonstrated at the course he went on in France three years previously.

"This is what you will use instead of smuggling out the documents," said Viktor. "All you have to do is have the document under a strong light and make sure you are at least eight inches above it and then shoot the pictures. The camera focusses automatically at that range. Here's a box of miniature films you will need. Now let me show you how to load the camera."

After the demonstration of the loading and unloading, Victor said, "All you have to do is send the exposed film in the post to this address." He gave Tom a small piece of paper and suggested he hide it on his clothing, such as with a pin under his jacket lapel.

"If you use the camera there will be less chance of being caught. I will see you in two weeks here at the pub to see how you are getting on. Don't let us down, otherwise there will be hell to pay!"

And he pushed Tom out of the car and drove away.

20

When Tom reached his room after his meeting with Viktor Gorev, he lay on his bed and a sense of panic overcame him. He had a raging headache caused by the stress he was feeling. His life had become a relentless nightmare from which he couldn't wake. His existence had been a persistent series of misfortunes that had been set in motion by his simple desire for social justice for the downtrodden and forgotten poor people in Britain. His quest had led him naively into the hands of evil, self-serving, power-hungry individuals who had no regard for the people they purported to represent.

Once again he tried to think through his dilemma because he was so conflicted. If he didn't cooperate with the Russians his career was over and he faced both espionage and indecency charges because of the photographs. This would result in jail time on both counts. He supposed he could fess up to Mr. Johnson, the head of security, who was rumoured to be from MI5. But, he rationalised, what he was doing was helping an ally fight the Germans so it wasn't really espionage. He knew this was a weak argument. Perhaps MI5 would understand that if he came clean. But why would they understand his rationale and give him a pass?

And then there were the Russians. They would never forgive

him and, he believed, would take an awful revenge on him and might even murder him. Like many other communist believers, he had been fooled into thinking that Russia was a shining light leading the way ahead to a more egalitarian society. He still believed in true socialism but the Russian version of it was anathema to him. All the purges and the continued subjugation of the Russian people who had suffered under the Tsar and now under an elite group of power-hungry men led by Stalin. They used bully-boy tactics to subjugate their people. There was no democracy or choice. It was how Hitler had come to power by sheer brute force.

What was more important to Tom than anything else in the world? His work, nothing else. So he would have to continue his espionage career and just hope he wouldn't be caught.

He got out a hidden bottle of Scotch and poured himself a large glass. Soon, aided by the alcohol, the self-pity started. It overwhelmed him and his thoughts turned him into a blubbering mess. Thankfully, he fell fitfully asleep, but his cataclysm followed him even there.

The following morning, Tom dragged himself out of bed and made it to the cafeteria just before it closed for a breakfast of strong tea and a corned beef sandwich. His breakfast helped make him feel a little better, although he still had a thumping hangover.

When he eventually sat at his workstation in the laboratory, his supervisor, Brian Ackerman, came over to him with some files. Brian was a friendly and outgoing man who Tom personally warmed to and respected for his astute technical abilities.

"God, Tom, you look like death warmed up. What did you get up to last night?" Brian asked, smiling.

"I had some bad news," was all that Tom could muster in response.

"Oh no. Do you want to talk about it?"

"No."

"Fine. Please take a look at these calculations in these files and check them for accuracy. We are going to start developing a prototype of the equipment and I want to make sure everything is alright. Oh, by the way, tonight is our singalong evening at the Blue Bell. I hope you'll be on form by then and I'll see you there."

Tom groaned inwardly. He'd forgotten about this. Every Saturday night they had some sort of entertainment, which included him playing some jazz for them. This week it was going to be songs from Gilbert and Sullivan operettas. He supposed it would help him overcome his current funk.

At this time, the Russians were eager to get their hands on any information about the H2S radar system that was being developed at TRE. This had become a priority for them and was why they were putting a lot of pressure on Tom.

The RAF had chosen night bombing as it afforded the bombers better protection from German fighters. However, the major drawback was that night bombing was inaccurate even with the blanket bombing technique the RAF had adopted. Aircraft would cover the whole area around a specific target in the hopes that some of their bombs would fall on that target. The need to develop some technology to improve accuracy was essential. Work on the development of the H2S was begun in January 1942 by TRE. This was a radar detection device that would allow bombers to see the ground at night and even on cloudy nights, thus enabling more accurate bombing.

In the next two weeks following his meeting with Viktor Gorev, Tom tried to photograph any documents he found. It was not easy because the H2S team were working around the clock and there was always someone there. Then one day his luck changed. The team had left one night for RAF Defford, some ten miles away from Malvern, where the Telecommunications Flying Unit was to test the prototype on a Halifax bomber.

Tom had found a small closet in the basement of the main building where he set up a desk lamp so he could take his photographs. He was not worried about being caught because he knew the routine of the security guards. The night the team was away, he gathered up as many documents he could find and took them to his clandestine studio and began photographing them. When he'd almost finished, he heard voices coming down the steps to the cellar. Tom turned off the light and closed the closet door and waited. Had he been discovered?

He heard the voices of a man and woman, and he looked out of the crack in the door at the couple. As soon as they reached the bottom of the cellar the couple began kissing and fondling each other, and soon they were partly undressing each other while lying on a blanket that one of them had brought. Then the woman whispered, "Have you got any johnnies, Bill, because I won't let you do it if you haven't?"

"Come on, Marge, be a sport," said the man.

"No! You don't have to bear the consequences if I become pregnant. You can make me come if you like but not that way and then I'll do it to you."

After a few minutes the woman came to a climax as she started to breathe heavily, cry out and squeal with delight. Then it was the man's turn.

All the time Tom was in his closet, he found the whole incident very amusing and he wondered who they were. After a while the couple got up, dressed and left. Tom continued his work photographing as many documents as he could.

Robert waited for the report on Tom Pearson, which was being compiled in London. He was pretty certain that Tom was his target, but he also carried out examination in the meantime of others, including the administrative staff. Also, he had the RAF police carry out snap searches of work areas, and some of the staff's digs. They had found nothing. Even with the search of Tom Pearson's room at the Blue Bell Inn they came up empty. He had the RAF guards vary the timing of their patrols and still they didn't catch anybody, except one night, to the amusement of the guards, a couple making out in the filing department.

However, what Robert had succeeded in doing was to anger

everyone and there was a clear reluctance to cooperate with him as a result, but he still persisted. He had someone from the Watchers department at MI5 spend a few days mixing with TRE's staff in their off time in pubs like the Lamb Inn and the Unicorn Inn and at social events, like dances, in the hopes of picking up information or observing any suspicious activity. Nothing came of it worth noting. This made him more convinced that Tom Pearson was the Russian agent.

Robert went to London to report to Maxwell Knight on his findings so far in the investigation at TRE.

"I'm pretty sure that Tom Pearson is our man and I would like to interrogate him further, sir. Perhaps I can shake him enough to make him confess," Robert said.

"I've read the report on him that our people did and it sounds to me you're right," said Maxwell Knight, reading a file in front of him. "He comes from a poor family in Jarrow where his grandfather was a communist trade union organiser and under investigation by MI5. When he was at the University of Leeds he was member of their socialist society. He helped out with the Jarrow Crusade in 1936 and, we believe, was recruited to the communist cause by a Jane Harcourt. We had her in our crosshairs until she disappeared. Her real name is Lady Penelope Weston.

"Tom Pearson applied for a passport in 1939 and must have gone abroad then. He isn't a member of the Communist Party of Great Britain or ever has been, as far as we can tell. If you see it from the Russian point of view, he would be an ideal recruit because of his research work in which we know they are interested.

"I think we can turn this man so he feeds misinformation onto the Russians. Perhaps he will lead us into finding other like-minded scientists, especially the members of Relativity Society."

That Saturday night was a time for relaxation and entertainment at the Blue Bell Inn. A group of scientists from TRE had formed an acapella group which gave weekly concerts. In addition, Tom Pearson was to give a recital of both classical and jazz piano pieces.

The small pub was crowded, although Robert Johnson was able to find a corner seat because he had come there early. He, like the rest of audience, was entranced by the performers, considering they were all amateurs. He was amazed at Tom's piano skills and he was interested to see how absorbed he was in his playing. Robert was among the enthusiastic audience to call for encore time and time again.

When the concert had finally finished and the audience was on its way home after time had been called in the pub, Tom went out to the car park in search of Viktor Gorev so that he could hand over the latest film he had shot of the H2S project. It was pouring with rain and Robert pulled on his raincoat and hat and followed Tom into the rain-soaked car park. He pretended to go and collect his bicycle at the side of the pub. As he walked past a parked car he saw Tom talking to a man. In the dark, he couldn't quite make out the man's features but made a mental note of the car's number plate.

Tom sat in the front passenger seat talking to Viktor, who seemed pleased by the information Tom had given him on the previous films he had shot. Then he looked up and saw Robert glancing at them as he walked past the car.

"Who's that?" Viktor demanded of Tom.

"Oh no! It's Mr. Johnson. He's the head of security and probably from MI5. He's seen us. What are we going to do?"

"Just calm down. I'll deal with him. Just carry on as normal and no one will be any the wiser."

Tom got out of the car and returned to the pub and to his room.

In the meantime, Robert was busying himself by pretending to pump a tire on his bicycle as he watched from the shadows of the building.

"What's wrong, old chap? Got a puncture?" said a voice behind him.

Robert turned and saw Brian Ackerman, Tom's supervisor.

“It’s just a slow puncture and if I pump it up it’ll get me home. I’ll have to repair it tomorrow.”

“You’ve picked a bad night to have problem.” Brian thought to himself, and it couldn’t have happened to a better man. Serves the bugger right! Brian’s digs had been searched by the RAF police and he, like most of his colleagues, had come to resent Robert Johnson.

Brian pulled his bike from the rack, put on his trouser clips and rode his bike out of the car park onto Guarlford Road as he headed back to the centre of Great Malvern. The rain was coming down hard as he set out, so visibility was bad.

Viktor Gorev sat in his car and waited, with his windscreen wipers struggling to give him some visibility. He saw a man on his bicycle ride past and he instinctively knew it was his quarry, Robert Johnson. He waited a few minutes and then followed him down the quiet country lane. There was no one on the road so he picked a spot near a corner and drove his car at the bicyclist. The man went flying in the air and landed on his head on the hard road. Viktor then backed his car over the prone body to make sure, and then got out and checked the man. Once satisfied he was dead, he went back to his car and drove away.

21

Robert Johnson watched from the bicycle shed as Viktor Gorev's car drove slowly out of the pub's car park. It soon disappeared from sight in the sheets of rain which made visibility nearly impossible. Robert waited to see whether the rain might let up but, after a few minutes, it was clear this wouldn't be the case. He sighed and pulled up the lapels of his raincoat and turned the brim of his hat down; he began to cycle back to his room at the Abbey Hotel in Great Malvern.

The only good thing about his two-mile journey back to the hotel was that it was mostly a downhill ride, but the poor conditions because of the rain meant that he had to go slowly. As he rounded a bend he almost ran over a prone figure lying in the middle of the road. He put on his brakes and came to a grinding stop, just avoiding crashing into a ditch at the side of the road. Leaving his bike, he walked back to the prone figure, kneeled down and, when he turned him over, he recognised Brian Ackerman.

Robert felt for a pulse, but it was obvious that Brian was dead. His keen sense could see that Brian hadn't been just knocked off his bicycle, but someone had run over him twice. When he looked closely, he could see two muddy tyre marks on his raincoat that went across Brian's chest. Robert realised that the poor man had been deliberately killed.

He moved the body to the side of the road so no one would run over it and then cycled back to a telephone box near the Blue Bell Inn. He called for the police and an ambulance and then went back to the curve in the road where the body lay. The rain was beginning to ease off and Robert sheltered under an old elm tree.

As he waited for the emergency services to arrive, Robert began to wonder who would do such a thing and why. He then realised that he was supposed to leave the pub before Brian if he had not wanted to see what Viktor Gorev was up to. Maybe the Russian thought the man on the bicycle was him. But how did he know who he was? Maybe Tom Pearson had pointed him out as they sat in the car. Once the Russian realised he had killed the wrong person he would be targeted again.

A police car arrived about half an hour later and a sergeant climbed out of it. Robert told the sergeant what he knew and the identity of the victim, but he didn't mention his murder suspicions or about the car he had seen leave the pub. After giving his particulars to the policeman, he cycled back to the hotel.

He called Maxwell Knight to report the incident and was told to call a halt to his assignment and return to London the next day.

The next morning he met with Dr. Rowe and said that MI5 had been able to plug the leak but gave no details. He spoke to Flight Lieutenant Channing and told him in confidence that the leak had apparently been in London after all. Robert knew the flight lieutenant would give away the information to others at TRE and, by doing this, Tom Pearson's role would remain confidential. Robert urged Flight Lieutenant Channing to keep a tight lid on security at TRE because foreign agents could well turn their attention to the research establishment.

Back in London Robert Johnson met Maxwell Knight at his office in Dolphin Square and they agreed that they should move on Tom Pearson. "I want you to take him to a safe house rather than the interrogation centre at Latchmere House because I'm pretty certain there is a Russian mole in MI5 and if we are going to turn him I don't want the Russians to know because he would be useless to us."

Robert Johnson returned to his office at MI5 headquarters in St. James's Street and began sifting through the papers that had accumulated on his desk since he had been in Malvern. He was not aware of anyone entering the office until he heard him say: "So the wanderer has returned. How was your sojourn in Malvern?"

Robert looked up to see Anthony Blunt standing in the doorway. "It was boring. I was asked to tighten up the security system there which I did. Now I'm back here looking for another project. How about you, Anthony, what have you been up to?"

They talked for another fifteen minutes about projects and office gossip and then Anthony Blunt had to leave, purportedly for a meeting. As he left, he invited Robert to a cocktail party at his flat the following night and then, before Robert could say no, he was gone. He did not like Anthony Blunt one bit. It was his prissy manner and his patrician condescension that bothered him. Whenever he saw him, he always had many piercing questions for Robert and he felt like he was getting the third degree. Anthony Blunt had been appointed to the department responsible for counter espionage which was mainly focussed on the German threat.

* * *

A week later, Tom Pearson received a telegram from Patricia Pearson, his stepfather's second wife, saying his stepfather was sick and asking for him. Tom was reluctant to go to Durham to see him but eventually decided he should try and repair his relationship with the man. He was given grudging permission from Dr. Rowe for three days' time off to visit his stepfather.

Tom caught the next train to Paddington in London. When

he arrived there, he looked for the Underground which was to take him to Kings Cross, the major train terminal that served the north of England. As he walked along the station concourse he was approached by two special branch policeman.

"Mr. Pearson?" one of them asked.

"Yes."

"We want you to come with us."

"I've got a train to catch and I'd thank you kindly to let go of my arm! I don't know who you are and I'm not going anywhere with you."

"We're from Scotland Yard and you will come with us," the man said forcefully as he pushed a pistol hard into Tom's ribs, which made him wince with pain.

At the main entrance to the station there was a car waiting and Tom was bundled into it. He was taken to a safe house in Harrow, which was in North West London. He was quickly shoved through the front door and taken to the basement and handcuffed to a chair.

The basement room had threadbare furniture. In the middle of the room there was a table with two chairs, a couch that had seen better days and a made-up bed in one corner. As Tom looked around the windowless room, he could see a sink and lavatory in an alcove.

He was left sitting at the table for at least thirty minutes before two men entered the room, one small and the other large. The small wizened one introduced himself as Richard Binder whilst the other no-named man stood by the door. He was large and muscular and was clearly the muscle.

Richard Binder unlocked Tom's handcuffs and sat down facing him. He was an owlish-looking bespectacled man. He looked the archetypical accountant that he used to be before he became one of MI5's most successful interrogators. His big ears were his most outstanding feature that stood at right angles on his bald head. However, his looks concealed a thorough and detail-orientated mind, and he was a man who had an ominous presence about him which demanded respect from those he grilled. Some of his spiteful critics said he had a Napoleon complex. This was probably somewhat true, but he got results.

He was carrying a large file which he threw down on the table with a thud.

Tom was scared out of his wits by this ominous presence and he did not look directly at Richard Binder. His worst nightmare had come to pass. The British security services now suspected him. How should he deal with this latest predicament? Defiance was a possibility. He could try and hold out as long as possible. They probably don't know much anyway and want to trick him into a confession. Well, it won't work.

"I'm sorry about our little deception about your stepfather, but we had to get you here without anybody suspecting that you were a spy because we need to talk to you," said Richard Binder in a conciliatory tone.

"Well, it worked, didn't it!" responded an angry Tom. "I don't know why you dragged me here in the first place!"

"Yes, it did work. We took a bit of a risk because we didn't know whether you already knew that your stepfather had actually died two years ago of bladder cancer."

"It was bloody deceitful of you. There was no reason to trick me that way! Anyway before you go any further I want a solicitor."

Ignoring Tom, Richard Binder continued: "It was not as deceitful as you have been, working for a foreign government. I see you've been a busy little bee for the Russians. I wonder why?" he said in a more hard-edged manner.

Tom did not answer his question but continued to vociferously demand a solicitor.

"You are not allowed one. The War Powers Act gives us the right to interrogate you and that's what we are going to do even if I have to use the services of Jeffrey over there to help me," Richard Binder said, pointing to the guard by the door. "Now we can do this in a friendly way or we can use the unseemly method. It's your choice. Either way, you are heading for a secret court trial and the gallows, so it's best if you could get things off your chest, so to speak, before the inevitable happens."

Richard Binder let that information sink in, although his mention of the gallows was only meant to frighten Tom because usually spies were sentenced to prison. However, he was met by a venomous glare from Tom, who was beginning to realise he had no room to manoeuvre. This was just what Richard wanted.

"What's it like working for that thug Viktor Gorev?" Richard Binder asked. "He was the one, by the way, who killed your boss, Brian Ackerman." Tom reacted internally with horror at this and it was only the flutter of his eyes that gave his reaction away.

"I don't know what you are talking about. Who is Viktor Gorev?"

"Let me refresh your memory then." And, with a sigh, he selected two photographs from his file and threw them over the table at Tom. They were pictures taken both in the pub in London and in Viktor's car.

Richard Binder continued: "How was the gorgeous Madelaine in Paris?"

"What?!"

"We've had you in our sights since you began meeting with Alexei Dorokhin. These Russian agents are so easy to follow. They have no trade craft worth talking about. You were followed when you left for France and your spot of training at the farmhouse in Sergy. You see, it's useless denying your culpability, don't you think?"

"But why didn't you stop me before now?" he asked.

"For the simple reason that we wanted to see who your contacts were and who else was in this nest of spies."

An ominous silence followed as Tom computed the odds stacked against him. Then suddenly he began to cry despondently and confess about all his work for the Russians, which seemed to cascade out of him. In his misery, he felt a relief that he was telling someone something that had been bottled up inside for a long time. He tried to rationalise his reasons for his treachery. He told them of the blackmail photographs of him the Russians had. Richard Binder had become his father confessor. He listened patiently for over an hour as Tom poured out his soul to this owlish man who seemed to know everything about him.

"What I want you to do right now is to write everything down for me. I mean everything, right from your contact with Jane Harcourt at university. Contacts, however minor or great, and all the friends you have made on your malevolent journey are of interest. Think of it as a PhD thesis on your experience spying for the enemy. If we are satisfied, maybe we might be able to save you from the gallows," said Richard Binder sternly as he handed Tom paper and a pen. "I will see you in the morning. Jeffrey will bring you some dinner."

For the next five hours Tom poured his angst into the statement he was making, hoping it would save his life. He didn't know that his minders at MI5 had other plans for him that would spiral his life down even further.

Tom didn't sleep at all that night, except he dropped off to sleep about six in the morning and was awoken when Jeffrey arrived with a big mug of tea, a boiled egg and some toast. Tom was exhausted and looked dishevelled. The noises of the night had played their part in his distress. First of all it was the honk of a car, then two drunks had a fight and finally he heard a woman scream. All this took place in the street outside and helped to jangle his nerves, which were raw anyway.

An hour later, Robert Johnson entered the room carrying the same thick file.

"Good morning, Tom. You look bloody awful. Didn't you sleep at all?"

"No, Mr. Johnson," Tom replied morosely.

"I'm sorry to hear that. I read your report and I was impressed with the thoroughness of it. Now, because you have been straight with us I'll be straight with you. We want you to continue to feed the Russians information via your microfilm. I will give you the film I want you to pass on to them. It will give them the information they want, but it will be doctored so they will have just enough to whet their appetites to want more."

"You mean I will be working for MI5 and spying on them. Suppose I won't?"

"You have options, of course. You can spend fifteen years in Dartmoor prison breaking rocks or at worst be hanged for treason. You could, of course, carry on with your career and work for us at the same time."

"Now you put it like that I have only one sensible choice."

"Yes. Look, this is a long-term project. With Russians making great strides in the war against Germany and the likelihood that we will invade Europe before long with help from the Americans, it means this war will soon be over. The most likely adversary after the war will be Russia and they will want to dominate Europe. They will probably be hell bent on getting our secrets. We have to stop this happening so we need to plant people like you, who they trust, so we can thwart this threat."

"But you know I'm a socialist, so how do you know you can trust me?"

"We understand your political leanings but, correct me if I'm wrong, you believe in democracy, don't you? Do you want to see a Russian-style government in this country? If they're allowed to take over Europe that's what will happen. Now we know that you got tangled up with the wrong people, so correct that and work to keep democracy alive. Also, ask yourself, what would your grandfather have done in your shoes?"

Tom was surprised that Robert Johnson had brought up his grandfather but didn't react to this.

"Now, by the station in Malvern there is a stone wall which has partly fallen down. At the very end the wall is intact. Count four stones to the left and between the fourth and fifth stones there is a crevice. If there is a blank piece of paper in it we want you go to church," he said with a laugh.

"Church, Mr. Johnson! You must be kidding!"

Robert Johnson smiled: "I'm not. There is a local vicar who is at Christ Church in Malvern. He has agreed to pass film on to you for you to give Viktor. Check the wall each day to make sure there isn't a message from him. If I need to meet with you, I'll contact you at work. If you need to contact me in an emergency here's the number to call. Memorise it and throw the paper away."

Robert and Tom spent another two hours going over more details of Tom's assignment, particularly the TRE projects in which they believed the Russian government would be interested.

Robert Johnson walked Tom to the Underground station at Harrow and Wealdstone. When they reached the station, Robert handed Tom a package. "This is the first microfilm for Viktor. Good luck. We'll be in contact."

Tom caught a Bakerloo line to Paddington station. From there he caught a mainline train that got him to Malvern at about four that afternoon. On his journey back to Malvern he felt a sense of relief having come clean with MI5 and was glad he would be starting what he saw as a new chapter in his life. Little did he know he had swopped one predicament for a much more threatening one.

22

NKGB Headquarters, Lubyanka Square,
Moscow, Russia, July 10th, 1943

Vsevolod Merkulov, head of People's Commissariat for State Security, known as the NKGB, was sitting in his large but sparse office at the infamous Lubyanka. This building, which was so feared and loathed by the Russian people, was a well-known prison, interrogation centre and execution site for both the NKVD, responsible for internal security, and the NKGB, the forerunner of the KGB, responsible for international spying operations.

The commissar's office was non-committal in that it didn't say anything about its powerful occupant. The room was dominated by a large six-foot square mahogany desk, which had been in one of the Tsar's minister's study in the Kremlin Senate building. Other than this impressive piece of furniture, the room consisted of two tables piled high with files and other files were stacked on the floor around the room. There were no decorations such as paintings, photographs or family pictures to be seen. The walls were painted in a sterile grey and the floor was covered in cheap linoleum. There were no chairs for visitors because the commissar wanted to intimidate them by making them stand and pay attention to him.

There was small window behind the desk from which the dark and foreboding city could been seen from this sixth-floor perch.

Forty-eight-year-old Vsevolod Merkulov was a brooding man, very reserved and humourless. He was not a person for small talk and was very demanding of his staff, commanding absolute loyalty. He was not tall in stature, maybe five feet eight or nine, with a square face and broad nose. Behind his back people called him 'dough face'.

Vsevolod Merkulov had just that month been made commissar of the NKGB by Joseph Stalin, a role he had briefly had in 1941. Previously he had been the deputy head of the NKVD reporting to notorious agency's head, Lavrentiy Beria, who was responsible, with Stalin, for the mass murder of Russian citizens throughout the 1930s and 1940s as well as the massacre of Polish officers, policemen, intelligentsia in 1940, known as the Katyn Massacre.

There was timid knock on his office door.

"Come!" Vsevolod Merkulov growled.

The door was opened by his assistant, a small, bespectacled man in his mid-fifties who was carrying even more folders.

"Here are the files you asked for, Commissar. Comrade Fitin is here. Shall I ask him to come in?"

"Of course, you fool. Don't let him stand there."

His assistant scuttled away and a few seconds later Pavel Fitin walked in carrying a folding chair because he knew of the strange habits of his superior.

Pavel Fitin was the head of the NKGB's first directive, responsible for foreign intelligence. He was a tall, thin man with swept-back hair and was a smartly dressed in a plain dark double-breasted suit. His intense, brown eyes focussed laser-like on whomever he was meeting. His intelligence and ability had enabled him to climb the intelligence agency ladder at a young age and survive the Stalinist purges of the late 1930s. He almost came unstuck in 1941 when he had warned Stalin of the imminent German invasion of Russia. This information he had gathered from a number of sources in Europe and the Far East. Stalin did not believe any of the information about Operation Barbarossa because he believed it was a Western disinformation plot aimed at sowing discord between the Germany and Russia. Fitin was only saved from arrest by the German invasion on June 22nd, 1941.

Pavel Fitin was one of the most successful foreign intelligence officers in Russia at that time. He had set up a vital network of Russian agents in Britain and in the United States of America and was currently attempting to get his spies to infiltrate both countries' atomic bomb research establishments. At thirty-six years old, he held the rank of Lieutenant General and had become head of the Soviet's first directorate for foreign intelligence in 1939.

"Congratulations on your appointment, comrade!" Fitin said as he walked in and sat down on the chair he had brought with him.

"That will do, Pavel. I want to talk to you about our agents in Britain and America. I've just come from a meeting with Stalin, Beria and Kurchatov." Igor Vasilyevich Kurchatov was the director of the Russian atomic bomb project and the leading scientist in Russia.

"They want us to double our efforts to obtain atom secrets and not through your five Cambridge agents. They don't trust them because, despite the information they have passed to us, they haven't come up with any Western spies here in Russia. That is impossible. There must be Western spies here."

At this time there was a growing suspicion by the Russians of the infamous Cambridge Five spy ring in Britain that they were in fact double agents. The five, all former Cambridge students in the 1930s, consisted of Guy Burgess and Donald Maclean at the Foreign Office, Anthony Blunt at MI5, Kim Philby at MI6 and John Cairncross at Bletchley Park. Despite the good information that was being fed to the Russians, it was ignored. One of the reasons for Russian suspicion of them was they hadn't revealed any British agents in Russia. In fact, there were none, although during the Cold War in the late 1940s and onward, the British did develop agent networks in Russia.

The information the Russians were getting from the Cambridge Five was so voluminous that Moscow Centre, as the headquarters of the Russian spy agencies were colloquially known, suspected they were getting false information. The purges of the 1930s had made Stalin's henchmen frightened of their own shadows and this state of paranoia made them suspicious of anything coming from Western sources.

Pavel Fitin explained to Vsevolod Merkulov that he had made some progress in breaking into thc Manhattan Project in the United States. "Most of the good and reliable information we are getting comes through our contacts at Tube Alloys, the British atomic research operation at Birmingham University. What is important is that our main agent has been transferred to Columbia University in New York to work on the Manhattan Project with the Americans. I expect to get some useful information from him."

"That sounds promising," said Vsevolod Merkulov. "How are you getting the information to us in Britain?"

"I want to expand our sources in Britain. There is a group of leading British scientists called the Relativity Society who have been feeding us useful data. I'll put pressure on them to give us more on atomic developments. We've been in touch with a Professor Cottrell at the Victoria University of Manchester who heads up this group and he has organised a really important scientific spy network for us. It's now time to expand their work."

* * *

Viktor Gorev took another swig from his bottle of vodka. He was in his small room in the basement of the Russian Embassy at 13 Kensington Palace Gardens, London. He was seething with resentment. The NKGB resident, Anatoly Kamenev, had marched him before the Russian Ambassador, Ivan Maisky, who had berated him about his killing of a scientist in Malvern. He was threatened with being returned to Russia in disgrace and put on trial for incompetence. Thankfully, he had been confined at the embassy as a punishment and put to work as a filing clerk in their registry. He was also restricted to the embassy for the next six months. While he chaffed at his treatment he was relieved that he hadn't been shipped home.

Reluctantly, men like Viktor were recruited by the Russian security services after the 1930 Russian purges, which had decimated their ranks. The men and women they recruited at this time were mostly sub-par and would never have been added to their ranks in former years. Viktor had been a local policeman in Ubisa, a small town in Georgia, Russia, and had a reputation as a brutal officer who got results because of this. This was noticed and he was soon recruited by the NKVD on the recommendation of an uncle who had been in Lenin's Cheka. Despite his bestial qualities, Viktor was intelligent in a reptilian way. He had a good ear for foreign languages and after time at the NKVD training school in Moscow, he was posted to Britain.

The more Viktor thought about it the more he wondered who had squealed on him. "How did they find out that I had killed someone? Yes, the car was dented but there was no blood or hair on it and I had told the embassy's transport mechanic that I had hit a deer and to please keep it quiet from the bosses. As an inducement I gave him a bottle of Scotch I had stolen from the stores. No, it wasn't him. It was probably that weakling Tom Pearson who I thought I had under my thumb. He was the only one who knew. He probably tipped off that security man, what was his name? Ah yes, Robert Johnson. I bet they are in cahoots. Well, I'll bide my time before I expose them. First I need to get back operationally and then I can expose the double agent in our midst. There's no point doing it now because it would sound like spiteful malice and no one would believe me."

In fact the tip-off to the embassy came from a Russian agent inside MI5.

* * *

Tom sat at the back of the church in Malvern and waited for the evensong service to finish. Finally, the twelve or so parishioners began to file out. He routinely checked the old wall by the station as Robert had instructed, and about two weeks after he returned to Malvern from his interrogation by MI5, there was a message from the vicar.

Seventy-year-old Reverend Martin Daniel made his way slowly up the church nave from its transept heading towards the main door. He saw Tom sitting in one of the back pews and gave him a warm smile. He sat down next to him: "I've been expecting you, Tom. Here's an envelope for you from your friends." They sat and talked for a while before the vicar said he had to go.

The package was the first of three Tom had received. However, he hadn't been contacted by Victor Gorev or anybody from the Russian embassy for some time and this puzzled him. He called Robert to let him know and the packages stopped being delivered.

After the murder of his boss, Brian Ackerman, Tom was promoted to head up Brian's old section. At last he was enjoying his work at Malvern for the first time in many months. The development of the H2S radar system was behind schedule and he had been pulling all-nighters to get the work done. This was normal in the intense atmosphere of work at the Telecommunications Research Establishment and Tom relished the intellectual challenge his job gave him. He was happy and contented.

Tom's scientific reputation had also grown and he had often been asked to give seminars at various universities. It was no surprise then that he received a letter from his mentor, Dr. Young at the University of Leeds, inviting him to a conference in London. He would be part of a panel that would discuss radio frequency modulation to graduate students and faculty from three universities. These conferences gave him the opportunity spot students the TRE might recruit as they continued to expand their war-time operations. The conference was taking place at his old university, Imperial College in London. He was looking forward to visiting his old stamping ground and meeting some of his former professors.

After his talk, Tom was invited to dinner with the other speakers including Richard Cottrell, Professor of Theoretical Physics at the Victoria University of Manchester. After dinner Professor Cottrell cornered him.

"I would like to have a private word with you. Would you join me for an after-dinner drink at a pub called The Hare? It's just around the corner."

"Certainly, Professor," Tom replied, wondering what this eminent man would want with him.

They left the college and walked north towards Hyde Park. On a side street tucked away in a cul-de-sac was The Hare. It was a small hole-in-the-wall pub which was frequented by only local residents. They found a small table hidden in an alcove and Professor Cottrell went to the bar and bought two brandies.

"I think we deserve this after our busy day," said the friendly professor, as he sat down. "Cheers. Tell me, Tom, how's TRE and that rogue Jimmy Rowe?"

"Working hard as usual. We have a number of projects on the boil, as it were, sir."

"Such as what? The H2S radar system?"

"I'm afraid I can't tell you," said an uneasy Tom.

"That's fine," Professor Cottrell said with a smile. "I understand your need for secrecy. Look, let me put my cards on the table. I know you've been working for the Russians and I have been asked by them to contact you. Viktor is no longer in the picture so you won't be worried about his thuggish ways anymore. I would like you to continue to feed information to me so I can pass it on to our friends."

This news hit Tom like a proverbial sledgehammer. First, he thought he was free of his spying and could just focus on his career. Now that sick feeling came back. Secondly, what was an eminent scientist like Professor Cottrell involved in spying for the Russians?

"You're a spy for the Russians?" Tom blurted out incredulously.

"I wouldn't say that. There are about six of us senior scientists in Britain who believe we should level the technology playing field to help the Russians combat the Germans for one thing. We meet every two or three months to discuss the latest technology developments. We are concerned that the Russians could be overwhelmed by the Germans and want to give them technology to help their cause. The other is that, when this war is over, and it will be soon, we want to prevent further confrontation by enabling every major country to have the same military means as each of the others. Thus there will be a stalemate and the result would be a forced peace that each potential combatant will have to recognise."

"But what will happen if some country secretly develops a weapon?"

"That's where we scientists come in. We pledge to reveal any nefarious plans to the other major players. I have had secret talks with scientists from Russia, the Unites States and numerous other countries at the various conferences I've attended, and they have all agreed to this plan of action."

Tom thought that what he was hearing was so naive that he wondered at the professor's sanity. Why would scientists in Russia even contemplate cooperating with Western scientists in this way, considering their police state and the control that was exerted by the government? It would be extremely foolhardy for anyone to be seen cooperating with Western scientists unless they had been sanctioned by the government for intelligence work.

What Tom didn't know was that Professor Cottrell had been a member of the Communist Party of Great Britain in his student days at Oxford University in the late 1920s and he had resigned his membership in order to take up university appointments. He was still a radical communist at heart and the other professors in the 'Relativity Society' were those he knew from their past communist affiliation.

"A penny for your thoughts, Tom," said the professor after a few moments of silence.

Tom thought quickly and replied, "I'd be happy to help out, but there isn't much going on right now that I could give you."

"How about the experimental V1 flying bomb that crashed and the important technical report of it that some of it was smuggled to England from Denmark, as well as photographs? We'd like copies of these."

"But that's been handled by Dr. Jones and his team at Air Ministry in London."

"Copies have probably been sent to Malvern for TRE's comments. See whether you can get hold of them."

Development of the V1 began in earnest in Germany in 1939 at Peenemünde on the island of Usedom in northern Germany in the Baltic Sea and it was the first unmanned rocket ever developed. This unguided missile had a range of only 160 miles and delivered a 1,870 pound warhead. This was causing indiscriminate damage to London and south-east Britain. It was first used in 1944 and missiles were fired at London from launch sites in Northern France and the Low Countries.

"Also, Tom, do you know anybody at Tube Alloys at Birmingham University? We have one good contact there, but I need another source," asked the professor.

"No, I don't." Tom knew about Tube Alloys only in general terms because it had been brought up at meetings with Dr. Jones and other government scientists, and he had been sworn to secrecy about the project.

"Pity."

Tube Alloys was the code name for Britain's secret nuclear weapons development project which was started in 1940 at the

University of Birmingham, and the operation was eventually transferred to the United States in 1943 because of the fear of a possible German bombing in Birmingham. Also, fighting a war was expensive and the substantial cost of the project meant that Britain could not shoulder this burden. The combined work by British, Canadian and American scientists was called the Manhattan Project and led to the successful production of the first atomic bomb.

Tom left The Hare pub that night in a quandary. For him the plot to give Russia secret technologies such as radar and other conventional weapons was one thing, but information on nuclear weapon development was a bridge too far. From the little he knew, this was a weapon that should not fall into the hands of those monsters in Moscow. He understood the need to help the Russians beat the Germans, but what about after the war? Would this espionage continue to enable Russia to become the most powerful country among the allied nations? A cold shiver went down his spine when he thought about what he knew of the communist system in Russia and just how evil the system was. It would brook no challenge from others, not even the Americans.

When Tom got back to Malvern, he called Robert Johnson on the telephone number he had been given.

23

Robert Johnson put the telephone down after his conversation with Tom Pearson. He felt elated. At last he had found the leader of the Relativity Society who had been feeding scientific information to Moscow Centre. Now the question was, how he was going to trap the group and stop their espionage?

His enthusiasm was damped by Anthony Blunt, who stuck his head around Robert's office door. This man had become a nuisance as he was always trying to draw Robert into his circle of friends. Although he had been to one of Anthony's 'soirées', he didn't enjoy himself because many of the other guests were snobs, artificial and pretentious. He swore never to go again.

"Hello, Robert, you look like the cat that got the cream!" observed Anthony Blunt.

Thinking fast, he replied: "Well, I've just landed a date with a woman I've been interested in for some time." He knew that would throw Anthony off the scent because he was a gay man with not the slightest interest in women. "I'm taking her to the Dorchester for dinner and a dance, and we'll see what else after that," he continued, elaborating. "What can I do for you, Anthony?"

"You are so crude sometimes, Robert. Anyway, I was just going down to registry for some files and as I passed your office, I was wondering how things were going with you as I haven't seen you since that cocktail party I had at my flat. I hope you enjoyed it."

"Yes. I found the company very illuminating."

"Anything much going on in your department?"

"Just a lot of dead ends, I'm afraid. I suppose that's the nature of the job. We've had a few bites with the British Nazis we're watching and some of them have been 18b'd." Regulation 18B of the Defence (General) Regulations 1939 allowed for the interment without trial of people suspected of being Nazi sympathisers.

"What about the Russian spies? Any news on that front?"

"Nothing. That's one of our dead ends. Anyway, we don't think there's any problem there worth worrying about." Robert knew that it was important to give him as little information as possible and to make it sound convincing.

The following morning Robert went to see Maxwell Knight at his Dolphin Square office and filled him in on the details of Tom Pearson's findings.

"What do we know about Professor Cottrell, apart from him being Professor of Theoretical Physics at the Victoria University Manchester?" asked Maxwell Knight.

"He is independently wealthy. His father made the family's money during the Great War as a munitions manufacturer from Bradford. His parents both died in the 1920s and he inherited a fortune. He had won a scholarship to University of Oxford and, after graduation, worked for a time at the Clarendon Laboratory, which is part of the Department of Physics. When he was there he joined a socialist society and was a member of the Communist Party of Great Britain. His membership was dropped after he received his PhD at Oxford in 1925. He joined the Victoria University Manchester in 1930 and was promoted to his present position in 1935," reported Robert.

"Ump. He probably dropped his communist party membership so he could find a job. We need to find out when next meeting of the Relativity Society will be. Your contact would be the best person to find this out. I don't think there is any harm in him giving the information on the V1 because I'm told by Dr. Jones there isn't much of importance to reveal to the Russians.

"You must arrange to have the professor followed so we can keep a check on him. Don't use the department's watchers because we don't want prying eyes to know what we are doing otherwise the birds will fly away. I've got contacts with some freelance and retired watchers you can use. I'll contact Chief Inspector Raymond Jarvis of Special Branch in Manchester and you can brief him on your operation. He can be relied on to keep his mouth shut."

The following week was busy for Robert setting up the operation against the Relativity Society. He spoke to Chief Inspector Raymond Jarvis on the telephone and told him about the operation. He briefed Maxwell Knight's freelance watchers and they began the task of following Professor Cottrell. Soon their quiet patience paid off and they were able to take photographs of him meeting with the NKGB resident, Anatoly Kamenev, in a park in Manchester.

Tom contacted Professor Cottrell with the excuse that he was having difficulty getting the information on the V1 rocket. The professor said he must have the information for a meeting of the group in two weeks when they would meet at his house. With this information, plans were made to wiretap Professor Cottrell's home. They decided that his study and dining room were the places where the meeting would likely take place.

A week later, a workman's van turned into Upper Brook Street in Manchester and pulled up at a semi-detached house. Two workmen dressed in overalls and carry tool bags got out and walked up the path to the front door. They were just about to ring the doorbell when the door suddenly opened and a man came out in a hurry.

"Who are you and what do you want!" demanded a flustered Professor Cottrell.

"Sorry to bother you, sir, but we're from the gas board." The man showed an identity card. "We've been asked to check all gas inlets and appliances for leaks and potential safety hazards. With the bombing we've had here in the last few weeks it could have shaken loose a lot of brackets."

"You'll have to see my housekeeper Mrs. Jennings. She will let you in. Mrs. Jennings!" he called out. An old motherly lady appeared from the back of the house. "Could you help these men out? I'll be late for my lecture otherwise." And with that he was off, striding down the street.

While one of the men chatted with Mrs. Jennings, the other got busy pretending to check the gas inlet and the basement pipes. They made their way into the kitchen, which was in the basement, where the friendly old lady was making a pot of tea and offered them a cup.

"That would be great. I'm dying for a cup," said one of them.

They made a show of checking the stove and then asked Mrs. Jennings whether there were any gas appliances upstairs.

"Well, there is a gas fire in the professor's study."

"What about the dining room?"

"No. Except two wall gas lights which aren't used these days."

"I'll just run up and do a quick check," said the lead workman. "You stay here and enjoy the tea, Fred, I won't be long," and he winked at the other man when Mrs. Jennings' back was turned.

"Tell me, how's your family after the air raids?" the remaining workman asked Mrs. Jennings to distract her from thinking about his supervisor who had gone upstairs.

"Well, dear, my daughter Dotty had a near escape two nights ago. Her husband is in the army abroad and…" She spent the next ten minutes talking and by that time the lead workman had returned, having put devices on the study telephone and under the dining room table. As they took their leave of Mrs. Jennings, they walked back to the street and climbed back into the van where there were two other men, a wireless technician and a special branch sergeant.

The technician turned on his equipment and was satisfied that all the circuits were working properly. The sergeant and the technician began to monitor the equipment and didn't expect anything to happen before the professor returned. They were due to be relieved at five in the evening and settled in for a boring surveillance operation. Meanwhile, the two workmen went to the mainline station in Manchester and caught a train back to London.

Professor Cottrell didn't return to his house until six that night. He had the dinner Mrs. Jennings had left him and then went to his study to work on some papers. About eight that night he received a telephone call from his Russian contact, Anatoly Kamenev. The police started their recorder.

"Anatoly, you shouldn't be calling me here. What if you are being watched?"

"Don't worry about that, Richard, I'm calling from a pay phone in Hammersmith and I shook off the people following me. Something has come up and my bosses in Moscow want to get any information you can on a German rocket they are developing called the V2. Maybe the British have got some material on this. Apparently, experiments are being carried out at Peenemünde on the Baltic coast of northern Germany."

"Hmm. I'll see what I can find out and let you know at our next meeting."

The German development of the V2 rocket was almost completed in late 1943 and the Russians were keen to get their hands on any rocket research. The first successful test was in 1942 at Peenemünde. There were problems with the gyro compass system so research on the weapon had been delayed. The British were unable at this time to get any details of this weapon as none had been fired at Britain or the information of it smuggled out of Peenemünde by allied agents.

"One other thing, which has some urgency," said Anatoly Kamenev. "We need to know about the research that is secretly being carried out the University of Birmingham into a big bomb which would destroy a whole city at a time. We know the Americans have a similar project and are working with the British.

Also, we need to know about the German heavy water project that was given to the British by the Norwegian Jomar Brun. Do you know anything about this?"

"I heard a rumour but I'll have to get in contact with someone I know at the university to see whether I can get you the information."

"When is your next group meeting?"

"Next Wednesday."

The transcripts of this telephone call were sent to London that night by courier and Robert Johnson met urgently with Maxwell Knight.

"We'll have to move on this group before they cause more damage," said Maxwell Knight, sucking on his pipe. "I'll have to get clearance from Petrie, but that shouldn't be a problem." Sir David Petrie was the director general of MI5 at this time.

Early that Wednesday morning Robert Johnson was sitting in the van with Chief Inspector Jarvis watching Professor Cottrell's house. They weren't sure of the time that had been set for the meeting but guessed it was late morning. At about ten thirty-two men turned up with overnight bags and when they disappeared into the house, the police turned on the recorders that would pick up their conversations.

As the men settled down in their seats in the professor's study they began to talk about projects that were being worked on for the war effort. One man admitted that he was able to get a file on the research that was done of the German Lichtenstein night fighter radar system. He handed it to Professor Cottrell. A crew of a Ju 88 night fighter had defected from Germany and had landed in Aberdeen, Scotland, in May that year. The information gained on the system had enabled British scientists to combat the success of the German night fighters.

"Jeez!" exclaimed Chief Inspector Jarvis. "I've never heard such obvious criminal statements. Let's go and get them right now."

"Let's see what the other men say first and then we've got them all," replied Robert Johnson.

A third man then began to talk about the advancements that had been made in atomic bomb development at Tube Alloys since he had last reported. Handing Professor Cottrell a file, he said a further report would be made at their next meeting as improvements were being continuously made, especially those by the Americans.

"Got you!" exclaimed Chief Inspector Jarvis, and a broad smile came over his usually inscrutable face. Then Professor Cottrell began to talk about what his Russian contact needed and the group discussed the best way to get the information they needed.

"Let's go and get them," said Robert Johnson.

Robert, the chief inspector and two of his men left the van and went up to the professor's front door and rang the bell. Mrs. Jennings answered the door and was pushed out of the way by Chief Inspector Jarvis as he charged towards the professor's study followed by Robert. As he entered the room the men looked up at him in astonishment and were shocked that they had been caught red-handed.

"Gentlemen, I'm Chief Inspector Jarvis of Special Branch and I'm arresting you all for contravening Section 2 of the Official Secrets Act. You are accused of providing secret information to a foreign power and other acts prejudicial to the public safety or the defence of the realm."

And so all three men were handcuffed and led away. They didn't say a word. Other than Professor Cottrell, one was a physics lecturer at the University of Glasgow, one a professor of chemistry at London University and the other an undersecretary from the Air Ministry in Whitehall.

A few days later, Robert Johnson was sitting in his office going through papers when an angry Anthony Blunt marched in.

"I'll tell you a lot of people around here are furious with you and Maxwell Knight. Keeping your operation against the scientists secret. Who do you think we are! We're your colleagues with a common purpose and that is protecting this country. You lied to me! How could you do that?!"

Robert looked up at Anthony and calmly said: "It was an operation that had the blessing of the director general and was carried out with a minimum of people in the know. We didn't want the information to fall into the hands of the wrong people. Anyway, we got the traitors. You know, traitors to our country are the worst kind of people. I'd put them all against a wall and shoot them. Now, if you'll excuse me, I have work to do to make sure they will all spend time on Dartmoor."

Anthony Blunt went red in the face, opened his mouth to say something and then thought better of it. He left quickly. He knew he had to let Moscow Centre know as soon as possible.

24

RAF Defford, February 6th, 1944

Tom Pearson was now in his element. He had shrugged off the depression and anxieties caused by his misadventures into the dark, macabre world of espionage. His contacts at MI5 had kept their word and not charged him with any crime. He was now free and much more focussed on the development of electronic countermeasure devices, which were designed to trick and deceive enemy radar systems, particularly those of German night fighters. These fighters were wreaking havoc on the British night bombers and so the developmental work on a countermeasure response had become extremely urgent. As a result, Tom was working long and arduous hours.

One particular Sunday afternoon, he was at RAF Defford making last-minute adjustments to a radar system which was to be installed in a Wellington Bomber the next day for a series of trials. There had been last-minute glitches in the equipment which had to be put right before the field tests began. He had sent his exhausted team home because the completion of the work was in sight and he could make the final adjustments by himself.

Trials on aircraft were the culmination of the design and

experimentation work at TRE. It wasn't until the scientists were satisfied that a system was made available to all units of the RAF. This practical work was carried out at RAF Defford, which was some ten miles from Malvern. The Telecommunications Flying Unit, as it was called, had some fifty or so different aircraft, which the scientists used to test their systems. Just as with an operational station, the aircraft came with aircrews and ground and administrative staff. There were some one thousand personnel at the station, which was commanded by a group captain.

As night fell, Tom found another problem with the device and he was resigned to working late into the night to fix the new snag. He turned the lights on and continued with his work and gave no thought to the blackout. It wasn't long before the door to the hut opened and an officious-looking young corporal of the Women's Auxiliary Air Force, known as WAAFs, came in.

"Come on, sir, you can't let Gerry see your light. This just won't do. What are you thinking?" she scolded as she closed the heavy curtains. Tom blushed as he looked up at the very attractive corporal.

"I'm sorry, Corporal. I got so involved with my project I wasn't aware it was dark." He smiled sheepishly.

"You boffins are all the same – forgetful. I would be surprised if you remembered to brush your teeth and comb your hair this morning when you got up," she continued, but more kindly.

"Well, actually I haven't been to bed in the last two days. I've napped at my workbench for a couple of hours at a time, but that's all."

"I don't expect you've eaten, have you?"

"Well, not really."

"Oh! How can you expect to function properly if you don't eat and sleep?" she said in kind, motherly way.

"Well, I have to finish this project to test tomorrow."

"What does it do? It seems very complicated to me."

"With this device, if it works, bomber command would be

able to avoid having so many planes shot down by German night fighters. By the way, my name is Tom Pearson from TRE."

The corporal smiled: "I'm Fiona Shelby."

Tom spent the next half hour explaining his radar device to Fiona. During their conversation, he found out she was from Norwich and had joined the WAAFs the year before after she graduated from a girls' high school there. She was supposed to go up to university but had decided that she would serve her country first and then, after the war, study biology, which was her passion. So she understood Tom's laser-like focus on his project. During their conversation she pummelled him with a lot of questions and showed a real interest in his project.

Fiona was not beautiful or ugly. She was short and muscular and had the appearance of a fit athlete. In fact, her other passion was rock climbing, which surprised many of her boyfriends when they got to know her. Her WAAFs uniform didn't do credit to her full figure, but she had a gentle face that always had a warm, inviting smile. Her father and mother regarded her as the family tomboy. She was the youngest member and had two sisters and a brother ahead of her.

Fiona looked at her watch: "Crikey, look at the time. I'd better go otherwise Flight will be after me. He sent me over here some time ago. See you around, Tom!" And she was off.

Tom was captivated by Fiona. What a whirlwind of a girl she was, he thought as he continued his work. About an hour later Fiona suddenly reappeared, startling Tom. She was carrying a large plate and a steaming mug of cocoa. On the plate were two large corned beef sandwiches.

"Now get this inside you, Tom. No arguments. You need looking after if you are going to help our boys in blue." As she walked back to the guardhouse, Fiona felt fascinated by this scruffy, unshaven, tousled-haired man in his ill-fitting clothes. She admired his seeming tenacity with his complicated project and his determination to see that it worked.

As the weeks passed, Tom and Fiona spent what little spare time they had going to concerts laid on for the military by professional entertainers, plays in Malvern's Winter Gardens and dances arranged as a regular social event either at RAF Defford or at TRE. They enjoyed each other's company and found that their sense of humour was very similar. She had also insisted that he buy new clothes and, after much prevarication by him, they spent a Saturday at a men's shop in the high street in Great Malvern.

Tom found that their relationship had helped him psychologically, in that his dates with Fiona had taken him momently away from the rigors of his work. The members of his team at TRE had noticed that he was less cranky and more collegial since he had been going out with Fiona.

One evening in April Tom was meeting Fiona in their favourite pub. Tom had got there early and was sitting at the bar when Fiona came in. He could tell something was bothering her and waited while she ordered a drink.

"What's on your mind, Fiona? You seem a little preoccupied. Has that flight sergeant been after you again?"

"No. I've got some good and bad news to tell you. First, I've been promoted to sergeant as of tomorrow."

"Fantastic. We have to break out the champagne and celebrate."

"Not so fast, Tom. I'm being transferred to RAF Uxbridge to the headquarters of No. 11 Group RAF and I leave here on Wednesday."

The news hit Tom hard and he didn't know what to say. At first he thought selfishly about what he was going to do without her. Would she remember him when she was among all those fighter pilots? These thoughts flashed through his mind before he pulled himself together and told himself not to be so self-centred: "That's a great opportunity for you. You must be very excited."

"Well, I am, but the thought of not seeing you so regularly upsets me. But I realise with this war on we shouldn't quibble about the transfer because other people are making bigger sacrifices."

"Look, Uxbridge is a north-western suburb of London. I visit the Air Ministry there on a fairly regular basis. We could see each other then. The Underground runs from Uxbridge into London so it will easy to meet. So cheer up and let's open that bottle of champagne!"

RAF Uxbridge played an important role in the Battle of Britain in 1940, not only in providing fighters but also as a central planning area of the campaign. The station was to become an important element in the D-Day landings (Operation Overlord) on June 6th, 1944, and the subsequent air campaign over Germany.

* * *

NKGB Headquarters, Moscow

Pavel Fitin slammed the telephone down in a fit of bad temper. He had just got word that his much-vaunted scientists' network, the Relativity Society, had been wrapped up by MI5. All the members of the group had been swept up, including their sources at various universities and at government research establishments. It was a complete disaster.

Fitin now had to report this to his boss, Vsevolod Merkulov, and was dreading his reaction, although the man's attention had been focussed recently on the impending invasion by the allies of Normandy. The Russians had been putting pressure on Britain and the United States for the last three years to open up a second front on Germany and, much to Stalin's chagrin, this did not happen immediately. Through their sources in Whitehall, the Russians had found out that the invasion would take place sometime in June after a big build-up of armed forces. Now it was on, a sense of relief permeated the halls of the Russian security services because Stalin and his henchmen were delighted the invasion at last was going to happen.

Pavel Fitin walked up some stairs to the sixth floor and told

Merkulov's assistant, he wanted to see his boss. Merkulov was standing by the window in his office looking out onto Lubyanka Square when Fitin was ushered in.

"I heard the news that your network of scientists has been discovered. What are you going to do about it?" Merkulov demanded.

Fitin was surprised that he knew about that. Clearly the man had sources within Fitin's department and he wondered who that was. He answered confidently: "Start again. We have a good source in America now who was transferred there from Birmingham University and Tube Alloys. He is feeding us information on the Manhattan Project and I will build my sources on that side of the Atlantic. Frankly, there is more fertile ground there than in Britain."

"What have you done about finding who the leak was in Britain? We need to find out who it was and eliminate him as an example to others. It will send the message that we won't stand for any dissent and we will come down hard on anyone who is treacherous," he said, raising his voice.

"I will replace our NKGB resident at the embassy in London with someone who will get the job done," Fitin responded confidently.

"I hope you're right, Pavel, because Beria is now following your progress."

* * *

Russian Embassy, London

A month later, Viktor Gorev stood to attention in front of Anatoly Kuznetsov. He knew this man and why he should be afraid of him.

"I have come here to clean up the mess you and comrade Kamenev caused. Now you are here rather than in Moscow because you are to be given the chance to make amends for your errors.

But make no mistake, I do not like people who screw up. Another mistake and you will be housed in one of our Gulags or, if I have my way, you will be shot. Do I make myself clear?" Kuznetsov said, staring with his cold grey eyes at a very contrite Viktor Gorev.

"Yes, comrade."

"Good. Now I want you to tell me all about your activities before your banishment to the archives department. Why did you kill that British scientist?"

"I was meeting my contact at the British Telecommunications Research Establishment in Malvern. We were sitting in my car outside a pub that was frequented by many of the scientists from that place. We were talking when a man passed by and my contact recognised him as head of security at the research establishment. According to our sources, this man was from MI5. The man looked at us as he passed and must have recognised my contact. I watched as he walked around the side of the pub where bicycles had been left and I presumed he was going to cycle back to his room in town. I knew I had to deal with this person to protect my contact. Now you have to understand, it was pouring with rain, and I mean really pouring, and the visibility was zero. I told my contact to go back to the pub. When a man of the same size, wearing the same type of hat and raincoat cycled by, I followed him in my car at a distance. At a quiet spot in the lane I drove my car into him. When I went back to check, he was dead. I found out much later that it was not the MI5 man."

"So you said that the MI5 man recognised your contact, so I wonder if he turned him to work for British security after that episode with the dead cyclist? What's your contact's name?"

"Tom Pearson. You have his file on your desk."

Anatoly Kuznetsov shuffled the files on his desk until he found what he was looking for. "Ah! Not only was he passing information to you but later fed information to Professor Cottrell, who is now languishing in a British prison. I wonder if this is our leaker."

Viktor Gorev thought that that was what he thought too. He

had suspected Tom Pearson for some time but kept his thoughts to himself, not wanting to annoy his superiors and not wanting to take the blame for not suspecting Tom much earlier when he was in contact with him.

"I want you to get in touch with Tom Pearson as if you wanted to restart your contact with him now that the scientific network is not operational. Once you've made contact, have him followed and see who he contacts. Then we'll know whether or not he's our man."

* * *

Now Tom was miserable without Fiona. He had been writing to her once a week and she had replied. They hadn't had time together since she left because she was extremely busy as D-Day approached. Finally, they had planned to meet in London when he was up there for yet another committee meeting at the Air Ministry. They planned to spend the night together after visiting the Savoy Theatre.

Tom reached London on a Thursday evening and, once he had checked into a small hotel, he went for a drink and a sandwich at a pub he knew. As he sat down at a corner table another man joined him. He looked up as the man sat down and recognised Viktor Gorev. His heart sank.

"What do you want?" Tom demanded.

"That's no way to treat a colleague."

"You're not a colleague and never have been. I'm done working for you."

"I think not. I've still got those photographs and I will use them. Now I want you to get me information on those radar projects you are working on. I'll come by the pub in Malvern next week. You better not let me down." Viktor Gorev got up and walked out.

Tom was in a panic. His worst fears had returned. When he

got back to the hotel he called Robert Johnson and they arranged to meet for lunch the next day. Viktor waited outside the Air Ministry, having followed Tom from his hotel in the morning. At noon, Tom left the ministry, walked into the Strand and entered a restaurant. Through the window Viktor saw Robert Johnson get up from a table and greet him.

The trap was sprung!

25

Despite Tom's fear of retribution from Viktor Gorev and the dread of interacting with the Russians again, he was determined to put these thoughts in the back of his mind and enjoy his brief time with Fiona. He had booked a room at the St. Ermin's Hotel in Westminster and they had met there for a drink in the bar before dinner and the theatre.

After the play had finished, they walked with the theatre crowd from the Savoy Theatre down to the embankment and to the Charing Cross Underground station. They were busy talking and walking arm in arm and didn't notice that they were being followed. On their way back to the hotel they were to take a District Line Underground train to St. James's Park station. The hotel was only a few minutes' walk from the station.

Tom had enjoyed the evening and was looking forward to spending the night with Fiona. And he guessed that she felt the same way. This would be their first time making love in private without being concerned about being seen, as they were when they went behind the dance hall at RAF Defford. It was a quick fumble that had given them no pleasure before a wolf whistle had interrupted their incompetent groping.

Charing Cross Underground station was crowded with

theatre-goers going home, and Tom and Fiona stood arm in arm at the front of a group of passengers awaiting the arrival of the train. Suddenly there was roar in the tunnel as the train approached. Just as it was arriving at the platform, Tom felt a violent shove in his back. As he and Fiona were arm in arm they both fell towards the incoming train. Fiona screamed and fell in front of the train, and Tom's head caught the side of the first carriage as the train braked hard. The deafening sound of metal on flesh and bone was gruesome as the train slid to a halt.

After an eerie silence, a woman screamed as the crowd stood back in horror at the macabre scene. The only person moving was a man running up the stairs towards the station exit. No one noticed him as they were all staring at the front of the train and at the prone, unconscious figure lying at the front of the platform.

After a few moments, the white-faced driver of the train opened the door to his cab and staggered out. He was violently sick in front of everyone. He groaned: "I didn't see her. Oh my God, I can't believe this!" And he started to sob.

The duty stationmaster rushed down the stairs to the platform and ordered one of his staff to turn the emergency electricity switch to off. Then he announced to everyone: "The fire and ambulance brigades are on their way as well as the police. I would request that everyone return to the station ticket hall because the police will want to talk to you."

Just then Tom began to stir. The impact of hitting the train had knocked him out and he felt his head, which was covered in blood. He slowly and painfully sat up and began to ask anyone who would listen where Fiona was.

The stationmaster walked up to him. "We have the emergency services coming here right now, sir. Please sit still, otherwise you might hurt yourself more."

This seemed to agitate Tom. "Where's Fiona!" he screamed.

"I'm afraid the young lady you were with fell in front of the train," he answered, reluctantly.

Tom staggered to his feet and teetered towards the front of the train, pushing the stationmaster aside, and looked down at Fiona's trapped and mangled body. He swayed and was caught by the stationmaster, who lowered him to the ground.

Two police constables arrived and started to usher the passengers up the stairs to the ticket hall, and as they did, a hysterical woman shouted: "He did it! He pushed her in front of the train! I saw him with my two eyes. Murderer!"

"Now come on, Jess, you didn't see anything. Let's go upstairs," said a worried man who was her husband.

"Yes, I did!" she shouted, as she was manhandled up the stairs by her embarrassed husband.

The firemen had arrived and had started to jack up the front of train to extract Fiona's crushed body. It was a gruesome job. The men had got used to dealing with bodies during the Blitz in London in 1940 and 1941, as well as the occasional air raids after that, and had become somewhat hardened to the task. Still, most of them had never become indifferent about what they did.

Tom sat down on the platform in a daze. He couldn't remember anything. Who was Fiona? He kept on shouting her name. Who was he, if it came to that? What was he doing here and why were all these people running around? It was all a mystery to him.

He got up slowly and began to walk towards the stairs and the exit. No one noticed him leaving because they were too busy working on the train. When he reached the street, he turned left and continued to walk east along the Thames Embankment. To where, he didn't know, but he knew he had to. Something was driving him. He didn't know why or what. Was it a survival instinct that forced him away from the scene of such horror? He knew he had to keep walking no matter what. Years later when he thought about it, he realised it had been the right decision.

Tom crossed the road and stopped to look at the swirling River Thames which was at high tide. The churning brown water with its eddies had a mesmeric effect on him as if it was inviting him in.

The honk of a car brought him back to reality and he continued his walk towards Blackfriars Bridge. He climbed the stairs up to the bridge and began to walk across it. When he reached the centre he stopped to look back at Westminster which was in darkness, but he could make out the outline of buildings such as the Shell-Mex office block when he looked upstream. The outline of St. Paul's Cathedral dominated the skyline when he looked the other way. After pondering the sights for a while, he walked to the guardrail and looked down at the river some forty feet below him. After a while he had become almost hypnotised by gyrating water. It was so inviting.

Then he heard a voice: "'Ere, it's not worth it, mate." He turned around and saw no one. Was he hearing things?

"Things can't be that bad, can they?" the voice continued.

"Where are you?" Tom asked.

"Over here, chum. Come and take the weight off your pins. You look all in."

Then Tom saw him sitting on one of the bridge's stone seats in an alcove. He walked up to the man and sat down beside him. "I'm Dick Tabard," he said, and offered Tom a drink out of his whisky flask. Tom took the flask and took a swig. "I don't know who I am. I think I've been in some kind of accident."

"It looks like it. Have you had that cut on your head taken care of?"

"I don't think so."

"Hmm. You better come home with me and my missus will fix you up."

"What are you doing here all alone on this bridge?" Tom asked.

"Oh, I often come here these days to look at my city and weep about the bomb damage the Germans have done to it. It's going to take long to put things right, once we win the war. We don't get any air raids these days, although where I live in Southwark we live in fear of further raids. It's difficult to get that fear out of your mind."

Dick Tabard must have been in his late forties and was a cockney through and through. He was born and brought up in Southwark, got married there and it was where he reared his two children. He was a strong-looking man, with muscles developed over the years of manual labour for the borough of Southwark. He was dressed in heavy denim trousers and a heavy, workman's jacket, which had leather on the shoulders and down the back. He had a cheerful face that had a bulbous nose topped off by a bushy moustache.

He continued: "Most of us in our street haven't got homes to go to. Mine was blown up in 1941 and at first we lived with neighbours then their house got hit. After the borough let me go because of their money troubles, I got a job as a porter at Covent Garden so I'm making some money, but we spend the nights in the crypt at St. George the Martyr church. The vicar has organised shelter for the neighbourhood and it is real communal living. We have a canteen and some nights they lay on plays, all sorts of entertainment and we have singalongs. It's not too bad, but sometimes I wish for the privacy of my own home," he said ruefully.

They each took another swig of the whisky from the flask and then got up and walked off the bridge down Blackfriars Road into Southwark. The scene that met Tom's eyes was the utter devastation of the houses, or what was left of them, on the streets they walked along. What was incredible was that while some of the buildings looked untouched, others were completely decimated. Dick explained that the worst of the bombing was not so much the high explosives, although they were bad enough, but the incendiary bombs which were used to create widespread fires that burned houses and people.

As they approached St. George the Martyr church, Tom could see some of the damage that the church had received in the Blitz, particularly the roof, as well some of its facade. Dick led the way down to the crypt which was organised into dormitories and a small canteen. He introduced Tom as 'Bob' to various people, including his wife, Margery. They sat down with a cup of tea in a corner of the canteen and chatted as Margery took care of Tom's head wound.

That night Tom slept well under a blanket he been given and on a spare mattress made of straw. He was exhausted from his bitter experiences of the night before, and when he awoke late the next morning, he saw that most of the people were up and starting to set off to work. Dick was nowhere to be found and Margery explained that he had left at five for his job at Covent Garden.

Tom sat in cafeteria eating a bun and drinking tea when a young priest came in and greeted everyone with a loud good morning. Everyone there, including the children, waved and smiled at the ebullient priest. He was a man a little older than Tom, heavy set but neatly dressed in a tailored jacket, carefully pressed grey flannel trousers and highly polished shoes, which denoted his years as an officer in the Coldstream Guards. Old habits die hard. Under his jacket he wore a black shirt and a dog collar. No one knew why he had left the army to be a priest and he had never volunteered a reason. He worked hard for the people in the parish and everyone appreciated this, and his upper-class upbringing was never an issue for them. They took him at face value and he had earned their undying respect.

He walked up to Tom and held out his hand to shake Tom's: "I'm Raymond James. Everyone here calls me Father Ray. I heard you joined us last night, Bob, but that you have a memory problem. Well, maybe we can help you. Dr. Dixon, our local GP, will be here soon and he can take care of you, especially the horrible cut on your head. We don't want it to be infected. Now, tell me what you remember."

"I'm afraid not much. I remember walking out of a tube station and then stopping on Blackfriars Bridge, where I met Dick. How and why I got there is all a mystery."

"Hmm. I notice from your accent you're from the north of England. Yorkshire? Do you remember anything about your childhood? Your parents or grandparents?"

"Nothing comes to mind. Wait a minute, I do remember my grandad, though. He was a union leader and took me to football games and we used to go fishing. I don't remember the town, though."

"Well, don't force it. Take your time and things will start coming back."

"Right you are, Vicar. I would like to contribute somehow because I don't want to be a sponger on these wonderful people. Is there a job I can do to help out?"

The Reverend James thought for a bit: "Do you know anything about radios? We have this big wireless which we use to play dance music at our social evenings. It's on the blink and only works for a bit and then stops."

"Let me take a look at it."

Tom spent the rest of the day taking the radio to pieces, soldering parts and then reassembling it. He was amazed at his knowledge, which seemed to come naturally to him. By the time he had finished repairing the wireless it was four in the afternoon. When he switched it on, it sprang to life, and he tuned it to the BBC. An announcer was reading the news. At the end of the bulletin he reported: "There is still no news of the British scientist who went missing last night after being involved in a train accident at Charing Cross District Line station when a woman he was with died. If anyone has information on this they are encouraged to contact their local police station. Now the weather…"

Tom wondered who the man was and Reverend James, who also heard the broadcast, wondered whether the mystery man they called Bob was the missing scientist.

* * *

Russian Embassy, London

"You idiot!" screamed Anatoly Kuznetsov, the NKGB resident, at a trembling Viktor Gorev. "You can't get a simple instruction right! I have no time for you. Take him away!" he ordered two of his men who were standing behind Viktor. They frog-marched him into a cell in the basement.

Viktor was shaking with fear. He expected to be sent back to Russia to his execution. Two hours later his cell door swung open and Kuznetsov's men returned; they marched him up the basement stairs and manhandled him into a van. They drove to the Battersea Power Station, where there were some bombed-out warehouses on the River Thames. They forced him to kneel on the edge of a dock.

All the time, Viktor was whimpering and pleading for mercy.

One of the men pulled out a revolver and screwed on a silencer, then aimed at the back of Viktor's neck and squeezed the trigger. His body fell into the river with a splash.

26

Rotherhithe, London Surrey Docks, May 2nd, 1944

Johnny Campion and Vincent Smith were best friends and then became orphans at the age of twelve. Both their parents and the rest of their families had been killed during the Blitz on the Surrey Docks in 1941. It had been a miracle that neither of them had been at home on that fateful day. They had both been playing soccer in nearby Dulwich when the sirens announced yet another raid. They dived down into a public shelter and when the all-clear sounded they made their way home to find that both their homes and their families were destroyed.

Since that terrible day, they had lived in the ruins of one of their homes and been able to eat at a Salvation Army canteen. They earned a few shillings by collecting scrap metal around the bombed-out buildings and along the River Thames when the tide was out. It was amazing what the river left behind when the tide was out, and at this particular point junk was trapped on the Rotherhithe side of the river because of a large bend in the river.

The boys walked along the beach as they searched for scrap metal. Sometimes they were lucky and found old prams or a bicycle, but today they were out of luck. Then Vincent spotted a large, old sack, or at least it looked one, but when he got closer he saw it was a body.

Both boys were somewhat immune to being shocked when finding grisly things like dead cats or dogs and even the occasional person who had committed suicide by throwing themselves off nearby bridges such as Tower Bridge or even London Bridge.

"Blimey, it's another stiff! We'd better go and get old Jock," said Vincent. Jock was the nickname they had given Police Constable Hamish Fraser, who was from Glasgow but had been brought to London by his English wife some fifteen years before because she was homesick for London. He was the bane of the boys' lives, always chasing them and threatening them with arrest. But there was unsaid mutual respect on both sides and they felt they could always go to him if they any problems. It was a love-hate relationship. For example, when they found a German bomb in the mud, PC Fraser was very concerned about their safety and had insisted on buying them some tea and cake at the Women's Voluntary Services mobile canteen, which had been set up in a nearby street while the army diffused the bomb.

While Vincent ran off in search of PC Fraser, Johnny stood watch over their find.

* * *

Robert Johnson sat in his office at MI5 making repeated telephone calls to the police and Special Branch. He was at a loss to know where to search for Tom. He had got him involved with working for the security services and he felt responsible for his safety now that the Russians were seeking to avenge the destruction of their scientific spy network.

The telephone rang which made him jump. It was Superintendent Brian Brill from Special Branch. When Robert heard his voice he anticipated bad news: "The police in Southwark have found a body which was washed up when the tide went out on the Thames. There's no ID on it but it could be your man. The body is in the mortuary at Guys Hospital. I'll meet you there."

Any mortuary is a sad place, when so many lives have come to an end and the authorities need to officially determine their identity and cause of death through post-mortems. Also sad was the number of unclaimed bodies that were stored ready for burial in a pauper's grave. This was especially heart-wrenching during the war when the sheer volume of the dead swelled. The Guys Hospital mortuary was similar to other mortuaries throughout London. It was white-tiled, smelt heavily of disinfectant and lined with body storage units. There were a number of bodies on gurneys waiting to be examined when Robert Johnson and Superintendent Brill walked in with the senior pathologist.

As they walked to a gurney the doctor gave his report. "This man has been shot in the back of the head. Death would have been instantaneous. The body had been in the river for over a week. There was no ID on him but we looked at the fillings of some of his teeth and determined they were done somewhere in Eastern Europe. Maybe Poland, Ukraine or even Russia. That's as close as we can be." Robert was relieved to hear that news.

They walked up to a gurney and the doctor pulled back the sheet covering the body. Although the fish and eels had been busy, Robert recognised the man. "His name is Viktor Gorev. He works at the Russian Embassy. I'll have to let the Foreign Office know you have his body. They will contact the embassy and make funeral arrangements. As it is murder, the police must be involved," said a relieved Robert Johnson.

* * *

Tom had by now been in the shelter in Southwark over a week and had been accepted as a temporary East Ender. His memory hadn't improved and he wondered whether psychologically he didn't want it to get better. Tom had gone down to the Rotherhithe public baths on Deptford Lower Road with the other men to wash and bathe, and it was then he had decided to grow a beard.

He was enjoying himself among these wonderful people and was doing something useful for them. Despite their outgoing joie de vivre, though, he could see and sense the trauma of their existence was written on their faces. Every so often, and with increasing occurrence, there would be an angry spat that would break out between individuals or groups about their living conditions or someone would come back drunk from the pub and cause trouble. Anger would spill over and the Reverend James had to step in as peacemaker.

He had made friends with many of the residents and had helped out with babysitting for some of them when they had to go somewhere or when they went to the pictures, which, other than the pub, was the only entertainment available to them. It was when a group came back from one of these trips that his identity was questioned. At the pictures, and before the main film, British Movietone News was shown and one of the segments in the newscast was a short story about a missing scientist that showed a picture of him. Several of the residents who went to the pictures talked to Reverend James about the identity of the man they all knew as 'Bob'.

The next morning, as Tom was sweeping up after breakfast in the canteen, Reverend James approached him. "Bob, we need to talk. Let's grab some tea and sit over there." When they had settled down, the vicar said: "We have been able to discover your true name. At the pictures last night there was piece about you and in this morning's paper there was also a story with a photograph." As the vicar said this, he spread on the table a newspaper clipping that had the headline 'Missing Scientist Sought'. There staring up at Tom was picture of himself, but without the beard.

Tom's memory by now had begun to slowly return. He knew it was inevitable that his identity would be discovered at some point, but he was quite happy to enjoy his new life as long as he could.

But now the time had come to face the prospect of it happening as the cat was out of the bag now.

"I still can't remember anything. This article says I am a leading scientist, but in what? It says I have contributed to the war effort, but how? What do you think I should do?" he asked, sounding sceptical.

"I think we need to go to a police station and tell them who you are. Who knows, you might have family wondering where you are. Maybe you have a wife and children who are frantic about finding you. We just don't know. Once you know all this then you can make a choice about where you want to be," said Reverend James.

"I suppose you're right," replied Tom morosely.

Tom went with the Reverend James to Carter Street police station and told the desk sergeant who he was. He waited in an interview room for two hours before a tall, smart man came in and greeted him like a long-lost friend. Robert Johnson was so glad to see him, although Tom wondered who he was and couldn't remember ever knowing the man before.

Reverend James asked to speak to Robert Johnson in private. When they were out in the corridor he explained to the man Tom's condition.

"What I want to tell you is absolutely important for national security and extremely confidential," Robert Johnson began. "Do I have your word that nothing will go any further?"

"In my last career, I had to sign the Official Secrets Act as part of my duties in military intelligence and I'm sure it's still in force," said the Reverend James with a smile.

Robert Johnson was taken aback. What was a military man doing here as a vicar? He put his natural curiosity behind him and continued: "I'm from MI5 and I've known Tom for some three years. Tom had worked with me to expose a Russian spy ring. His injury was a result of him being attacked in an Underground station two weeks ago. A Russian agent was trying to kill him. He managed to murder the girl Tom was with but Tom was lucky. It was important that we take him to a safe place out of the reach of the Russians so he can recover from his ordeal. They are hunting him."

"But this a safe place. No one here would betray him," said Reverend James.

"How many of your flock or their acquaintances belong to the Communist Party? We know that a call has gone out for members to look for him."

"I see what you mean. I know of several men who I've banned from this shelter because of their very radical views that were upsetting some of my parishioners. They would certainly turn him in."

"That's why we must get him away to a safe house."

They went back into the interview room where Tom looked at them and said: "What have you two been hatching?"

It took over an hour for them to convince Tom to leave the shelter. Reverend James finally convinced him to go with Robert Johnson and to trust him. They left the police station and drove to a safe house in Hounslow that was on the west side of London.

Robert Johnson left him in the hands of Richard Binder, who had originally interrogated Tom when he was recruited to help MI5. This time the old man was kindly and started to show Tom many photographs from his past at Malvern in the hope that this would jog his memory. This did not work and it was decided that he would be transferred to a private clinic known to Maxwell Knight in Sennybridge in Wales.

Finally, two weeks later, his memory began to return. It flooded back when he was shown a photograph of Jane Harcourt who had seduced him at university and taught him about the delights of a close, intimate relationship, however upsetting this particular relationship turned out to be.

* * *

On June 6th, 1944, the allies made their long-awaited D-Day landings in Normandy. The invasion had been a success, although there were a tremendous number of casualties, especially among the Americans at both Omaha and Utah beaches where German resistance had been stiff. The allies were now at this time attempting to breakout of the Normandy region, and this wouldn't be achieved for several weeks.

The British people were joyous that at last the fight had been taken to the Germans after nearly five years of being pounded by their Luftwaffe. However, this joy was short-lived, as concerns about the casualties became paramount. In the first assault there were at least ten thousand casualties, of which four thousand soldiers and airmen died. The long, hard road to German defeat had begun.

The Russians were attacking the retreating Germans from the east and were taking revenge on the Poles and then the German civilians. The allies were all now in a race to Berlin and Stalin, in particular, saw an opportunity to dominate Europe through his conquests of eastern and central European countries.

* * *

Robert Johnson was happy that the allies were at last making a move. The clubs and pubs in London and southern England were empty, and the campgrounds were deserted as the troops had embarked en masse to France. However, Robert still had many issues to settle with espionage in Britain, especially from Russia. He, like Maxwell Knight, was convinced that there was an agent in MI5 who was feeding information to the Russians. He suspected Anthony Blunt, or one of his minions, was the leak, and he had been extra careful about securing documents. But reports had to be typed and sent to MI5's director and its senior staff. This was the Achilles heel of the operation.

Robert knew he was often being followed and he just assumed

this would be the case every time he left the office. On one particular day, he stepped out of his office building on his way to visit Tom Pearson in Wales when he spotted his usual tail as he walked across St. James's Park. He knew he had to lose the man following him, but he had trouble doing so. Whoever was trailing him was very good and was not the clumsy, unsophisticated tail he had been used to in the past. He caught several buses and even dived down the Underground to appear at another entrance. But there he was. It occurred to him that he was being tailed by a team of people. Eventually he went into a jeweller's shop in the Burlington Arcade and the owner, who had previously worked for MI5, got one of his assistants to put on a coat and hat and pretend to be an interested customer. Meanwhile Robert was ushered out of a back door of the shop and took a taxi to Paddington Station. There he caught his train to Cardiff.

Sitting in the train as it pulled out of the station, he began thinking about the intensity of Russians' determination to find Tom. They were being paranoid. Why were they interested in seeking revenge on a fairly low-level agent? It didn't make sense. Perhaps Tom's 'crime' was more serious than Robert had thought. Then he remembered what an old diplomat in Moscow had told him. He had said that the Russians by nature, and particularly the new communist regime, were mistrustful of anyone and believed the rest of the world was always planning to dominate them. They had a national inferiority complex and were determined never to be the victims of any international intrigue. It made sense to them to eliminate anyone who crossed them, however small the slight might be.

Robert realised he'd have to warn the staff at the clinic that he must be alerted to any strangers seen in the vicinity or asking for Tom. But he was about to move Tom elsewhere and perhaps there was no necessity to do this.

He knew the news he was bringing was likely going to cause Tom great stress and anger, and he was not looking forward to their meeting.

He found Tom in the gym at the clinic and was pleased to see a great improvement in his health. The staff at the clinic had done a wonderful job of helping him and he was ravenously reading the physics magazines and books he had been given. He greeted Robert with a smile and strong handshake. They went onto a patio outside the clinic that looked over the Brecon Beacons National Park. There was no one there so Robert could talk freely.

After small chit-chat and when a waitress brought them tea, Robert got right to the point: "Tom, we have to talk about your future."

"I can't wait to get back to Malvern. There's a lot I want to do. I've been thinking about some projects and I have written several notes." Then he saw the look of gravity on Robert's face. "What's wrong?"

"The current situation with the Russians is so serious that they will kill you the moment you set foot in Malvern." Then Robert told him about the tail he shook off in London on his way to visit him and that this showed how serious the situation had become.

"So what am I going to do!" demanded an angry Tom. "If I can't do the work I love what's the alternative? I might as well kill myself. I've got nothing left in life!"

"I understand it's painful, but what's the alternative? What I'm going to suggest is something that you can do to contribute to the future of physics without running the risk of being killed. Because you haven't got much choice if you want to live," Robert replied aggressively.

As Tom began to realise his predicament, he began to ruefully speak: "You have no idea how I feel so how could you 'understand' me?! That's rubbish and you know it! You people got me into this. I should have ignored you."

"No. You got yourself into this mess by working for the Russians against your own country," Robert replied calmly. "We only gave you the chance to avoid prison. The question is, do you want to live to a ripe old age or not? You have to make a choice because the Russians will make sure you don't see your next birthday if you go back to Malvern. We can give you protection from them only if you do as we ask. I suppose one day, when this has blown over, you could work again for a government research lab or go into academia. But in the meantime you have little choice in the matter."

After a few minutes of silence and contemplation, Tom said: "All right, what's the plan?"

"First, we have changed your name to Charles David DeFreis and you will be the new maths and physics teacher at Kingsmeade School. The headmaster is a friend of Maxwell Knight so there will be no questions asked. This is a private school of about five hundred boys and it's near the small village of Kintbury. This is just west of Reading in Berkshire. There is no accommodation for you at the school, so we've arranged for you to live on a renovated canal barge which is tied up on Kennet and Avon Canal, a short distance from the school."

Robert opened his briefcase and produced two certificates, one for an undergraduate degree and the other for a master's degree in physics from the University of London, both in Tom's new name.

Just then a shot from a rifle rang out and a bullet hit a column on the patio. Both men dived for cover.

27

A second shot rang out and the bullet ricocheted off the table where they had been siting. Robert drew his Webley pistol and said calmly to a very frightened Tom: "When I start firing keep low and run to that door!"

Robert then fired four shots in the direction he thought the gunman was. He knew that his pistol was no match for someone with a rifle but his shots would at least keep the gunman's head down while they made their move.

As they crashed through the door to the main building, a third shot rang out and Robert felt a searing pain in his side. He hadn't got time to look. He shouted at a very startled nurse to telephone the police and report that they were under attack. She picked up the telephone receiver and after several seconds of tapping the cradle she said the line was dead.

Just then a man arrived with a large basket with loaves of bread and rolls. He was completely unaware of the drama that was unfolding as he began to walk to the kitchens to deliver his supply.

"Quick, Tom, follow me."

They ran out of the front door and jumped into the baker's van. Robert began to slow down and it was then that he saw the blood. He said nothing to Tom but cursed to himself. Thankfully the man had left his keys in the van. Robert gave it a few desperate cranks and the engine started. They drove at speed down the half-mile-long drive until they reached the main road and turned towards the town of Sennybridge.

"There's an army camp near Sennybridge and that's our best bet to elude the Russian hit squad. I used to be at the camp in my military days when we trained for the Great War. Since D-Day it's probably quiet, although I imagine they still have recruits there," he said, fighting back the pain and trying to be as positive as possible for Tom's sake.

After a while as they drove at speed towards Sennybridge, he looked in the van's rear-view mirror and spotted a car following them.

"Hold tight, Tom! We've got company!"

The car following them was about a quarter of a mile away and was closing the gap between them. Robert increased the van's speed and took a sharp corner sideways. He was determined to put as much distance between them as possible, but the pain of his wound restricted his physical actions. Also, the trouble was that the van was old and slow, and he knew they would catch up with them easily.

Then lady luck was shining down on them. A tractor pulling a plough was coming out of a field and had just started to enter the narrow road. Robert swerved around the tractor almost driving into a ditch, but it cost him with a stabbing agony in his side and he was now having difficulty focussing. He blinked hard in order to try and improve his vision, but everything was now out of focus. He knew the tractor would slow their pursuers down for a while, but it was nearly two more miles before the army camp.

As they came over the crest of a hill they saw the camp before them. They also saw the car pursuing them. Now it was a matter of luck if they made it to the camp, but as the gradient was downhill now they were able to keep ahead of the pursuers.

Robert swerved the van into the front gate of the camp and a very angry corporal with a rifle came out of the guardhouse.

"Oi! You can't come in here!"

Robert struggled out of the van, gripping his stomach, and in a weak voice said: "I'm Major Robert Johnson. Who is your commanding officer?"

"Colonel David Burgess, sir," said the astonished man, coming to attention and then rushing to catch Robert as he nearly fell.

"I know him. Call him and get him here, now!" he said in gasps as the pain burned inside him.

The corporal lowered Robert to the ground. He laid there in a foetal position clutching his stomach. The corporal reached in his coat, took out Robert's wallet and looked at the ID.

"Shit! MI5. I'll call him right away, sir. Also, I'll get a medic."

"You see that black car over there." Robert spoke with a great deal of difficulty and was gritting his teeth. "Get two of your lads to arrest them. They have been pursuing us and are German agents. One of them shot me."

"Right you are, sir. Barnes and Jones, fall in right now and bring a towel from the washroom!" Two soldiers appeared from the guardroom and were ordered to arrest the occupants in the car. As soon as they started to run towards the car, it took off at high speed.

All this time Tom just stared at Robert. He couldn't believe his friend had been shot and had driven the van, and at such break-neck speed. He was woken from his trance by the corporal: "Perhaps you should take this towel, sir, and put some pressure on his wound to stop the blood. I'll go and make some phone calls." Tom mechanically did as he was told.

As Tom tried to staunch the bleeding, Robert gave him a wintery smile and slowly croaked: "Tom, always remember never to trust anyone, especially from MI5. There are too many traitors there. The only exception is Maxwell Knight. He'll see you right. Be careful, for God's sake." Robert closed his eyes. His breathing got more difficult and raspy until it stopped altogether. Just then two army medics arrived and began to examine Robert. They looked up at Tom, who realised at once that Robert was dead.

Tom felt an arm around him; someone gently lifted him to his feet and was guiding him to a vehicle. Colonel David Burgess sat Tom down in the staff car and drove him to the officers' mess. There he got him a brandy: "There you are. This should help you. When you're ready you can fill me in on what happened."

"I've got to call Maxwell Knight at MI5," was all that Tom would say.

* * *

December 20th, 1945

World War Two in Europe was over and the 'Cold War' was about to begin with the conquering allies now at odds with each other. Russia had occupied half of Germany, most of eastern and central Europe, and was threatening other European states. The threat was real and the Western nations were concerned that a third world war might break out, pitching the Russians against their former allies. As a result, the spy agencies in Britain, the United States and Russia were working overtime to find out the plans of each of the potential combatants. Suspicions of each other grew to new heights of irrationality, especially on the Russian side as their national persecution complex kicked into high gear.

Over eighteen months had now passed since Robert Johnson's untimely death. It seemed to Tom that Russian interest in him had waned because no further attempts on his life had been made. Needless to say, he had not let his guard down and took evasive precautions wherever he went. Maxwell Knight had also appointed Charles Ingram as his 'minder' and successor to Robert Johnson. Apart from a brief meeting at a safe house in London, Tom had only met Charles Ingram once, although they spoke on the telephone every six weeks or so, just to check in.

The NKGB resident at the Russian Embassy in London,

Anatoly Kuznetsov, and Tom's nemesis, had been ordered not to continue with plans to assassinate Tom even after Russian Ambassador Gusev was called into the British Foreign Office. He was given a lecture by the British Foreign Secretary, Ernest Bevin, about the attack in Wales that had killed an MI5 agent and the finding of Viktor Gorev's body in the Thames. He was told that the 'wild west' activities of his staff had to stop, otherwise there would be serious diplomatic repercussions. The ambassador denied that Russia had been involved but Ernest Bevin did not accept his protestations.

Anatoly Kuznetsov was extremely angry. He was a communist fanatic and was determined to carry out his instructions from Moscow Centre but decided that he would wait a while and look for an opportunity to strike. He knew that ambassadors didn't last very long and maybe the next man in the job would be more inclined to let him finish his assignment. Tom Pearson had gone to ground anyway so it would take some time to find his new location.

The focus of Moscow Centre had also changed to more concentrated espionage in the United States, particularly on the Manhattan Project, which was the name given to the development of an atomic bomb. Russia had several agents working on the project as key scientists, who had been leaking information to Moscow for its own atomic project.

In the meantime, Tom, now known as Charles David DeFreis, was enjoying his teaching post at Kingsmeade, the boys' private school, for over a year now. Despite his frustration at not being allowed back to TRE he realised that the trauma of the attempts on his life in London and Wales meant he couldn't return to his former life. The pupils at the school he taught at were, on the whole, bright and challenging. He was able to help prepare some of the brightest ones for university careers. The boy's enjoyed him and sought him out either for advice on careers or often for more mundane adolescent guidance.

Tom lived on a canal barge on the Kennet and Avon Canal and cycled to the school every day along the canal's towpath. He met many people walking their dogs on the towpath and had made friends with most of them. Life was beginning to feel normal.

He had taken up again his passion for jazz and played twice a week at his local pub. His musical career had then morphed into many gigs, first in Reading at a club called The Raven after one of the pub's patron heard him play. He was soon also playing at small, intimate clubs in Bath and Bristol as word got out about his talent. But he had refused appearances at large, well-known clubs in London because he didn't want to be recognised by anyone, including his old friends from Malvern.

Then one day he received an emergency call from Charles Ingram at the school. According to Ingram, MI5 had been able to intercept wireless traffic between the Russian Embassy in London and Moscow. It turns out that a Russian mole inside the security services had discovered Tom's location and the embassy had requested permission to execute a plan to eliminate him. Ingram advised Tom to leave his present location and go to a 'safe' house in Manchester to await further instructions.

When Ingram rang off, Tom sat in the staff room and thought out his own plan. He decided to disappear and not have contact with anybody, particularly anyone at MI5, because the agency was clearly compromised. Wherever he went, the Russians would soon find him. No, he would have to go on his own terms. He was also determined to hit back at his would-be assassins, so he made plans to avenge Robert Johnson's and Fiona Shelby's deaths. This was a different Tom now. He was dispassionate and calculating as he planned his revenge.

First he had to find accommodation. He booked himself into a pub which was in the village of Radley, some three miles away, and rented a car at a garage in Reading. He packed two suitcases of clothes and personal items and stored them in his room at the pub. He then filled two milk bottles with petrol from the barge's tank and put a rag in each. He hid his Molotov cocktails in some bushes near the barge. And now he was ready.

Three days later, Tom was looking out of the window of the staff room when he saw two men in a car talking to one of the boys. Tom left the school by a back door and took a short cut across a field to the canal. He got to the barge before the men and opened the hatch and turned on a radio so it looked like he was there. He then hid in a ditch and watched as the men approached. They cautiously looked around and then climbed down into the barge with guns drawn. Tom crept up to the barge, lit the two Molotov cocktails and threw them down the hatch; he closed and locked the hatch door. There was a mighty explosion as the barge caught fire. He heard the screams of the two men inside as he walked away and he saw an anguished face looking at him out of one the portholes. After a while the screams of agony stopped. The barge sank to the bottom of the canal, leaving just the top of the cabin showing above the water.

Satisfied with his work, Tom got into his car and drove away. Two days later he called Charles Ingram at MI5 to let him know he was still alive and wasn't one of the bodies Special Branch had found. But he refused to say where he was and promised to call in occasionally. That was the last time he was in touch with Charles Ingram.

28

Tom wanted to get away from the scene of his crime as fast and as far as possible. During his drive to Reading railway station and his train ride to London, his mood swung from anxious to depressed as he recalled what he had done. He had become an animal, just like them, and he didn't like it one bit.

Where was he supposed to go? With all the activity of the last few days he hadn't thought this out. He knew he needed somewhere which would be a sort of oasis that would give him time to recover and decide what he was going to do for the rest of his life. He remembered reading an article in the school library in a magazine called *Country Life* about Lincoln and its picturesque cathedral and medieval area. And so he decided, somewhat irrationally, that Lincoln would be his sanctuary.

Late that night, Tom checked into the White Hart Hotel in Lincoln as Duncan Patterson. The hotel was near the cathedral in the historic part of the city.

He spent three days walking around the historic parts of the city and sat in the cathedral contemplating his future. He enjoyed sitting in the vastness of the cathedral and found it gave him the solace he so desperately needed.

After the days of contentment, he had made up his mind

what he was going to do. There was no chance of getting back into research for either the government or for a university, as he had burnt his bridges with scientific colleagues. They would never forgive him for his work with the Russians and MI5. He had to find somewhere that was not high profile because he strongly believed that the Russians were after him to liquidate him. He realised that teaching at a school was the best way to work in the subject he loved. He could even use the school laboratories to do experiments and write research papers anonymously.

But to get a job he needed to present his university diplomas to potential employers. He realised that he needed several diplomas with different names so that he could move around the country if he felt threatened. He'd have to call Maxwell Knight, who was the only person he trusted at MI5.

Tom called Maxwell Knight from his room. Before he told him what he wanted, he heard a definite but faint click on the line. It was being tapped. Maxwell Knight also heard the click and told him to call back on his secure line from a call box and he gave him the number. When they finally talked, Tom asked for copies of his diplomas under certain names and arranged to have them sent to his bank in Leeds.

"This will take about three weeks to organise. Call me in three weeks on my secure line," Maxwell Knight said.

Tom left Lincoln the following day and moved to Durham, where he found a furnished flat. After three weeks, Tom called Maxwell Knight and arranged to pick up the diplomas at the Midland Bank in Leeds.

He arrived in Leeds and walked to the university. He was amazed at the new buildings that were going up all over the campus. He booked into the Old Griffin Hotel. That evening he walked to the Pack Horse pub. As it was the summer holiday period, there were no students at the pub. He bought himself a beer and sat at one of the tables. A group of men came in and among them was a familiar face, Frederick Thomas. He had been the chairman of the university's Socialist Society when Tom had been to a few meetings.

"It's Tom Pearson, isn't it? What a surprise to see you after so many years," Frederick Thomas said, taking a drag of his ever-present cigarette. "What are you doing these days?"

"Not much. I'm teaching at a boys' school."

"Where?"

"Near Reading. And yourself?"

"Oh, I'm the local secretary of Amalgamated Union of Operative Bakers here in Leeds. Are you involved in politics anymore like you were here?"

"No, I gave that up years ago."

"Weren't you going out with Jane Harcourt, our well-known communist recruiter?"

"Yes, for a while."

"Didn't she recruit you to the cause?"

"No. That's the reason we broke up," said Tom, lying.

"So what are you doing back here at our alma mater? Not looking for a job, are you?"

"I was in Jarrow clearing up some of my father's affairs and I decided that I'd come here to see the old place since I was nearby."

"So what did you do during the war, Tom?"

"I was in the Royal Signals, helping with their communications needs," he said, lying again.

"That's interesting. I heard you were with the Telecommunications Research Establishment doing work for them."

"Oh, yes. Where did you hear that?"

"It was in the alumni newsletter. How long are you going to be in town?"

"A couple of days and then I'm heading back to London."

"You'll have to excuse me, I've got to run as I have a union meeting to go to." And with that he beat a hasty retreat.

As Tom walked back to his hotel that night, he had a strange feeling he was being followed. Every time he looked back there was no one to be seen. He began to wonder if he was being paranoid. No one knew he was in Leeds except for Frederick Thomas, who he had just met. He still had this feeling and decided to take precautions.

Instead of heading back to his hotel, he walked to another hotel, The Victory. He walked into it and up the stairs as if he was going to his room. He then took the staff stairs at the back of the hotel and left by a side door which led into an alley. As he walked cautiously along the side street towards the front of the hotel, he spotted his tail, who was standing in the darkened entrance to a shop watching the front of the hotel. The man was none other than Frederick Thomas.

As Tom was peering around the corner of the hotel, he didn't hear anyone coming up behind him. He turned too late as the cosh landed on his head and he lost consciousness. He was vaguely aware of his hands being tied behind his back and being thrown in the back of a van, which was driven for at least an hour. When the van arrived at its destination he was dragged into a building and thrown into a room. The door was then locked.

Tom was recovering some of his consciousness when the door to his prison was opened and in strode Frederick Thomas.

"Well, well, well. Now we have the traitor. I guess your time is up. We are just waiting for the arrival of Anatoly Kuznetsov, the NKGB resident from the Russian Embassy in London, who plans to take care of you personally. According to him, you've led them on a real goose chase, killing some of his agents and revealing to MI5 a network of agents. You have been a bad boy. We were warned that you might visit the university and we were on the lookout for you. Now here you are."

"I'm sad for you, Frederick, because you've chosen the wrong cause to follow," said Tom as he shook his head in an attempt to clear it. It hurt like hell, but his thoughts were becoming clearer. "Yes, I helped the Russians, but I soon realised their ambition was no different than that of Hitler's. I was naive, I suppose. They will fail and take people like you down with them. I think you and these acolytes who have helped you should read George Orwell's fantastic new book called *Animal Farm* which summarises the wicked ways of the Russians. It will open your eyes. Tell me, how did you get involved with them?"

"I suppose it won't hurt to tell you, seeing as you are going to die tomorrow. If you must know, I was one of Jane Harcourt's recruits. When she left, I became the Russians' talent spotter. I must say I had a great deal of success over the years."

"Just for interest, where are we?"

"We are in an abandoned farmhouse on the North Yorkshire Moors. So you can shout as much as you like and no one would hear you. Now I've got to go so I can meet Anatoly Kuznetsov off the London train. See you in the morning. Oh, by the way, one of my colleagues will be outside all night in case you want room service!" And he laughed at his own joke as he left.

Tom got shakily to his feet and started to inspect the room he was in. They had chosen it well. It was an inside room with no access to the outside except through the one door. He heard his guard outside who had an oil lamp and a battery radio blaring some big band music. He realised morosely that he was stuck and in a lot of trouble. There was no way to escape except by deceiving his guard.

He began to call out to attract his attention. He banged on the door with his feet. Finally, he heard the man calling out, telling him to shut up. Tom continued to bang around. Finally, the guard opened the door. He was enormous and as big as a professional wrestler. He didn't say anything as he came in and as he approached Tom he punched him full in the face. Tom collapsed unconscious on the floor. When he finally gained consciousness, he found he was tied up around the legs and there was dirty rag in his mouth. And the loud music kept playing.

Tom didn't really sleep that night. He was in such pain as

the ropes were chafing on his arms and ankles because they were bound so tight. His swollen face ached where he'd been punched. He was bleeding from several cuts. As a result, the night had become nightmarish. As the dawn came up, the light of the day poured into the room through the underneath of the door and he felt the sun's heat begin to warm his prison cell.

About two hours later, he heard a man arriving at the farmhouse. Eventually the door swung open and he was grabbed and dragged into another room. He was forcibly pushed down on a chair and his hands were tied behind the chair. As he looked up, he saw Anatoly Kuznetsov sneering at him in utter contempt and disgust.

"So this is the traitor. He doesn't look like much but the damage he has done to our cause is intolerable. What have you got say for yourself, scum!" said Anatoly Kuznetsov with an angry scowl on his face.

The gag was wrenched from Tom's mouth. After he swallowed and licked his lips, he said with a smile: "You and your master Stalin are really mirror images of Hitler and Himmler. Your cause will never win, just like theirs, and it's likely to be cast as a failure into the dustbin of history. You will likely kill me, I don't expect anything else, but I'm not frightened of you. You personally are also doomed when they call you back to Moscow and I will be there in hell to welcome you!" He laughed out loud.

Tom's response so infuriated Anatoly Kuznetsov, who began punching his face frenetically. Tom's face was soon a bloody, swollen mess and he had lost consciousness again. With the help of Frederick Thomas and the large guard from the night before, he was dragged outside towards a well which was in the middle of the courtyard.

"When I shoot him, throw him down the well and then clean up here," said Anatoly Kuznetsov. "Now make him kneel and I will shoot in the back of his head like we Russians do with all traitors."

Anatoly Kuznetsov drew a luger from a holster under his armpit and took aim. There was a sudden explosion and he fell to the ground dead with a gaping wound through his skull.

At first, the others just looked in shock at the body in front of them. And then a voice commanded them to get on the ground spread-eagled. About half a dozen uniformed police officers appeared from one of the outbuildings and began to search and handcuff the suspects. The sergeant who had fired the shot that killed Anatoly Kuznetsov came out from his hiding place behind an abandoned tractor carrying his Lee-Enfield .303 rifle with its telescopic sight and examined his handiwork.

"Excellent work, Sergeant," said Superintendent Brian Brill of Special Branch. "Now can we get Tom to hospital ASAP?"

A week later, Tom still was in hospital in Leeds recovering from the beating he had received. At first it was touch and go that he would recover, but slowly he began to pull through. At visiting time, Superintendent Brill appeared with the customary bunch of grapes that always seemed to be given to hospital patients whether they liked them or not.

"How are you doing, Tom?"

"They say I'm making progress. I can't wait to get out of here, though. I tried walking today which wasn't a good idea because I fell and sister gave me a hard time. What I want to know is how you appeared so suddenly on the scene."

"We always had Anatoly Kuznetsov in our sights, but when he suddenly left the Russian Embassy in a hurry we knew something was up. We knew that he was determined to find you and was beside himself when you killed two of his men. My men followed him on the train to Leeds and they saw him meet up with that little shit Frederick Thomas. The next morning, we followed them to the farmhouse at a distance and were able to stop them executing you."

Two weeks later, Tom was released from hospital and spent a month in a nursing home in Scotland receiving physiotherapy.

While he was there, he sent a copy of *Animal Farm* to Frederick Thomas, who was in Leeds Prison awaiting trial for attempted murder, kidnapping and espionage. He sent the book with a notecard that simply said: "Enjoy."

29

Harrogate, Yorkshire, England, January 15th, 1999

"Where the bloody hell is he?" demanded an exasperated Donald Jevons, thc managing director of a privately owned crematorium near Harrogate, Yorkshire. The young priest at his side looked upset. "Sorry, Vicar, for swearing, but he drives me to distraction."

They were standing outside the entrance to the crematorium's chapel in the crisp winter air awaiting the arrival of a deceased man's hearse. It was the first cremation of the day and timing was important, as services had been planned for just about every hour until three that afternoon. It was vital to start on time because any delay would affect the timing of every following service and cause unnecessary anxiety to his clients.

This first service was to include live organ music and the funeral directors had given Mr. Jevons a list of the hymns to be played, which he had left on the organ for the organist. Most crematoria services only included piped music and occasionally the mourners would ask for live music. Donald Jevons had hired an eighty-three-year-old organist who had been highly recommended by a local vicar some years before. Robert Radcliffe was good at his job and

Donald had received many compliments from mourners about his playing, but he was always infuriatingly last-minute in putting in an appearance. And today there was no sign of him.

Donald Jevons was the grandson of the founder of Whispering Pines Crematorium and the firm's current owner. He was a tall man at about six foot three inches and as thin as a rake. He always had a grim, straitlaced expression on his face and nothing seemed to worry him, except Robert Radcliffe. He was of a mind to fire him, but finding someone to replace him would be difficult and, after all, he was cheap.

The priest, Reverend David Deakin, was in his vestments ready to take the service. He was shivering in the cold even though he had put on two sweaters that morning and was wearing long underwear. The hill, where the crematorium sat, was exposed to the raw wind off the Yorkshire Moors, and the damp cold at this time of year really got to the two men's bones.

"He knows the service starts nine and it's five to right now. We don't have many services where the family wants an organist. You'd think he would be here on time," Mr. Jevons bitterly complained to the priest.

Just then, down the hill, they saw the funeral cortege making its way slowly along the winding, half-mile driveway towards the crematorium. When it was about a hundred yards from the entrance to the chapel, the organ began to play Chopin's Funeral March.

"I'll kill him!" Donald whispered to the priest.

Reverend David Deakin couldn't help smiling. He knew Robert Radcliffe and his wry sense of humour, and the joke he had perpetrated on Donald Jevons that day was typical of him. With the shortage of priests, the Church of England had been forced to amalgamate many parishes which before had had their own priests. Reverend Deakin was in charge of four parishes and Robert Radcliffe was the organist for two of them.

To say he knew Robert Radcliffe was a bit of an exaggeration.

When he was appointed to run the parishes some five years before, he had 'inherited' Robert Radcliffe. He knew he lived near the village of Darley in small, isolated cottage that looked out onto Nidderdale, which was part of the famous Yorkshire Dales, consisting of wild rolling moorland of hills and river valleys. The vicar had never been to his house as Robert Radcliffe was a bit of a recluse, although he was an outgoing choirmaster when he ran choir meetings and practices at the church. But nobody had ever set foot in his home.

When the funeral service had come to an end and all the mourners were in the garden of remembrance viewing the floral tributes to the deceased, Donald Jevons marched up to Robert Radcliffe and angrily demanded to know why he had been late. Robert Radcliffe stopped gathering his music and looked up at him with a mischievous grin.

"I wasn't late, Mr. Jevons. In fact, I was here at eight thirty so I could look over the material I needed for the service."

"You weren't in the chapel at ten to nine. So where were you?"

"I was in the break room having a cup of tea with the lads who work behind the scenes. I was in position at five to nine when you were outside."

"Next time report to me when you arrive so I know you're here." And with that Donald Jevons marched out of the chapel.

Robert Radcliffe smiled and had enjoyed riling Mr. Jevons. He thought he was a pompous bastard who needed putting in his place. There were many of his type around these days in positions of power, or so they thought, from the people at the bank, the local council offices, to this crematorium. Mr. Jevons ruled his crematorium by barking orders at people and, as a result of his lack of people skills, he was always losing staff. He blamed them for the high staff turnover and not himself. It didn't matter to Robert because he was called upon to play at funerals on a very few occasions so he could put up with being bullied by Mr. Jevons.

"Now, now, Robert, you shouldn't rile him that way," said an amused Reverend Deakin, who had come up behind him.

"I know, but I can't help myself," Robert Radcliffe said with a mischievous grin on his face.

"I'll see you on Sunday at St. Mark's."

"Yes, I'll be on time." And they both laughed.

Despite his jovialness, old age had caught up with Robert. These days, he was very stooped and walked with a cane. He had untidy grey hair and wore glasses with strong lenses. He finished tidying up his papers and closed down the organ cover. When he took off his cassock in the changing room at the crematorium, it was clear that his clothes had seen better days. His green jacket sat very loosely on his shoulders and it was obvious that he had lost weight since he had bought the jacket and corduroy trousers.

In truth, Robert was a very sick man, although no one knew, except his doctor in Harrogate. He had a cancer which had infected his lungs, although he had never smoked. According to Dr. Davis, he only had a few months to live and the doctor had advised him to make sure his final wishes were made in a will. Robert had never been married, had no children that he knew about and no relatives. So, when he made out his will, he turned over his entire estate, such that what it was, to the University of Leeds, where he got his undergraduate degree in physics, and to Imperial College in London, where he had earned his master's degree sixty years previously. Both universities were where he had had his happiest, though troubled, memories.

Robert walked slowly to his car, an ancient Austin A30, which he had bought in 1961 and was looked after by a local garage, whose owner enjoyed working on it. It was midday when he reached his home after he did some grocery shopping in Darley's village shop. He had an idea for a jazz piece he was writing and wanted to get it down before he forgot it, which happened a lot these days.

With his move to Yorkshire some twenty years previously,

he felt safe from his pursuers, safe enough to take up more public appearances as a jazz pianist. This had resulted in at least one television appearance on a variety show and gigs at various nightclubs. Since his retirement from teaching in Harrogate five years ago, he had spent his time composing jazz pieces and several had been published. He felt fulfilled.

His other preoccupation was his physics books, collecting papers written by leading scientists in the field and reading avidly numerous scientific journals. After all, he had a master's degree in physics awarded to him in 1939 and he kept up his interest in electronic communications. He was fascinated by the new wave of personal computers and the development of a thing called the internet. Recently, he had bought a personal computer and had it connected to the internet, and he spent many hours researching all sorts of topics.

He was living off a pension from the British government, money he had inherited from his mother and savings he had scraped together over the years. He still had a contact in Whitehall. The original man from MI5 had been killed and his successor had retired long ago, and he was given his third – or was it his fourth? – officer to contact if needed. They never bothered him and he certainly didn't need them.

Robert spent the final day of his life that Saturday doing chores in the morning and then, bundled up against the weather, he went to watch Harrogate Town Football Club playing a local derby game against a team from the nearby town of Thirsk. By half time, he was feeling unwell, so he went to the club house and had a cup of tea to warm himself before driving home.

He got home at about four and lit a fire in his living room. Soon he warmed up. He poured himself a large scotch and sat in his chair and started to reminisce about his life and his loves. Then the pain started and he put his drink down. It got worse and he couldn't move. Soon he just drifted away. He had, at the end, many acquaintances but no firm friends or family. His life had become lonely after he had taken many wrong turns and made many bad choices.

Sunday came around and the Reverend Deakin was concerned because there was no sign of Robert Radcliffe. He usually had a pre-service practice with the choir, but he was nowhere to be seen. One of the choir members was a music teacher at the comprehensive school in Harrogate and so the vicar asked her to play at the service.

After the service, Reverend Deakin went around to Robert Radcliffe's home and knocked on the front door. Getting no answer, he went around to the back and peered through the window. There was Robert sitting in his chair motionless with a glass of whisky on the small wine table next to him. He looked as though he was asleep. The back door was open so the vicar went in. He felt for a pulse on the seemingly sleeping man and could find none. He was just sitting in a chair next to a long-gone-out fire. He knelt down by the body and prayed.

He then went to a desk, picked up his telephone receiver and called emergency services for an ambulance. He reported that there was a deceased man and the operator said she would send the police as well. While he waited he started to look around Robert's study, trying to understand his mystery organist. On the wall was a master's degree certificate from Imperial College, London, made out to someone called Thomas C. Pearson, and one under the same name for an undergraduate degree from the University of Leeds. Since nobody visited him, Tom had felt confident about hanging his diplomas with his real name in his inner sanctum.

The vicar was stunned by his discovery. So that was why he was so secretive. He was living a double life. But why?

Tucked under one corner of the blotting pad on his desk was a business card with a man's name and what looked like a home address in London and a telephone number. There were two other cards in the opposite corner of the blotter. One was a solicitor and the other his doctor. But other than that, there was no address book or correspondence to indicate any next of kin or pictures of family hanging on the walls.

The ambulance arrived, followed closely behind by a uniformed police sergeant and a constable in a squad car. The paramedics officially determined that Tom Pearson was dead and asked the police sergeant whether they could remove the body. It was clear that there wasn't anything suspicious, no struggle, no evidence of foul play, so the sergeant gave his go-ahead.

The vicar stood by the door as they carried the body out on a stretcher. As the ambulance pulled away he said reflectively: "Goodbye, Robert Radcliffe, or should I say Tom Pearson."

* * *

Fifty-year-old Brian Horricks was the one person in the office at MI5 who enjoyed Mondays. It got him away from his wife and their house in Woking, a suburb south-west of London. The weekends were purgatory because the couple always fought about really minor things, but it always boiled down to money. His wife of thirty years or so was tired of not having enough money to enable them to go on holiday or live without always counting their meagre savings before they spent it.

Marilyn Horricks wondered why her husband worked for the government on such a meagre salary considering he had a master's degree in engineering from the University of Loughborough. She didn't know he was with MI5 and thought he worked somewhere in the Home Office, the British government's justice ministry. She didn't want to know any of his colleagues and was happy with her circle of friends in Woking.

Brian Horricks always liked to get into his office early so he could read the newspapers and go over any cables that had come in the night before. His junior officer, Amanda Barret, tended to come in five minutes before the start time of nine o'clock. She was part of the intake of recruits three years previously and was nearly ready for her first assignment. Amanda was an Oxford graduate in modern history and had applied to join the agency soon after graduation. She had spent a year of gruelling interviews that examined every nook and cranny of her young life. Finally, she was deemed suitable and had begun her training, spending time in various departments. It was like an apprenticeship and all the time she was monitored and judged.

Brian's telephone rang. It was a solicitor who he didn't know from Harrogate telling him that Thomas Pearson, alias Robert Radcliffe, had died. The man had left instructions that Brian was to be called if something should happen to him. He thanked the solicitor and rang off. He picked up the phone again and called Inspector Raymond Dannell of Special Branch. That was the arm of the Metropolitan Police, which, among many of its intelligence responsibilities, worked closely with MI5 to arrest and prosecute suspects on the agency's behalf.

"Ray, Tom Pearson has finally kicked the bucket! Could you get the local police to seal his cottage while we take a look inside? I'll go up there today. Can you be there too? It's near Harrogate in a village called Darley."

"So the old bugger finally died. What is it, forty years since our predecessors turned him? Was there any sign of foul play?"

"It doesn't look like it."

"So he escaped the wrath of the KGB. Well, I'll be darned. Don't worry, Brian, I'll be there. I wouldn't miss this final chapter for anything. See you in Darley."

As Brian put his telephone down, Amanda walked in and switched on her desktop computer.

"Don't settle in because we're going to Yorkshire. Grab your overnight bag and let's go. I'll brief you on the way. Let me just say you will witness the final chapter of the one of our greatest World War Two coups that led to the trial of some dozen Russian agents and the closing down of a major spy network."

"Are we still fighting the war then?"

"Not anymore. But I want to make sure there are no loose ends."

They spent the next two days going through every room in the house and took away only a few papers mainly for the files. After a post-mortem, they returned to Harrogate a week later for Tom Pearson's funeral and were surprised at the turnout of his acquaintances from the area. The vicar had placed an obituary in *The Guardian* newspaper using Tom's real name and had announced his death at church services. For the MI5 officers there appeared to be no one of interest there except an old lady who stood by herself at the graveside for a long time and clearly was not a local because she had no interaction with anybody.

Inspector Dannell got one of the local police officers to find out who she was. It turned out she was an old university friend called Megan Rafferty who had seen Tom Pearson's obituary in *The Guardian* newspaper.

After Tom Pearson's funeral, Brian Horricks and Amanda Barret of MI5, and Inspector Dannell of Special Branch, were just taking a final look around Tom's cottage. Brian and the inspector helped themselves to some scotch, but Amanda refused to join them. Brian sat in Robert's chair and raised his glass.

"I'd like to toast Tom Pearson, our wily spy of many aliases, who had become a bit of a legend in his time in the service." The two them raised their glasses.

Brian continued: "You know, Amanda, even the very name he used was a lie. Robert Radcliffe was an alias that he had adopted over two decades ago. He had had several names over the years as he kept ahead of his real or imagined pursuers. His first new name had been Charles David DeFreis when he taught at a boys' school near Reading. When he lived near Peebles in Scotland it was Geoffrey Adams and in Cornwall he was known as Brian Darrow. Maxwell Knight at MI5 had manufactured degree diplomas with his new name on them so that he could continue to teach. That was the only contact he had with the agency and, when Maxwell

Knight retired, we had no trace of him. He certainly didn't let us know where he was living, although he telephoned us occasionally, but his calls ceased twenty years ago. I was given the files on him and was nominally in charge as his minder.

"As time passed, he realised, I suppose, that his enemies had given up looking for him and he was able to keep Robert Radcliffe as his permanent name. He reckoned his NKGB antagonists had died or had been purged and no one at the Russian security agency was bothered about pursuing such an ancient case as his."

Brian hesitated and then said: "God bless you, old chap! Thanks for your service."

They closed the front door of the cottage and left for London.

As a conscript to a forlorn cause, Tom Pearson had been trapped by evil men and had not been able to pursue his dreams of scientific stardom, which his talent had foretold. He had atoned for his mistakes but couldn't shake free from his past. And so it was that he died alone with no one close to him to mourn his death, except for Megan Rafferty, who he had not seen since his university days, but she was at his funeral.

Epilogue

Ironically, Tom Pearson's fear of his Russian pursers, that continued to haunt him, was an illusion. The NKGB's and then the KGB's interest in him had dissolved with death of Stalin in March 1953. After much infighting among the Politburo members, Nikita Khrushchev became leader and by December of the same year Lavrentiy Beria, former head of the NKVD, and Vsevolod Merkulov, head of the NKGB during the war and the man who had been pressing for Tom's elimination, had been tried and executed. Pavel Fitin, responsible for international operations at the NKGB, was luckier as he was just dismissed with no state pension.

Maxwell Knight left MI5 in 1956 and worked for the BBC on radio and sometimes on television as a commentator on nature. He was a passionate naturalist all his life and had a reputation during his time with MI5 of keeping exotic animals in his London flat. He also was the author of some thirty-two books about nature and two detective novels, as well as numerous magazine articles. He died in Reading, England, in 1968.

In 1964, Anthony Blunt was accused of being a Russian spy and was given immunity from prosecution in return for a full confession. He was one of the 'Cambridge Five' network of

Russian spies who was working for MI5, MI6 and the Foreign Office during the war. He was a special assistant to Guy Liddell, who headed up MI5's counter-espionage division who had been tasked with finding and arresting spies in Britain, particularly the Germans and to a limited degree the Russians.

His role was made public in 1979 in the House of Commons by Margaret Thatcher, Britain's Prime Minister. He had been Professor of the History of Art at the University of London, director of the Courtauld Institute of Art and Surveyor of the Queen's Pictures. He was also knighted in 1956 by the Queen. He was stripped of his knighthood and other positions when his treachery was made public. He died in 1983.

Try as he might, Anthony Blunt was unable to penetrate the operations of Maxwell Knight, mainly those that were related to Russia. Robert Johnson was one of Knight's men, but, like him, he had been tight-lipped and wouldn't reveal any information.